# A WISH IN TIME

*A Novel*

## LAUREL BRADLEY

iUniverse, Inc.
New York Lincoln Shanghai

# A Wish In Time

iUniverse books may be ordered through booksellers or by contacting:

iUniverse
2021 Pine Lake Road, Suite 100
Lincoln, NE 68512
www.iuniverse.com
1-800-Authors (1-800-288-4677)

ISBN-13: 978-0-595-40948-8 (pbk)
ISBN-13: 978-0-595-85307-6 (ebk)
ISBN-10: 0-595-40948-2 (pbk)
ISBN-10: 0-595-85307-2 (ebk)

Printed in the United States of America

To Janet for the smiley faces, the "yuck"s the hours spent editing, and the unfailing friendship. Thank you!
And to Tom for countless reasons.

# Chapter 1

# Kirkinwall, Scotland, 1718

Magda McClellan waited in the stuffy, dimly-lit church while her fellow Sunday worshippers filed out. Father Toddy stood at the door looking stern as he bid the three-dozen parishioners to keep their heavenly father in their hearts all week. Most of his congregation avoided meeting his eye as they mumbled, "Good day, Father."

Magda was the last out the door. She held a handful of her full blue skirt and yellow overskirt as she stepped over the threshold.

"When are ye gonna drag yer Davy in with ye, Magda?" the priest asked.

Magda widened her eyes and looked incredulously at her uncle, her bonnet shading her face.

"All right then," he admitted. "I ken the answer as well as ye. He'll come when there isna so much fire and brimstone in the sermons that none of God's mercy peeks through." He frowned, staring at his niece. "How is it ye can say so much and not open yer mouth?"

"It's because ye ask her questions ye ken the answer to," Davy said, coming down the street to join them on the path in front of the church. He smiled, his gaze caressing the small body of his wife, round with child. "I missed ye this morning, Acorn," he said, drawing her to his side. "Ye were gone when I woke. Where did ye get to so early?"

Magda's brown eyes twinkled as she smiled. "I'd summat special to fetch fer yer breakfast, husband."

"Why do ye always call her Acorn?" Father Toddy said, interrupting what looked to become an intimate moment between husband and wife. "She's small and brown to be sure, but acorns are bitter nuts fit only for boars and kine. Magda is sweet and mild—more a hazelnut than an acorn."

"Aye, she's small and brown," Davy said, winking at his petite wife before turning his eyes to her rounded belly. "But not normally as round as a ripe acorn nor as bitter to the taste." He tugged gently on a nut-brown curl that escaped her bonnet before continuing. "But that's not why I call her Acorn." He stood up straight, looking down on the hefty cleric. "I'm a big man, Father. My sons will be big as well. Big as oaks—tall, sturdy and strong. And they'll all sprout from this little bit of a woman." His soft brown eyes smiled at Magda. "My Acorn."

Father Toddy cleared his throat. "Ye should have been a bard instead of a carpenter."

Davy's chuckle was deep and warm. "I think not, Father. My poetry and stories would not keep a man my size well fed."

"Speaking of food," Magda said, looking at her husband. "I doubt me uncle has broken his fast, and I know we havena. Perhaps he would join us at our table."

Davy laughed again. "Of course. 'Tis the Sabbath, so yer uncle must join us as usual. The only question is will it be mistletoe or ivy that rounds the oak today?"

"Still mistletoe," Father Toddy admitted. "As long as the laird wants his people to hear of Our Lord's wrath against sinners, I'll be the poisonous mistletoe rather than the gentle ivy."

"Mistletoe doesna hurt the oak," Magda said, slipping her small hand into Davy's large one.

"Aye, as long as ye mind the berries."

Once inside the small house nestled amongst the trees just outside of the town of Kirkinwall, Magda donned an apron and bustled around putting out the ham, bannocks, parritch, honey, and fresh strawberries for their breakfast.

"Strawberries," Davy said in awe. "I thought they were well done for the year. Where did ye find them?"

"I willna be telling ye; ye'll graze the patch clean, and there willna be any late bearers next year," she scolded, batting at his hand as he reached over her shoulder to help himself to the small flavorful berries.

"Left some for the fairies, did ye?" he teased.

"Hush, now," she scolded him, shooting a glance at her uncle.

Father Toddy frowned. "Canna fight superstition even in me own family. Yer da used to claim ye were a changeling, that nothing so small and brown could come from a big red man like he."

"But I look just like me ma," Magda protested, pulling butter from the cupboard to add to the spread adorning the table.

Her uncle grinned. "Her ma claimed she was a changeling too."

Davy laughed, gesturing to the priest to sit as he pulled out his own chair.

"And she might have been at that," Father Toddy continued. "She could charm honey from the bees and find berries out of season as well. Must be the fairy-stock." He pulled out a well-built chair and sat at the table.

"Fairy-stock, my eye. Gram wouldna have raised a changeling," Magda insisted, giving the table a quick look before sitting. "She'd have marched to the fairy hill and switched them back, make no mistake."

Her uncle shrugged, loading his wooden plate with food. "Could be the changeling Mary Margaret was less trouble than the original. I remember your ma cried solid her first six months and then, poof, like magic, she stopped and smiled, fit to charm the moon ever since. Could be my ma was so grateful for the silence, she'd have raised a piglet instead."

"Could be she did." Magda eyed her uncle's plate. "Are we to eat without thanking our heavenly father?"

Father Toddy blushed. "Of course not, but it be yer man's job, as master of the house, to say the prayer."

Davy laughed. "Oh, 'tis my job now, is it? I'll not mind the priest at the table, and he'll not mind my grace." He bowed his head and waited a moment for his wife and her uncle to join him. "Bless, God, the food on the table and those gathered around it, be they Adam's spawn or fair."

Father Toddy laughed. "Best ye stay out of the kirk until ye know if ye've wed a changeling or no."

Davy shrugged, helping himself to the food. "If ye let the fair folk in and hear their prayers, ye'll let anyone. Still, I'll wait 'til ye admit it before I'll darken the door."

Father Toddy sobered. "'Twill be a while, I'm afraid. Since his sister Gwen passed, the laird makes the Pope look lax. He'll not rest until he finds the person who is to blame."

"I thought 'twas clear whose fault it was," Davy said, buttering a bannock. "The Lady Gwen died after eating fruitcake made by Sanna's hand."

"The Lady Sanna she is now," Father Toddy said. "Rob married her with the McClellan's blessing—and mine too, I'm ashamed to say." He held off Davy and Magda's protests with a wave of his hand. "Could do nothing else. The McClellan called me to the castle, and I could do naught but obey. Any road, she was nearly as round with child as Magda here, and Rob claimed it as his own, conceived when he came to Kirkinwall to fetch the rents. He's managed to convince the laird that both he and Sanna were bewitched. Swears he'd not have broken his vows to Gwen else nor would his Sanna, being pure as snow."

"Hmmph." Davy's snort showed he didn't agree with Rob's assessment of the baker's daughter.

"Aye, just so." Father Toddy nodded. "Still, I'd not want to be the one that takes the blame. She's a sly one, that Sanna."

The thunder of hoofs approaching the cottage stopped all conversation inside. In a heartbeat, Davy's look changed from affection to trepidation. The English had caused too much trouble lately for a group of fast-moving riders to be ignored. If the riders were indeed George's soldiers bent on destruction, they'd fire the place and then murder those inside as they fled. There was no time to hesitate. He sprang to his feet. There was no place for Magda and Father Toddy to hide and no escape but a side window that was shielded from the path. Davy grabbed Magda and pushed her through the window.

"Run," he ordered her, as she dropped to the ground outside. "I'll find ye when I'm able."

She didn't hesitate, hiking her skirt and dashing behind Davy's workshop and into the woods beyond.

Davy didn't waste time watching her. He turned to the door, grabbing the broad axe that leaned against the doorframe, and rushed into the yard just as the riders arrived.

Eight men wearing McClellan colors pulled to a halt in front of Davy, scattering the chickens in the yard. They were armed with swords, broad axes, and flintlock pistols. One led a dapple-gray mare.

"Are ye daft, man? Come thundering in here like the bloody English," Davy scolded, recognizing the men of the guard.

"Put down the axe, Davy. We've but come to fetch Father Toddy," the leader announced from atop his dancing roan. "We've caught the witch."

Hearing his name, Father Toddy left the cottage and entered the yard. "And what witch would that be, Rory McClellan?"

"The witch what cursed Lady Gwen."

Father and Davy looked, but they didn't see a prisoner.

Rory answered their unspoken question. "She's been taken to Kirkinwall and tossed in the hole to wait for ye. The fiscal has sent for the laird as well."

"Who is she?" Davy asked.

Rory and several of his men made the sign against the evil eye. "They call her Auld Annie."

"She's a witch all right," a young member of the guard piped up. "Lived in a cottage in the wood surrounded by fairy rings and wild animals as tame as me dog. Heard tell they were innocent folk she caught unawares and turned to animals to keep her company. There were live rabbits under her cot and a crow on a chair by the table and …"

"That'll be enough, Dawin." Rory sent a scalding look at his young kinsman. Dawin subsided, frowning. Rory turned back to Davy and Father Toddy. "His sister ran off with a Campbell, but he thinks she's one of the rabbits."

"It came up, tame as can be, and nibbled at me boot," Dawin protested.

Rory stiffened, quelling Dawin with a look. An uncomfortable silence reigned for several long seconds. Finally, Rory said, "Will ye ride with us, Father?"

"Aye," the priest said, turning to Davy. "Give Magda my thanks for the fine meal, and tell her I'll look for her later."

Davy nodded, watching as the portly cleric mounted expertly, revealing a knife strapped to his calf. Davy wasn't surprised. Scotland was a wild land where cautious men were armed. His wife's uncle was wise not to rely solely on his cassock for protection. Davy watched the men ride away before heading into the woods to retrieve his wife.

He wound his way to their meeting spot and waited, knowing that she was somewhere nearby watching. Hearing a noise, he turned and looked up into the branches of a nearby tree.

"'Twas Rory and the guard. They came for yer uncle," he said, walking to the tree where Magda perched hidden amongst the leaves. He waited for her to pick her way down to the lower branches before reaching up and plucking her out of the tree and settling her on the ground. "Have trouble climbing?" he asked, gently criticizing her choice of hiding spots.

Magda nodded, straightening her skirts and accepting his criticism with a dull blush. "I keep forgetting how large I am."

"I'll make the cave bigger," he said, referring to their other hiding spot. "It'll have to fit you and the bairn before long."

"God forbid."

"Aye," Davy said, hugging her close. "Would that He did, but He doesna always."

Several years ago, a band of marauding redcoats loosed by the British to keep order in the Highlands during the Rising had laid waste to Kirkinwall. They'd butchered whole families—Madga's younger sister and parents amongst them. Luckily, Magda was not home during the attack, for she had been taking a turn working in the castle kitchens. Before they were even married, Davy had plotted an escape route, several hiding spots, and a safe meeting place in case the English came again. He had not taken Magda from the safety of the castle to have her die in a raid on their cottage.

She pulled out of her husband's embrace and then stood on tiptoe to give him a kiss on the cheek. "What did they want with Toddy?" she asked as they walked home a different way than they'd come.

"They found the witch who cursed Lady Gwen."

"Or who they'll blame for it," she said softly.

He frowned. "Not much we can do about it, I'm afraid. Toddy will call in the ecclesiastical examiners and wash his hands of it, no doubt."

"What choice does he have?" Magda said, defending her uncle.

"None. He's as much a prisoner to the process as the unfortunate woman they tossed in the hole."

"And who is the poor soul?" She shuddered, thinking of the hole Kirkinwall used as a holding cell for accused criminals awaiting trial. It was a deep pit topped by a grate. On hot days, the stench of misery and human waste rose from it even when it was empty.

"They called her Auld Annie. Said she lived in the woods surrounded by fairy circles. Which means she had a hut in a forest clearing same as many others."

"Do ye know her?" Magda asked.

Davy shook his head. "I heard tell of a wise woman who lives in the wood past Craig's Cairn and knows a bit of herb-craft, but I never had the cause to ask the way, having a wise woman of me own." He winked at her, hoping to lighten the worry that wrinkled Magda's brow.

"It's a sad day when innocent old women get blamed for the crimes of the young and wicked."

"Dinna fret. I'm sure she had her chance to be young and wicked."

Magda smiled at that. "And maybe she was. Still, it's her own sins she should be judged for and not Sanna's."

"Sins," Davy sighed. "It's crimes, not sins, that make the guard ride."

"It's both," Magda argued. "'Twere not for the sin, there wouldna be a crime."

Despite the merits of her argument, Davy shook his head. "Yer spending too much time with yer uncle, Acorn. The fey queen will hardly take ye back if ye talk of sins."

"I married me a giant. No fey queen will let me in her hill with a giant's get rounding me so." She caressed her rounded belly affectionately, smiling at her husband.

"Good," he said, swinging her into his embrace. "Then I've caught ye good."

"Aye," she said, hugging him back. "And I've caught ye good as well. The giants'll not take ye back with a changeling wife and bairn."

"Then we'd best make do with each other." He kissed the top of her head. "Good thing the guard came when it did. Yer Uncle Father was making short work of those berries ye picked fer me.

That afternoon, Magda walked to the workshop to join Davy. She brought her flute and her basket of knitting as she often did when her chores were done. Sunday afternoons were golden times they always spent together. Sometimes he'd come into the house, take her hand, and lead her off for an afternoon in the sun-dappled woods. Sometimes they'd sit in front of the fire and talk. Other days, like today, she'd join him in the workshop, playing her flute or knitting while he cut and carved, sanded and nailed, transforming raw wood into the high-quality furniture he was known for.

She loved the ordered peacefulness of Davy's workshop—the piles of lumber that lined the back wall waiting their turn, Davy's tools hanging neatly above the long workbench, and the box of sawdust and shavings meant for the fire. She loved the clean scent of raw wood mingled with the sweet scent of wax. She felt as much at home in the workshop as she did in front of her own fire.

"Ye can have the babe now," he announced as she entered, giving the cradle a final rub and then standing back so she could see. Sunbeams speckled with sawdust slanted through the large open windows to highlight the wee rocking bed.

"Oh," she gasped, dropping her basket into the rocking chair as she rushed to the cradle. She knelt next to it on the smooth-planked floor, running her hands over the glossy carvings of acorns and oak leaves that adorned the bed. It was a good-sized cradle, big enough to house a toddler or infant twins end-to-end. Tears filled her eyes as she turned to her husband. "It's beautiful."

"It'll fit our bairn," he said, his voice filled with pride.

Magda laughed, wiping away her tears. "Let's hope not."

Davy frowned. Magda eyed her belly and then the cradle. "At least not at first. I know ye expect oaks, but ye'll first have to be content with wee seedlings for a while."

Davy grinned. "Wee seedlings, then saplings, then oaks." He kissed her soundly. "And what took ye so long getting out here? I about polished this smooth waiting."

"I was putting a bundle together for the poor thing they've got in the pit."

"Auld Annie?"

"Aye. Ye know they willna feed her a thing without weevils. I think they keep a jar of the beasties in the fiscal's cupboard for that very purpose."

Davy laughed. "Dinna let Margery hear ye. She's mighty proud of her kitchen."

"I said they were in a jar, not running amuck."

"Aye," Davy chuckled. "That would calm her."

Magda ignored him, turning her attention back to the cradle. "It's a fine piece of work ye've done here, Davy." She rocked it with her hand. "I dinna know ye were working on it. I thought ye were carving one for Rob and Sanna."

"And I did." He nodded to a cloth-covered mound near the woodpile.

Curious, Magda crossed the room and pulled aside the cover. The cradle, another rocker constructed of fine oak, was much more elaborate than her child's smooth-lined bed. Angels with trumpets floated above fields of flowers inset in pale ash at the head while cherubs played with bunnies at the foot. Davy's trademark oak leaf was nearly lost in the clover at the bottom. She looked back at the elegant simplicity of their cradle, glad her babe wouldn't have to endure Sanna's monstrosity. She turned to Davy. "It's … it's … nice."

Truth was it was a bit much. Very much like Sanna herself. Rob had wanted something simple. He'd actually wanted to use the one his and Gwen's girls had slept in, but Sanna wouldn't have it. She wanted cherubs and rabbits and a riot of flowers for her son. Davy shrugged. "It's paid for."

"Well, that's good then," Magda said, covering Sanna's cradle and turning back to caress her own. "Ours is truly lovely."

By the time Magda and Davy strolled into town, the evening was nearly upon them. Davy carried the basket that held dinner to share with Father Toddy. The hot sun that had beaten down from a bright blue sky all day, intensifying the stench of the fly-ridden piles of horse dung that marked the cobblestone streets, was nearing the horizon.

They entered the village of Kirkinwall, lying in the shadow of Castle McClellan. They passed the church Magda had visited that morning—the one the town was named for. It was built into what remained of the old battlement wall that once enclosed the town before it got too large to be contained by the protective barrier. The town had originally been laid out like a small cross with the church as the top of the cross on the north end; the fiscal's house, the well, and the bakery flanking the public square; and the tanner and black smith sitting down the road a bit at the southern end not far from the loch. The cross's left and right limbs had been lined with houses, and a gated wall had surrounded the entire village. Now, however, other businesses and more houses had filled in the spaces between the arms and the head and foot of the cross. The wall had been mostly torn down and appropriated for use as building material.

As they reached the square, Lizzy, Sanna's mother, greeted Magda.

"The guard's got the devil's hand-maiden what killed the Lady Gwen. Thrown her in the hole to rot." The baker's wife, who was as plump and soft as twice-risen dough, grabbed Magda's arm. "They caught her surrounded by familiars and making potions plain as day. She was living in a croft that just appeared in the woods one day. And 'twas not a new one, though no one had ever set eyes on it before," Lizzy blathered, relieved to have someone to deflect suspicion from her daughter and her husband's bakery. No one had publicly accused Sanna or her family of the poisoning, but after Gwen died, purchases of bread and cakes from the bakery had fallen off while use of the public oven in the square had increased.

Magda patted the woman's hand sympathetically, thinking about the poor woman accused of the crime. Already stories filled with half-truths and lies had started to circulate. Most didn't make sense—crofts didn't just appear. Still, it wouldn't do to defend the old woman too loudly. It was one thing to sneak her food and water, but it was too dangerous to appear to support her after she'd been dragged through the village to await trial as a witch.

There were more people in the square than Magda had expected. Men and women stood in knots discussing the situation. She fingered the string that ran through a small hole in her skirts. The bundle meant for Annie was suspended on the other end beneath her skirts. She'd planned to stand near the hole to peer down at the accused as the others were, but she would release the string and drop the bundle.

She'd been certain that the initial fervor over Auld Annie's capture would have subsided by now. The laird had come and gone, declaring that justice would be done. Magda had expected that the townsfolk would have tired of the spectacle—what little there was with Annie in the pit—and gone home to their dinners.

Two men carrying a heavy ladder passed led by a third clearing the path. The fiscal and Father Toddy brought up the rear, both looking stern. Seeing his niece and her husband, the priest bobbed his tonsured head at them, and his countenance lightened.

"Good even'. Glad to see ye, Davy, Magda. We were just about to send someone for ye. We've need of some stout planks."

Davy raised a brow in question. Surely it was too early to make a scaffold to hang the poor woman.

"We have to move the witch," the fiscal informed Davy. "The hole's walls are falling in. We need to shore them up."

Davy nodded. "Ye've men enough to get her out, I trust."

"Aye," the fiscal said, watching as John the locksman marshaled the people back from the hole. The heavy ladder was lowered into the hole amidst much discussion from the audience as to whether they should just let the pit collapse and bury the witch, saving the time and the expense of the ecclesiastical examiners.

"Have ye a wagon ready?" Davy asked. He had his own and a team as well, but it would take time to walk home and get them ready.

As he spoke, a wagon driven by Rory McClellan and flanked by several members of the guard clattered into the square.

Davy set the basket on the ground near Magda's feet and swung onto the plank seat beside Rory. "I'll be back," he told his wife.

Rory twitched the reins, and the wagon lurched off.

"Where will they put her?" Magda asked her uncle, watching the gray head emerge from the pit.

"Michael's got a storeroom at the pub. They'll lock her in there."

"Feed her more than likely too," she said, glad that her small bundle wasn't needed.

Father Toddy shook his head. "Not likely. It's a change of location only. She'll not get more than she would in the hole. Might be less since the storeroom is clean and dry."

The storeroom might have been clean and dry, but Auld Annie wasn't. She was covered in mud and offal. The squalid condition of the pit had been made worse by the partial cave-in. She was so soiled that her guards didn't touch her, instead prodding her forward with sticks and a pitchfork.

"Best wait a while," Father said. "People will be heading home to their suppers now."

He was right. Once the prisoner was out of sight, the womenfolk bid each other good evening and left for their kitchens, pulling children and husbands in their wake. Soon, naught but the fiscal stood in the square.

He sauntered over to where Madga and Father Toddy stood. "I imagine Davy'll want to be helping with the hole once he and the boys get back with the wood," the fiscal said. "Margery will skin me alive if I dinna ask ye to sup with us. Ye too, Father, if ye've a mind."

"'Tis kind of ye, Alec," Toddy told the fiscal, "but, if I'm not mistaken, that wee basket at Magda's feet contains our dinner."

"Aye, 'tis," Magda confirmed. "But thank ye kindly for the invitation, and tell Margery I'll be by tomorrow with some eggs for her baking."

When they were alone, Father picked up the basket and carried it to the low wall surrounding the well. He set it on the ground. "We'll sit on the wall while we wait on Davy, shall we?" he said, hoisting himself onto the barrier.

When both were settled, Magda turned to her uncle. "Shouldna she be checked for signs?"

"For signs?"

"Marks of the devil."

He shook his head. "Now, Magda, you're not believing she's a witch, are ye?"

"Of course not." Magda frowned. "I was thinking of Auld Annie covered in mud and stinking. If she needed to be checked for the devil's mark, she'd need to be cleaned up a bit."

"Ah." Father Toddy smiled, nodding his head. "And who better to check than my niece who's been instructed in what to look for?" He slid from the wall, being careful not to let his cassock ride up too far. "I'll order the tub."

"And I'll fetch a vial of holy water from the kirk. Maybe we can prove her innocence tonight and save the poor thing."

Father Toddy frowned, shaking his head. "No, Magda. No matter what we do, ye must know that once the ecclesiastical examiners have been sent for, there will be a witch trial. If parish priests were judged capable of performing witch tests, there would be no need for the examiners. But we aren't. If I were to find her innocent of witchcraft and the examiner found her guilty, I would be judged to be bewitched. And that is not something I want to consider. Checking for a mark is different. I'll be helping the examiners, but not interfering. Not all witches are marked." He shook his head sadly. "Make her comfortable if ye wish, Madga," he warned, knowing his niece's tender heart well, "but dinna befriend the poor thing."

Father Toddy, Magda, the fiscal, and the guard stood to one side of the tavern's storeroom door as the serving girl approached with the key and a bucket of water.

"Wouldna catch me going in there," she told Magda, pulling the key from her apron pocket and fitting it in the lock. "I smelled her when they brought her in. She's a mess. And you'll not get her to take a bath. Witches dinna like water." She unlocked the door but didn't open it.

"Well, like it or not, she'll wash off the worst of that muck so we can look for the mark," Father Toddy said. "And it will take more water than this. Fetch another bucket or two and a washtub."

The serving girl lowered her eyes. "Yes, Father."

"Make it two buckets," the fiscal said. "Dawin here will help ye." He waited until they left before turning to Father Toddy.

"Yer sure this is necessary, Father? We could wait for the examiner."

"Aye." Father nodded. "Or we can find the proof we need and make their stay shorter. There's never just the one, ye ken, and they're paid by the day." He paused, considering. "Though, come to think, it's not the church's coffers the money comes from—it's the town's." He looked at the fiscal. "Maybe we should wait."

The fiscal blanched. "No, no," he said hastily. "We're already here, and Davy's said he'll spare us Magda a while. Let's just get it done."

He tugged open the door, swollen with humidity, wrinkling his nose at the smell of rotten food and human waste that greeted him. The pit had been used as a garbage heap and toilet when it wasn't being used to house inmates.

"Witch," he said, addressing the gray-haired wretch that huddled miserably between two kegs and a pile of boxes. "We're checking ye fer the devil's mark. I've a good God-fearing woman willing to do it out of Christian mercy and a group of men who'll gladly take over if ye give her a moment's trouble. Which will it be?"

"The woman," Annie croaked through a raspy throat.

The fiscal nodded to Magda.

"We'll say a prayer first," Father Toddy instructed, bowing his head.

Magda bowed her head as well and recited the words.

The witch didn't flinch or make a sound.

Dawin and the serving girl returned with the washtub and water. Two boxes had to be taken from the room and put in the hallway to make room for Magda and the washtub.

Finally, Magda was alone in the cramped room with Auld Annie. She placed a torn shift, cast-off gown, a sliver of harsh lye soap, and the stained bar towels for washing and drying on a box before loosing the string that held her hidden bundle in place.

"I've come to help ye," Magda told the old woman.

"Why?" The woman, who had stood when Dawin carried in the tub and buckets of cold water, now sank to the floor.

"Because I know ye dinna curse Lady Gwen."

Auld Annie shrugged. "It hardly matters." She cleared her throat. "I'll be hanged or drowned, burned or buried alive, whatever it is ye do to witches in this town."

"No," Magda protested. "Not if yer innocent."

"Are ye that naïve, girl, or are ye daft? Surely ye know that accused is guilty in cases of witchcraft."

Magda avoided meeting Auld Annie's eyes by bending to pick up the bundle from beneath her skirts.

The woman watched Magda untie the cord and lay out the food. "I was wrong," she finally said. "Yer just a kind thing, aren't ye?" She grabbed the chunk of bread and ripped at it with crooked teeth. She snatched up the cheese with her other hand and crammed it into her mouth, chewing hungrily.

Magda busied herself setting out the towels and soap while the old woman ate.

When Annie had finished her meal, she tugged off layers of soiled garments and piled them in a filthy heap until she stood in her ruined shift. It had been a serviceable one made of coarse linen that now held scents and stains that would never come clean. She undid what remained of her once-neat bun and laid a coil of thick gray hair over her left shoulder before wrenching off the clinging shift. The hair covered her left breast, but the pendulous right one hung like an empty flask.

Magda averted her eyes, wanting to give the woman some measure of privacy.

"This bath and change of clothes will be yer idea, yes?" Annie said, drawing Magda's attention, if not her eyes.

"I just couldna …" Magda began, but she didn't continue.

"Yer a good soul." Annie stepped into the shallow tub and wet herself with the cool water, shivering despite the stuffy heat of the storeroom. "I'll give ye a wish."

"Then I wish ye were found innocent and freed," Magda said, looking the woman in the eye.

Annie nodded, smiling to herself. "A rare good soul." She poured water over herself. Tiny rivers of water left tracks in the grime as they coursed their way down her flaccid stomach and bony legs. "I'll be found guilty, girl." She held out her hand for the soap. "What is yer name?"

Magda placed the bar in the old woman's hand. "Magda."

Annie nodded. "I'll be found guilty, Magda. It'll come out that I made summat for this one or that to prevent the bairn or cure a wart. And ye'll report this birthmark." She moved the coil of hair to reveal a penny-sized red mark on her left breast that would have been called a stork-bite on anyone not accused of witchcraft.

"I willna," Magda insisted, aghast.

"It willna matter if ye don't, except if they find out later. Then they'll say I bewitched ye, and they'll make ye and yer bairn pay." She soaped her body. "No, Magda. Give me a minute more to hear yer wish and then scream that I've a mark. Have yer uncle bless ye in front of the whole tavern and say a Patre Nostre loud and clear. That'll save ye sure."

"Couldna ye say a Patre Nostre and save yerself?"

"Nay, lass. I'm old. A few more seasons, and I'd be good as dead anyway. Let them have their fun. Death isna hard. It's over in an instant. Willna bother me in the least."

"But there must be something I can do?"

The old woman soaped her hair.

"Aye, and ye've done it. I'll grant ye a wish fer yerself then. Surely there's something ye be wanting?"

Magda shook her head.

"To be tall and fair-haired?"

Magda shook her head again. The poor woman was surely daft to think she could make Magda tall and fair-haired. "There's nothing I want but your freedom. I'm happy with me life." Magda used a bucket of clean water to help Auld Annie rinse off.

"Then ye'll keep the wish for later." Annie squeezed out her long gray hair and took the towel from Magda's hand. "Ye best hide yer bundle behind the box and then scream. It's time ye saw the mark."

Seeing the wisdom of concealing the food against sudden intrusion, Magda wrapped it back up and placed the bundle between two boxes, but she didn't scream. She wouldn't scream. She was here to help, not condemn the woman.

Annie seemed to understand. "Do it for yer bairn, Magda. Do it for me. I'll not get a chance to give ye yer wish if they burn ye alongside me."

Tears filled Magda's eyes. Annie was a sweet old woman who didn't deserve what was happening to her. "I canna." She wouldn't be the one to seal Annie's fate.

Annie put a damp hand on her sleeve. "Scream."

"Witch!" Magda screamed, shocking herself. "Witch!" The word erupted from her throat again, unbidden, like a compulsion. She stared uncomprehendingly at the smiling woman. "Witch!"

Annie nodded, pleased, as the storeroom door sprang open. The entire population of the pub was outside the door, craning their necks to see around Dawin, Father Toddy and the fiscal. Davy and the rest of the guard heard Magda and rushed into the pub.

Magda shouted "Witch!" once more before she regained control of her voice. As the compulsion left, she sagged against the wall, horrified by what she'd done. She huddled in a shivering heap, finally able to remain silent now that the damage was done. She couldn't look at Auld Annie. She felt ashamed as if she'd chosen this course. There was nothing she could say or do that would help the old woman now.

Davy elbowed his way through the crowd.

Annie faced the mob, defiant. She held the small towel in front of herself, shielding what she could. The cherry-red mark on her left breast shone like a beacon. She glared at the men.

Father Toddy cleared his throat and looked away from the nearly naked woman, nervous sweat sprouting on his brow. "It's the devil's mark to be sure." He plucked the cross from his chest and held it aloft. "In the name of The Lord God, Jesus Christ, I order ye back, bride of Satan."

Auld Annie laughed, but she stepped back.

"Take her soiled clothes and burn them," Father directed. "She may have charms secreted in them. And empty the tub. We'll leave no water for conjuring." When no one jumped to obey, he cautioned, "Be quick about it. I dinna know how long I can hold her at bay."

Dawin and two other men rushed to obey. Davy shoved his way into the room as well. He pulled Magda to his side and ushered her out.

"What happened?" he asked.

Someone answered for her. "The witch had a mark—the devil's face on her breast."

Davy searched Magda's pale face for answers. "Are ye all right then?"

"I'm fine," she said, blinking back tears.

Someone handed her a pint of ale. Someone else pulled up a chair. She sat, holding her drink with shaky hands.

Davy sat on his haunches in front of her, covering the cold hands that clutched the mug with his warm ones.

Magda's eyes burned into his with unspoken words.

Davy nodded. They'd talk later.

In a few minutes' time the tub was drained and the water gone, the storeroom door was locked and barred, and a lad was sent to the kirk to fetch rosaries and holy water to seal in the evil.

Father Toddy exchanged a glance with Davy when the boy returned.

"Come, Acorn," Davy said, taking the untouched pint from her hand and handing it off before pulling her to her feet. "Ye've a bit to do."

The crowd parted, and the couple returned to the storeroom door.

Father Toddy sprinkled Magda with holy water.

"God bless yer faithful servant, Magda, and her unborn child who, witnessing evil, remained pure in yer sight." Looking into her eyes, he pressed a rosary into her hand. As was expected, she brought the cross to her lips and kissed it.

"*Pater noster, qui es in caelis, sanctificetur nomen tuum. Adveniat regnum tuum. Fiat voluntas tua, sicut in caelo et in terra. Panem ...*" Everything seemed unreal. Magda heard herself recite the prayer in a clear, strong voice, but she felt disconnected—an actor in a role rather than a true participant.

She didn't feel normal through the entire door-sealing ceremony nor the strange reception afterwards. She didn't come out of her daze until she and Davy were walking home with a borrowed lantern held in Davy's hand to light the way.

"Did ye fix the hole?" she asked, holding his hand as they left the town. "I never thought to ask."

"Nay." He shook his head. "'Twasna worth the wood nor the effort. It would be like fixing a backhouse from below—had been used as one for too long to be anything else. Rory decided we'd dig a new one and was scouting the spot when ye called witch. Bless me if the hole dinna cave in just then. 'Twas the strangest thing."

They walked in wondering silence for a few minutes.

"What made ye call her a witch when ye were there to help her?"

Magda shrugged. "I dinna ken. I dinna mean to. It just came out. I saw the stork bite same as the rest, but I knew that's what it was. I was going to tell Father she was clean, but she wouldna have it. She ordered me to scream 'witch,' and somehow I couldna refuse. It was like a game with her. Said she dinna mind the dying and to let them have their fun. And she offered me a wish."

Davy stopped walking. "A wish? Does she fancy herself a witch then?"

Magda shrugged again. "I dinna ken, but I told her I was happy with my life and dinna want the wish."

"Well, that's good, then." He started walking again. "I'm happy with our life as well."

"And then she said a strange thing," Magda continued. "She said to keep the wish for later."

It took a couple of days for the examiners to arrive. Late Tuesday evening, the two clerics rode into Kirkinwall on a cart pulled by an overworked nag. The two stern-faced clerics were so portly they made Father Toddy look thin in comparison. They took residence at the fiscal's house while word of their arrival spread like wildfire.

Wednesday at noon, Auld Annie was pulled from the new thief hold for her trial. Despite her better judgment, Magda accompanied Davy to town.

"Ye'll be wanted as witness," he said.

"I trust they'll have witnesses a plenty. There's enough that saw the mark."

Magda didn't believe that Annie was the bride of Satan no matter what was said. She was an odd duck, no doubt a bit soft in the head, who knew about herbs, green medicines and forest lore like many of her generation. It was the fact that she'd not been born near Kirkinwall and had no man to stand for her that made her suspect.

Magda stood in the crowd with the rest, the sole compassionate face that Auld Annie would see had she looked up. The accused stood solidly on her feet between two armed men, not swaying with the hunger of days without food as Magda half expected, but rather looking bemusedly at Rob and the McClellan perched on their cushioned chairs beside the examiners.

It wasn't surprising that the trial was taking place in Kirkinwall square, nor was it a surprise that Laird Angus McClellan was at the trial since Auld Annie was being tried in the death of his sister, Gwen.

Angus refused to sit in judgment over Gwen's death. He clearly wanted to believe that his beloved sister's death had been the result of witchcraft instead of his brother-in-law's lust and Sanna's jealousy and greed. He'd ignored the rumors and sent men in search of a witch instead of blaming his best friend and that friend's new wife. His presence made Auld Annie's guilt almost a foregone conclusion, regardless of the examiner's proclamation. The line of witnesses recruited to testify against the poor soul would most likely never get a chance to speak.

Annie didn't spare them a glance.

Sanna came forward first, wrapped from head to toe in her husband's plaid so that not so much as a flash of color from her embroidered skirt or petticoat showed. She stood flanked by her mother and husband before the McClellan and the examiners.

She barely waited for the nod to begin before pointing at Auld Annie and announcing in a voice that turned heads. "There she is, the witch what killed poor Gwen and enchanted both Rob and me."

Sanna's mother interrupted, rushing to stand between her daughter and the wretched accused. She used her rounded body as a shield. "Please, sirs, my Sanna's in a family way and delicate. She shouldna be here with the witch. It isna safe."

A nervous rumble rose from the crowd as all eyes turned to the witch. Auld Annie stared at Sanna with a mild questioning look as if trying to figure out the chit's identity.

Sanna's eyes grew wide in feigned fright. "Dinna let her look at me. Please, dinna let her."

Rob stepped in front of Sanna, shielding her from Annie's view.

The crowd erupted in noisy speculation.

Angus McClellan rose from his cushioned seat and fingered the sword at his side. "That will be enough of that." His deep voice resonated through the crowd, stilling it. He turned to the accused. "Eyes down, witch, or I'll cut them out myself. We'll have no more bewitching here."

Annie gave him an insolent glare before turning her attention to the ragged hem of her dirty skirt.

"Sanna," Angus ordered, "continue."

Sanna came out from behind her husband, shaking. She was on trial as much as Auld Annie. "Ma and I were fetching water from the spring ..."

Sanna's mother interrupted again. "Auld Annie stopped me by the spring, telling me not to let Sanna go to the mill the day Rob came to collect the rents.

'Twas foolishness, so I sent the girl to see to the flour as always. Auld Annie stopped her on the way and stuck a cup in her hand, ordering her to drink it."

"Lizzy," the laird interrupted in a voice that was gentle, but firm. "I ken how worried ye are, but I'll be hearing it from Mistress Sanna."

Sanna nodded, pale-faced and nervous. She cleared her throat, squared her shoulders, and took a deep breath. "It's as Ma said. The witch stopped me and handed me a wooden cup, bidding me drink. I hadna been thirsty a moment before, but at her words I was dry as dirt." She shot a quick look at the McClellan to see how her story was playing thus far. His frown wasn't encouraging. She hurried on with the tale. "The liquid was bitter as sin. I wanted to spit it on the ground, but I couldna. Then, all of a sudden, me head felt thick and me ears rang. I could hear the old woman's voice in me head, saying words I dinna recognize but her lips never moved. I remember heading for the mill and then nothing 'til after I … er … we …" One glance at the laird's face, and she dropped to her knees. "'Twas witchcraft, sure. I wouldna … um … Rob wouldna." Her red face was pinched with agitation and wet with sweat. "We …" She swallowed hard and cried out. "It was the witch! 'Twas her curse that killed Gwen and her message that blamed the sweets."

She looked up at the laird, her hands clasped before her in petition, feeling as fearful as she had after she'd missed her courses two months running, as desperate as she'd been when she made the fruit cake, adding the ground pecans Rob's wife couldn't have.

"Half the castle ate that fruitcake." She glanced around at the crowd, her eyes pausing pleadingly on the castle residents. "All of ye ate from the basket and were fine. None got so much as a bellyache. But Lady Gwen, cursed by the witch, died writhing in agony with all of us, her loving friends and family, looking on, unable to do anything to ease her pain." She sobbed into her hands, desperate to cast her guilt onto the stupid old woman. "It was the witch."

For a long moment there was no sound but Sanna's sobbing.

Auld Annie started clapping her hands. "Well done, well done. Missed yer calling, ye did."

"Silence!" bellowed Angus McClellan.

One of the guards enforced the decree with a hard fist to Annie's stomach.

Lizzie rushed to her daughter's side, wrapping her arms around Sanna and easing her to her feet.

As his mother-in-law took care of his wife, Rob pointed to the gaping, breathless Annie. "Aye, she's a witch," he told the examiners, but he was looking at his brother-in-law, the laird. "She was jealous of Sanna's youth and beauty. She tricked her into drinking a potion that made her irresistible to the next man she saw and ripe for his seed. I would never have taken her else; ye know how much I loved yer sister. I've been a faithful husband and father these eighteen years. Fathered the three lasses. I'd not risk our love nor yer disfavor for a roll in the hay, no matter how comely the chit, but for the spell. And it was a spell, for not more than an hour had passed when the witch come up to me and told me I'd got a son on Sanna."

Angus McClellan addressed the examiners. "Ye've heard the testimony. Make yer decision."

Standing in the shelter of her mother's arms, Sanna sagged in relief.

One of the examiners, more concerned with garnering another day's stay in Kirkinwall than with dispensing any kind of justice, looked pointedly at the people lined up to testify. "There's more as want to have a say."

"If what ye've heard isna enough, then listen to some more," Angus said flippantly. "John Drover," he called to a man in the middle of the line. "Tell yer tale."

John had been prepared to say that Annie was a white witch, a wise woman who warned his sons to keep the sheep clear of the caves north of the swollen burn the day of the rockslide, but seeing the way his laird was leaning, he quickly changed his mind. "She has powers to be sure," he said, sweating. "Called a rockslide what buried several caves my sons and me used to shelter the sheep during storms."

"And dinna forget the devil's mark," a man who'd been in the pub Sunday night said. "Saw it with me own eyes, same as everyone."

Another man, thin and bowed, wearing a yellowed shirt, elbowed his way to the front of the line and then leaned heavily on a crooked staff. "She cursed me wife, she did." He pointed his stick at Annie. "Told me to dig my missus' grave deep, and me wife there in the croft making dinner. Said, dig it deep and dig it quick or me Jenny would become a haunt. The next day me Jenny fell to the floor making the bread." He covered his face with a large-knuckled hand. "The witch had cursed her dead."

A greasy-haired wench with freckles that Magda recognized as one of the older McNabb girls moved backwards in the crowd, obviously deciding not to testify after all. With the laird against Annie, no one with half a mind would be for her. So if Annie had helped the McNabb girls keep their whiskey-soaked father from touching them, it was best kept silent, lest something worse happen.

"She turned my sister into a rabbit," Dawin announced, only to be cuffed by his commanding officer.

Sanna hid her smile, wondering why she'd been so worried.

"His sister Betsy ran off with James Campbell, sir," Rory reminded the McClellan.

Angus McClellan nodded. He'd received the bride price from the Campbells.

"Well, if there is no one else," he said, in a tone that suggested he'd heard enough. "I believe ye can make yer judgment."

The two examiners put their heads together for a moment to confer.

The crowd erupted in excited chatter, all offering suggestions.

"She should be hanged for her crimes."

"Bury her alive!"

"Burn the witch!"

Magda held her breath, praying for a miracle. Davy pulled her close. It had been a mistake to let her come. Magda had always been softhearted and more so now that she was breeding. Watching the witch die would upset her. He started to lead her off toward home.

Before they'd gone more than a few steps, the examiners shared a nod of agreement and separated. "We'll test her by water."

"No," Magda mouthed in silent protest. Anyone who defended the old woman now would likely share her fate.

Magda pulled Davy's sleeve so that he lowered his head to her level. "Tell her I'm sorry."

Davy shook his head. "It's not yer fault, Acorn."

"Tell her I'll pray for her."

"Wouldna help. She's as good as dead."

"She needs to know somebody cares."

"I'll tell her nothing, and neither will you. We're going home. I should not have let ye come in the first place."

"No." Magda dug in her heels. "Leave if ye must, but I'll see it through. I willna let her die alone."

Davy rolled his eyes. Not much chance of the poor thing spending a moment alone until they tossed her in the loch bound crossways thumbs to big toes. Even now someone had brought a rope.

The crowd moved around them, sweeping them along to the loch south of town. The examiners and audience watched as John the locksman trussed her like a Sunday partridge. One of the fat examiners shouted a brief explanation, though everybody knew that if the water rejected her and she floated, she'd be burned as a witch. Only the innocent sank. Unfortunately, by the time that innocence was established, the person had usually drowned.

Auld Annie was dragged to the end of the dock and pushed into the water with a big splash.

Silence reigned temporarily as people jockeyed for a view of the dark water. Sanna was amongst them, trying unsuccessfully to hide her smug grin. When Annie didn't surface right away, a few began speculating her innocence. After several minutes, when the surface had calmed, John the locksman was directed to pull the poor innocent from the dark water. He yanked on the rope he'd attached to one of Annie's ankles for this purpose, and it came springing out of the water, flying through the air in a shower of droplets.

It took a moment for the meaning to sink in.

Annie wasn't on the other end as she should have been. Several fishermen jumped in to look for her, but they came up empty handed.

Sanna turned pale as death.

Auld Annie was gone.

Magda had a hard time getting to sleep that night, and then she was plagued with dreams. She sat up in bed, hugging her knees in the darkness.

"Tell me about them," Davy encouraged, rubbing her back until she relaxed enough to lean into him. He hoped that talking about her dreams would allow her to settle down.

Magda stared into the darkness, wrapping Davy's arms around her tightly.

"It's as if I am under the water seeing her. It's dark and cold, but she doesna seem to mind it. She laughs at the people on the dock. She disappears a moment. I think I must have blinked in my dream, because she's back in an instant. She tells me she knows just what to give me, what wish to fulfill, and then she's gone. She doesna fade. She just disappears." Magda pressed against Davy. "I'm afraid," she whispered. "I dinna make a wish, but she thinks I did. She's going to do something—change something—and I dinna want her to. I'm happy with me life."

"I know ye are. I'm happy with our life too. But, Acorn, it was just a dream, nothing more. It wasna a vision. Ye were not under the water with her. It was just a dream. Ye'll laugh come morning when ye wake up and everything is the same."

Magda nodded, shifting to rest her head against Davy's chest. "I'm sure yer right," she said, praying that he was.

"Of course, I am. Now try to get some sleep."

He slid down the headboard, pulling her with him until they were both lying down again. He kissed her hair and held her close.

She forced herself to relax against his warm bulk. She lay still, listening to his breathing as he drifted off to sleep.

She must have slept as well, because she awakened later with the premonition that whatever would happen would come with the storm. The wind was blowing outside their cottage, calling the storm to them. She felt it, like the gathering of power, with rising fear.

Magda slid from the bed and went to the window. The air had cooled from the day, and she felt chilled.

"It's early, Magda. Come back to bed." Davy's voice called to her from the warmth of the lumpy bed they'd shared.

Magda shivered in the darkness, pushing the wooden shutter open to stare into the night. "It's coming, Davy. I can feel it."

"The babe?" he asked, concerned. The ropes of the bed squeaked in protest as he rose. He swiftly covered the few feet to the window and his wife. "Surely not. It's too early."

Magda turned into her husband's arms, resting her cheek against his bare chest. "It's not the babe—it's the storm."

Davy squeezed his woman tightly. "Come to bed, lass. It's rained other nights. This one will be no worse. It's thoughts of Auld Annie keeping ye up. Dinna fash yerself. She was no more a witch than you or me—water test aside. There's no winning with them tests. Float and burn—or sink and drown. And she sunk. That means she was innocent."

Magda shook her head. "They dinna find her body."

"I'll admit that was odd." Davy bent his neck to kiss his wife's curly head. "But I dinna believe in witches and neither do you. 'Twas nonsense, her offering ye a wish. She can no more grant one than yer uncle Father can."

"I ken that," she agreed, although not convinced. She wasn't sure why she was worried. No one could grant the type of wishes Auld Annie suggested. No one could make her tall and blond or do anything that outlandish. Magda *knew* that. And yet, she was afraid.

"Auld Annie was touched in the head, but she wasna a witch." He gave her a brief squeeze. "Now stop this nonsense and come back to bed." With one arm wrapped around his round wife, he reached the other out to pull the wooden shutter closed before guiding her back to bed.

Once they were in bed, she snuggled next to him. "Love me," she said, pulling him close. "Love me, like it's the last time."

"Oh, I'll love you, woman," he insisted gruffly, sliding his hands up her body from knee to pregnant belly to full breasts and higher, dragging her night rail over her head. "But it'll not be the last." He pressed her into the husk-stuffed mattress.

# Chapter 2

# New York, New York 2002

Waiting for the minute hand to reach twelve, Maggie McDonald checked her watch for the fifth time in as many minutes. She sighed as she read its face. There were still nine long minutes to go until three o'clock. She bent her head back over her book and forced herself to reread the first paragraph again. It was futile. She couldn't keep her mind on the words long enough to understand an entire paragraph. She closed the book with a snap and tossed it onto the coffee table in front of her.

Maybe David was wrong, and the bronze would be hot enough to pour before three. Maybe her watch was slow. Deciding to check, she grabbed the handle of the flute case sitting beside her chair.

She tried to walk slowly, patiently, to her husband's studio in the back of the brownstone, but that, too, was futile. In less than a minute, she was tucking the case beneath one arm and tugging open the studio's heavy fire door. Instantly, the distinctive scent of hot bronze floating on a wave of heat greeted her. She shivered once as her body tried to adjust to the change in temperature. Smiling, she pushed the door closed and filled her lungs with the wonderful metallic-scented air. It didn't take more than a moment or two for tiny drops of sweat to form on her body and cause her crisp cotton blouse to begin to wilt.

David stood next to the smelting furnace on the far end of the large concrete studio. Dressed from head to toe in heat-resistant material with his head hidden beneath a welder's helmet, he looked more like a foundry worker than an artist, but that was part of the attraction. Working with bronze did more than yield art and add calluses to his hands and extra definition to his muscles; it was an extension of who he was. He brought the same patience, attention to detail, and passion to every aspect of his life.

Although David couldn't possibly have heard the door over the roar of the furnace and steady drone of exhaust fans, somehow he knew the instant Maggie arrived and turned toward her. Lifting the front of his helmet, he took in her tall, lithe form, appreciating the view as he crossed the room, pulling off his gloves as he went.

Maggie met him halfway, smiling up at him as she touched the front of his heavy leather apron.

"Couldn't wait, huh?" he asked, though the answer was obvious. She never could. She needed to be with him as much as he needed her there. It wasn't just the art.

"How hot is it?" she asked. Bronze melts at 1,850 degrees, but David refused to pour it until it was fully liquid and the thermometer read 2,150. Maggie had a hard time waiting, which was why she'd been trying to read in the living room instead of pacing the studio while David did the preparations.

In a lot of ways, David saw the final casting in bronze as a birth. A sculpture that began as an idea had moved slowly from sketch to model to rubber mold and wax casting, until eventually the ceramic shell was ready for the bronze. And while this birth into bronze wasn't the last step in the process, it was the most dramatic one. Maggie had been with him every step of the way. It was necessary that she be there when he poured.

"Two thousand." He took her hand in his automatically, unable to stand so close and not touch her.

"So … I'm late."

He smiled, absently caressing her knuckles with his thumb. "Later than usual." She usually arrived just as the bronze began to melt and pestered him to check the temperature every few minutes.

She squeezed his hand. "Go check."

He laughed. Still, he released her hand and turned back to the forge, pulling on his gloves as he went. The soft clang of his visor closing was lost in the midst of the ambient noise. He checked the gauge and turned to give Maggie the thumbs up, waiting until she uncased her flute on the large worktable below the skylight before he flipped off the burner.

Maggie blew the first notes of the sculpture's birthing song as David tightened the mold on the centrifuge and began to pour. The hiss of liquid bronze filling the mold joined the song. The sounds played together. The flute's melody seemed to add life and depth to the bronze, as if it were giving the golden liquid a soul as it took its new form. She played while the centrifuge spun into life, distributing the bronze to the sculpture's every hair, its every pore. She played while David shut down the machines and disrobed, hanging his protective gear on their hooks along the wall.

The flute called to him as he left his sculpture glowing red hot in its ceramic shell and crossed the room to her. It provided the soundtrack as he slowly peeled away her sweat-dampened clothes, but ended as he lowered her to the floor. A different kind of music replaced that of the flute, and a different fire kindled and burned as the newly born sculpture slowly cooled.

Days later, Maggie was on stage at Lincoln Center putting her flute in its case when her cell phone vibrated against her hip. She pulled it out of her skirt pocket and flipped it open.

"Is practice over?" Her husband's rich voice filled her ear, and she thought, for the thousandth time, how he could have been a radio announcer as easily as he was a sculptor.

"Just." She snapped the flute case closed and waved good-bye to a clarinetist friend. "How's your day been? Did Mr. Frank like *The Hunter*?"

"He loved it. Said I captured Sheba down to the last hair on her tail."

"That's wonderful! Where do you want to go to celebrate?"

"The clinic. Our results came in, and we are perfect candidates for that gamete *in vitro* procedure. They want to check your estrogen levels and get you started on Pergonal. They have an appointment in 45 minutes if we can make it."

"Forty-five minutes?" The list of errands she'd planned for that afternoon sped through her mind only to be discarded. They'd waited too long for the go-ahead to let anything get in the way. "I'll meet you in the waiting room."

"I love you."

Seven years of marriage hadn't diminished the warm glow those three little words brought to Maggie's heart.

"I love you too, David."

An hour and a half later, Maggie sat on the paper-covered examining table, wearing the clinic's thin cotton wrapper and trying not to fidget.

David rose briefly from his seat to squeeze her hand reassuringly.

Maggie smiled weakly in response. There was no need to be nervous. They'd all but been accepted into the program. Still, she had the desperate feeling that this was the last resort—that if this didn't work, nothing would.

The door opened to the knock of an elderly nurse in brightly colored scrubs. Her long gray hair was wound into a bun at the back of her head. She glanced at the clipboard in her hands.

"Seven years?" the nurse asked abruptly. "Ye've been wishing a long time for this bairn."

The nurse's heavy brogue took Maggie by surprise. That and her bedside manner. Normally healthcare professionals introduced themselves and made small talk before asking personal questions. This nurse hadn't done either. Worse, she was now looking at Maggie as if she required a more thorough answer.

"Well, ah …" Maggie stuttered. "We married young and didn't really try for several years. We didn't use anything to prevent a baby, though, either. We just figured I'd get pregnant, but it never happened."

"We've really only been actively trying for a year," David explained from his seat in the molded plastic chair next to the wall.

"Yer both twenty-seven," the nurse said, looking at the chart. "I'd imagine ye'd both give just aboot anything to have a bairn."

"Uh … yes," David said, hesitantly. This nurse's bedside manner was certainly lacking. She'd been abrupt and was now asking obvious questions. After all, they were in a fertility clinic about to spend thousands of dollars to become pregnant. Their desire wasn't really an issue. He looked at her nametag and changed the subject. "Uh, Annie, you have an interesting accent. Where are you originally from?"

The nurse smiled. "I hail from Scotland mostly. You come from there too originally."

David looked puzzled.

"Oh," Maggie said. "McDonald. David, she must mean your ancestors."

David shrugged. "I never really thought about it, but I guess they came from Scotland."

The nurse nodded. "Now then, this isna an easy thing yer wanting. Some's not meant to have children every lifetime, but if it be yer wish, and if yer willing to give up a bit of each other fer a while, I've a way to grant it."

She patted Maggie's stomach and abruptly exited.

Maggie and David exchanged confused glances.

"She was certainly … different," Maggie said.

"Different?" David stared at his wife in disbelief. "Nuts is more like it. 'If yer willing to give up a bit of each other?' What did that mean?"

Maggie shrugged. "I don't know. Maybe she's talking about the procedure. I'll have to stay in the hospital overnight. Or maybe she means after the baby is born."

"Who knows?" David shook his head. "I wonder how many patients she scares off with her demeanor," He snorted. "'I've a way to grant it!' Like she has some sort of magic."

A knock on the door, and a middle aged, heavy-set nurse came in wheeling an ultra-sound machine.

"Mr. and Mrs. McDonald, I'm Kayla, Dr. Angelo's nurse. How are you today?"

This nurse was all business, taking Maggie's vitals and asking the sort of things David and Maggie had expected from the first nurse.

"Do you have any questions?" Kayla asked.

"Will you be our usual nurse?" David asked. "No offense, but that other nurse, Annie, was a bit odd."

"Annie?" Kayla frowned. "Are you sure that was her name? We have an Amy, but she's off today. When did you speak with her?"

"Just before you came in," Maggie said, sharing an anxious look with David. "She was an old Scottish woman. Her name tag said, 'Annie.'"

"That's odd," Kayla said. "Did she examine you or anything?"

Maggie shook her head. "She just asked us some questions and …" Maggie shot a quick embarrassed look at her husband "… said she'd grant our wish."

"Grant your wish? Well, I hope we *can* grant your wish for a child. That's what we're here for. And the results of gamete intrafallopian transfer or GIFT are fairly promising—between 16 and 24 percent of those having the procedure end up conceiving babies. I certainly hope that you are among that percentage, but there is no guarantee. I want you to know that."

She'd already explained the procedure: the Pergonal regimen to promote the ripening of multiple eggs to be harvested, the semen sample that would be spun in a centrifuge to separate out the sperm, and then the implantation of both sperm and eggs into Maggie's fallopian tubes to fertilize there.

"It's a sound medical procedure that has had good results," Kayla continued. "And while full-term pregnancies and healthy babies are our goals for every couple, it is not something we can guarantee, no matter how hard we wish it."

"We understand," David said.

Kayla nodded. "That's good. Now, if you don't have any more questions, I'll go look for this Annie. The doctor should be in to see you in just a few minutes."

They picked up gyros and salad on the way home. The old house, tucked in between high-rise apartment buildings, was both their home and David's studio. The living room and entryway doubled as a small gallery devoted to David's work. Bronze children flew kites, read books, skipped ropes, and observed goldfish, while a bronze old man fed pigeons from a park bench. Each sculpture contained an acorn, David's signature mark, incorporated into the piece. Many also had oak leaves worked in, perhaps tucked in the grass or resting on a bench or shore.

As she passed through the living room on the way to the kitchen, Maggie ran her hand over the head of a petite curly-haired girl playing a flute while standing among the acorns and oak leaves. It was her favorite. David teased her that it was her surrogate child, though with Maggie's straight hair and long lean lines, the only thing about the statue that could be likened to Maggie was the flute.

"We'll get one of those pretty soon," David assured her.

Maggie purposely misinterpreted his comment. "We've a houseful of bronze children already," she protested.

He came up behind her, wrapping his arms around her waist. "You know what I mean."

"I know," she sighed, turning in his arms. "I can't help thinking about what Annie said about how not everybody is meant to have children."

"The woman was a nut. She said in every lifetime, too, if I remember correctly. Don't think about her or what she said." He kissed her forehead before releasing her to put the bag of gyros on the counter. "Dr. Angelo sounded encouraging, don't you think? He said that we're perfect candidates with our age and health. He seemed surprised that we hadn't gotten pregnant on our own since there's no physical reason why we couldn't. You have regular cycles, and the doctor assured me that my little guys are quite active." He got plates down from the cupboard and arranged the food on them. "I think this GIFT is going to do the trick. We're going to be one of the ones who get a baby." He looked at his wife and grinned suggestively. "Now that we know there's nothing holding us back, maybe we should postpone dinner and see if we can get pregnant the old-fashioned way."

A week later, Maggie was flat on her back having her eggs harvested. David stood beside the table, holding her hand.

"You don't have to be in here for this," she told him, feeling uncomfortable with her feet in stirrups as Dr. Angelo checked the ultrasound he would use to guide the needle used for harvesting the eggs.

"Yes, I do," David insisted. "I want to be with you every step of the way."

Maggie snorted. "You just want me to help you get your sample later."

He grinned wickedly.

"I need you," David cajoled. "A guy can always use a helping hand."

Three hours later, Maggie was being prepared for laparoscopic surgery.

"I'll see if they're ready for us and be right back," Kayla told the couple.

"I hope this works," Maggie said.

David squeezed her hand.

"Dinna fash yerself. It will." Annie appeared at David's elbow, wearing surgical scrubs. "It's still yer wish, isna, Magda?"

"It's Maggie," Maggie said.

"It's Maggie now," Annie said. "'Twasna always."

"Who are you?" David asked, looking around for a call button. "Are you supposed to be here?"

"Only if ye still wish to have a bairn." Annie put her hand on Maggie's arm. "It is still yer wish, isna, Magda?"

Maggie decided to humor the old woman and not correct the name again. "It's why we're here." She covered Annie's hand with her own. "But, Annie, why are you here?"

The old woman grinned. "Why, I owe ye a wish, dinna I? And no one will ever say Auld Annie doesna keep her vows."

"You don't owe us anything," David said.

"I owe Magda a wish and 'tis only now she'd tell me what she wanted. It will take a bit of doing, but ye said ye were willing to be parted a while to get the child." She grinned at Maggie. "Kiss yer man good now, Maggie, and know that when ye return to him, ye'll be with child."

"Uh … thank you," Maggie said, uncertainly. Annie was calling her Maggie again. She wondered why.

"Yer welcome, lass. Ye've always been the good sort, and I've been around long enough to know. Not many risk giving me comfort, but ye did. I'm glad to be granting ye this wish."

Kayla came in the room just then with another nurse.

"We're ready for you, Mrs. McDonald." She unlocked the bed's brake. "Mr. McDonald, you can go to the waiting room. I'll come get you when she's in recovery."

David was about to mention Annie, but when he turned to point her out ... she was gone. He shrugged it off—the old woman was strange, but harmless. She'd probably slipped out when the nurses arrived. The important thing now was kissing his wife good-bye.

He gave her a lingering kiss. "I love you, Maggie." He noticed the worried look in her eye, and he knew that Annie's visit had bothered her. He squeezed his wife's hand. "Everything will be all right. We're making a baby!"

She snorted a laugh. "I think I like doing it the old-fashioned way better."

"Everybody does," Kayla chuckled. "But sometimes this way is more efficient." She patted Maggie's shoulder. "Don't worry, Mrs. McDonald. This doesn't take very long, and you'll see your husband when you wake up."

Maggie was nervous as the anesthesiologist explained that she would be lightly sedated and might remember disjointed things later, but there would be no pain during the procedure and minimal pain after.

Oddly enough, she was less worried about whether or not the procedure would work and more concerned about what Annie had said. Who was Annie? How had she gotten in? And what about the separation she'd mentioned? The length of the procedure was too short to be termed a separation. Maggie routinely spent far longer in rehearsals than the operation would take.

She heard the anesthesiologist tell her to count backwards from one hundred.

"One hundred, ninety-nine, ninety-eight ..." She drifted into oblivion, still pondering Annie's strange words.

# Chapter 3

Maggie woke up to the feeling of her husband's big warm hand on her belly and a strange bumping and rolling inside her. She stiffened in fear. What was it?

"I wondered how long it would be 'til ye woke. Our son's a might active this morning. His kicking woke me up."

Maggie's eyes shot open at the sound of the stranger's voice. She jerked away from him. The bed rustled and squeaked noisily. Maggie froze, panicked. She was in bed with a strange man! She'd been in the hospital and now she was—

She looked around the dimly lit room. Now she was in a cabin. How did she get here? Where was David? She closed her eyes, willing herself to be calm. This was a dream, an anesthesia-produced dream. In a moment she'd wake up in the hospital bed with nurses and monitors and David standing at her side.

"What's the matter, Acorn? Your heart's racing like a captive bird's. Did ye have a bad dream again?"

Maggie opened her eyes again. She was still in the cabin. Pale morning light seeped around the shutters of a single window, barely illuminating the room that had refused to become the hospital room she'd hoped for. From her place in the bed, Maggie could see the window, a large wooden chest next to the wall and a rocking chair. It wasn't a dream. She scrambled from the bed as best she could with her unfathomably enormous belly only to discover she was naked. She grabbed the rough, linen sheet from the bed and covered herself, shaking. "Who are ye? Where am I?" she croaked.

Davy looked into his wife's eyes, startled to find them wide with terror. "It's me, Magda, yer husband, Davy, and yer home. Did ye have a bad dream?"

Maggie shook her head, backing away. This man was not her husband. He was huge—a giant with dark, scraggly hair that passed his broad shoulders. He was tall, at least a foot taller than she was, maybe two, and built. Not body builder built, just strong, hard working, could-beat-you-to-a-pulp-without-even-trying built. His arms and legs were like tree trunks. His chest was covered with a thick mat of dark, curly hair just like elsewhere—and she could see elsewhere since the man wasn't wearing a stitch of clothing either.

No, this man was definitely *not* her husband, and she wasn't letting him near her. She didn't stop her retreat until she backed into the wardrobe.

"My name is Maggie." She forced the words out of her cramped throat. "Maggie McDonald."

"This isna funny, Magda," Davy scolded as worry tightened his gut. He grabbed his plaid from the top of the chest and wrapped it around his waist, never taking his eyes off his wife.

"I'm not Magda," Maggie whispered.

"Aye, ye are," he said, slowly rounding the bed.

Maggie clutched the sheet, looking around frantically for an escape. She dashed diagonally into the room, tripping over a trailing end of the sheet as she put a rocking chair between herself and the man.

Davy stopped. "Hush now, lass. I'm not going to hurt ye."

"Stay where ye are," Maggie directed.

"Aye, I will, just dinna be dashing around like that. You're like to hurt yerself and the bairn."

"The bairn?" she repeated, wild-eyed.

"Aye, Magda. Dinna ye remember yer carrying our bairn?"

Maggie looked down at herself. Waist-length, curly brown tresses framed a large, pregnancy-swollen, sheet-covered belly that obstructed her view of her feet. She blinked at her abdomen in disbelief.

She was pregnant.

This was most certainly a dream.

She grabbed a handful of the dream hair that hung past her waist and pulled. "Ouch." It was firmly connected, that was for sure. But how? Her hair was short and honey blond. She swayed on her feet.

Davy caught her before she hit the floor. Muttering a string of Gaelic curses, he carried her back to the bed. He settled her there, more worried than he'd admit even to himself, and wondered what was going on. It wasn't like Magda to make a fuss for fun. He stared at his wife, swallowing heavily. She'd been worried last night about dreams and Auld Annie. Maybe this was another dream, and she wasn't quite awake.

He tucked the sheet firmly around her before pulling her into his lap and holding her securely. It wouldn't do to have her dashing about in a daze. He thought it best to hold her still until she was settled and herself again.

Maggie awakened with a jolt and a yelp.

"Hush, now," Davy soothed. "Yer all right."

Maggie struggled, fighting the strong arms that held her. "Let me go."

"I'll not have ye thrashing about nor dashing around bumping into things. Yer not quite yerself this morning, and until we've talked, ye will stay right here."

Maggie fought against the man despite the pointlessness of it. She was smaller and much rounder than normal, and he was even bigger than her muscular, six-one husband. She rammed her head into his chin, earning an earful of what first sounded like gibberish. But then, oddly, the words had meaning as if her ears were accustomed to hearing that language even though she wasn't. She found, strangely enough, that she knew the words to answer him in the same language. It was that, as much as the futility of escape, that quieted Maggie.

"I'm not yer wife," she whispered emphatically. The sound of her voice was odd to her ears. It was pitched higher than her own, and accented with a thick Scottish burr. She said "yer" when she meant "your." And, strangely enough, she seemed to be bilingual.

"I dinna know, Magda Mary," he said, trying to cajole her out of it. "You look like my sweet brown acorn ripe enough to burst."

"But I'm not. My name isna Magda. It's Maggie."

Puzzled, Davy narrowed his eyes. What game was this? "Maggie, huh?" he repeated, smiling as he decided to play along. "And what does me sweet Maggie want?" he asked, kissing her hair.

*Oh, God. He thinks I'm playing some kind of sex game,* she realized, panicking anew. "I want ye to let me go. This isna a game," she insisted, pushing at his arms. "I'm truly not yer Magda. I'm truly Maggie McDonald." Her voice caught as tears began to fall. "Please, please believe me," she begged, sobbing.

Davy froze, holding Maggie as she struggled and sobbed. "Blessed Mother," he prayed under his breath. What was going on?

"Please, please, let me go," Maggie begged.

"Hush, lass," he whispered to her. What did she say her name was? "Hush, Maggie. I swear I'll not hurt ye."

"Please, please, let me go," she repeated.

"I will, but ye must promise to stay on the bed."

"Let me go!" Maggie thrashed in his arms, pummeling him with her fists until he caught her hands and stilled them.

"Bless us," he prayed reflexively. "Are ye a changeling?" The thought chilled him.

"A changeling?" She knew that a changeling was. It was, supposedly, a fairy left in a human's place. Not that she believed it. This man didn't look fey, and she certainly wasn't. Which left … what? A dream? A nightmare? Insanity? "No." She fought against the thought with renewed vigor.

He tightened his grip. "Now stop yer thrashing, fairy."

"I'm not a fairy!"

"As ye say. Still, it's me wife's body yer wearing and me bairn inside of ye. I'll not have ye tearing around the room."

Maggie stilled, shoving down her panic long enough to look at herself. She couldn't deny the truth of his words. This wasn't her body. She wasn't petite or brown-haired or pregnant. She was tall, slim, blond and thus far barren.

"How?" She couldn't formulate a more detailed question with her mind in a panic.

"That I dinna ken, though I've a thought or two," Davy said, looking Maggie in the eye.

Maggie waited expectantly, but Davy merely stared at her.

"Are ye going to let me go?"

"Ye've not given yer word."

"All right," Maggie sniffed. "If ye let me go, I promise to sit still on the bed while we talk."

"All right then," he said, releasing her.

She awkwardly pulled away from him. It was difficult to move wrapped in a sheet, and her body was too round for her to maneuver as she'd like and remain covered. She'd promised to stay on the bed, and since the bed wasn't all that large, she could only pull away a few inches. Even then she had to fight not to slide back to his side. The problem was the bed itself. The mattress, stuffed with leaves or hay or something like it, was suspended from the wooden frame by a series of knotted ropes. It sagged wherever Davy sat, and Maggie had to struggle to keep out of the swale. In the end, she opted to sit on the wooden bed frame to maintain the separation.

The silence grew heavy as Davy watched her move as far from him as she could.

"Are ye settled then?" he asked when she'd succeeded in leveraging herself onto the bed frame.

She frowned at him, trying to ignore the knotted ropes pressing against her backside. "I thought ye were going to tell me what happened. How I got here."

Davy returned her frown. "I said I've thoughts about it, that's all."

She nodded. "Then let's hear them."

Davy shook his head. "Best not. Ye'll think me daft."

"Right," she replied sarcastically. "I'm God-knows where, sitting in a strange man's bed discussing why I seem to be in his wife's body. I think this whole thing is crazy or a dream. Or more likely I'm having an allergic reaction to the anesthetic and David is worried sick."

"David'll be yer husband, then?"

She nodded. "And if I'm with ye, then maybe yer Magda is with him. Think about that as ye hold me prisoner. Would ye want Magda held captive, dressed in nothing but a sheet?"

Davy frowned. "I'll not let ye run away with me wife and child, nor will I let ye harm them."

Maggie stilled. "Somehow I dinna think running from ye will get things back to normal." Tears filled her eyes. "I don't know if anything will. I willna hurt yer wife's body. It might not be mine, but right now I'm in it, and I feel everything it does." Tears spilled down her cheeks as she caressed her hard abdomen. "And I've tried too long to get pregnant to ever hurt a bairn."

"Did ye wish for a bairn, then?" He ached to take her into his arms and comfort her. Maggie or not, she looked like his Magda, and the sound of her tears tore at his heart.

She nodded. "Ye sound like that crazy nurse, Annie. She talked about me wishing for a bairn as well. Not wanting, just wishing."

"Annie?" Davy's gut twisted. His hands fisted in his kilt, and his voice grew in volume. "Ye ken Auld Annie?"

Maggie's eyes widened with fear at the vehemence of his tone.

"Ye ken Auld Annie?" he repeated, more quietly.

"I met a crazy old Scots woman named Annie two times."

"And she talked to ye about wishes?"

"Aye."

"And ye took one?" His eyes were crazed, angry and raw with pain. Maggie flinched at his words.

"David and I were at the fertility clinic ..." she explained, giving him the story verbatim as well as she could while he listened in confusion. "We thought she was crazy—harmless, but crazy. We never dreamed ..."

David had told her that Annie was harmless and not to worry, just as Davy had told Madga.

"We were wrong," Davy said, closing his eyes.

Struck by the despair in Davy's voice, Maggie leaned closer. "Who was wrong?"

"Yer David and I. We told ye she dinna have the power, and we were wrong. She gave Madga a wish for helping her, but Magda wouldna take it. She told Annie that she liked her life, dinna want to be tall and fair-haired, dinna want anything, but Annie told her to keep the wish and use it later."

"I'm tall and fair-haired," Maggie said, stunned. "Not now, of course." She fingered the rich brown locks. "But I was." She looked into Davy's pained eyes. "And she called me Magda."

"Who?" His voice was soft, deep, and tightly controlled.

"Annie. She called me Magda and told me she'd grant my wish for a child, but that it would mean David and I would be apart for a while. I thought she meant during the fertilization procedure. I dinna think this." She looked at the room and her belly. "I never imagined this."

Davy nodded, sliding from the bed. "Ye'll be wanting to get dressed, no doubt." He took a dress from a peg on the wall and laid it on the bed without looking at her.

"I'm sorry," Maggie said, feeling as if she'd stolen Davy's wife so that she could have their child. "I wanted my own child, not hers."

Davy looked at her then. "I ken that, lass. Dinna fash, Maggie. Ye dinna ken what the auld witch was about." Davy began to close the door behind himself. "No one did."

Alone, Maggie scrambled out of bed before turning her focus to her pregnant belly. She unwrapped the sheet and touched herself. Her abdomen was firm, almost hard, not soft as she had somehow expected. She could feel an extra firmness along one side and wondered what part of the baby was pressing there. She caressed herself and the baby within. The baby moved, and Maggie gave a startled laugh. This is what she'd longed for. She wished David were here to feel it as well, to feel their child.

She stopped abruptly, removing her hands from her belly. This was Magda and Davy's child, not her and David's. She felt like a thief. She stopped looking at the lush body she was in and scrambled into the long dress Davy had gotten out. She managed the layers with an ease that shook her. The body she was in was familiar with things her own wasn't. That realization was almost more than she could handle.

Dashing tears from her eyes, Maggie looked around the room. There was a queer dichotomy to everything. Things were comfortably familiar and frighteningly different at the same time. Part of her knew what was in each drawer before she pulled it open. Her hands automatically went to work remaking the bed while her mind was still shocked that the mattress was stuffed with straw and suspended from the bed frame by taut rope. Her hands found her shoes next to the wall by the head of the bed, not beneath the bed or in the wardrobe where she'd have looked for them if she had thought about it.

Maggie knew right where the mirror was and turned toward it without thinking, but she had no idea how she knew. Everything was familiar to her body, but none of it was familiar to her mind.

There was an instant of recognition when she looked into the mirror followed by a much longer period of discovery.

"Yer beautiful," she whispered to her reflection. The woman in the mirror was petite and pixie-like with fine features. She had eyes the color of fresh-dipped chocolates—a rich and shiny brown. They stared at Maggie with a mixture of fear, guilt, and admiration. Maggie blinked, and the woman in the mirror did the same. Long sable eyelashes, which always seemed to be wasted on handsome boys, brushed the ridge of her eyebrows. Maggie smoothed her fingers over finely arched eyebrows and knew that they had never seen tweezers and didn't need to. She touched her well-defined jaw from the delicate ears that lay close to her head to the slightly pointed chin. Maggie stared at the beautiful, expressive face, touching the small nose that turned up slightly at the end. She wondered what Magda would think of the face she now wore.

A knock on the door interrupted her thoughts.

"Are ye all right?" Davy asked through the door, obviously concerned that she was taking so long.

"Aye," she answered, the change in speaking patterns still surprising her. Her mouth automatically said things before her brain had a chance to think about them.

She sounded so much like herself that Davy thought that perhaps she'd returned. "Acorn?" He burst through the door in hopeful anticipation.

Maggie jumped back, clutching a boar-bristled brush in defense. "No!"

Davy stopped abruptly, his smile fading. "I beg yer pardon, Maggie. I thought …" His voice trailed off. He closed his mouth and swallowed several times before addressing her again. "Are ye ready to break yer fast?"

"Almost," Maggie said, her throat suddenly tight as she wondered if David would miss her as much as Davy obviously missed Magda. She ran the brush automatically through the thick, mahogany curls and felt the loss of her own husband. She'd been so distracted by the newness of her surroundings and her body that she hadn't spent more than a moment or two thinking about David. Would she ever see him again? Would she ever hear his voice and feel his touch?

Her hands automatically twisted her hair into a bun and secured it with pins while her mind catalogued the things she'd miss most if she never returned—their walks, their talks, their quiet times. They were so much a part of each other's life that she couldn't determine what she'd miss more and what less. Tears filled her eyes and spilled down her cheeks. She'd miss the loving and how they always spooned afterwards. She'd miss spending whole days in his studio watching him sculpt and playing her flute.

Closing her eyes in sorrow, she wondered if the GIFT had been successful. It probably hadn't been. If she were pregnant in her own body, she wouldn't be in this one. She wondered how David would react when he realized she was gone? How would Magda cope with Maggie's world? And how would she cope with Magda's?

"Enough," Davy said, interrupting her thoughts once again. "Fashing does no good." He started to reach for her hand, caught himself with a jerk, and then consciously reached for it again, grasping it firmly. "We've a problem to work on, Maggie-girl. Something we need to work on together, and we'd best get started." He led her into the cottage's other room, a combination of kitchen, dining room, living room, and pantry. She experienced the odd sense of knowing and not knowing she'd had since she'd awakened as Magda.

"I've set out what was left from yesterday," Davy said, leading her to the table. "I dinna ken what ye like."

Maggie sat for a moment in what she knew as her chair, surveying the table. There were bannocks and honey, ale, oatmeal, and a beef pottage. Davy had forgotten the butter just as David always did. She rose from the table to get the dish of butter from its niche below the floor where it was kept cool. She stopped halfway there.

"Maggie?" Davy went to her. "What is it?"

"I was going to get the butter," she said.

"Oh." He took a deep breath to banish the wave of sadness. He'd forgotten to put it on the table. He liked honey in his porridge, but Magda liked butter. "It's kept in a wee box below the floor with the milk and such to keep cool."

"I know." Maggie looked at him. "If I dinna think about it, just go get it, I know where everything is kept. Or this body knows."

Davy swallowed. "I'd imagine it does. Do something enough, and it becomes second nature." He opened the trapdoor and got the butter. "It will make it easier for ye to get along here."

She nodded, unconvinced. The knowing and yet not knowing was disconcerting. "Where is here?"

"Kirkinwall, Scotland, lass." He carried the butter to the table. "Come sit."

Maggie nodded, returning to her place.

"When is it?"

"1718"

She paled.

"And where are ye from?" he asked, but what he really meant was "Where is Magda?"

"New York, New York, in the United States. But that isna even a country yet." The thought flustered her. "New York will be a colony now, I guess. In America, er ... the American Colonies," she stumbled over the words. "I'm from the year 2002."

Davy swallowed hard. Magda was lost to him in a time and place that didn't exist. Tears pricked his eyes, but he blinked to clear them. "What is it like there?" he asked, when he could squeeze the words past the lump in his throat.

"Big. It's a city with millions of people. She must be so frightened."

Millions of people. There were maybe a couple hundred in Kirkinwall all told. He pushed away the thought of Magda's fear and his feelings of helplessness. "She's a brave lass, my Acorn."

Davy's words didn't reassure Maggie. She knew how frightening parts of New York could be even to someone who grew up there and loved it. And she had no idea if David would accept Magda the way Davy had seemed to accept her. David didn't believe in fairy magic. She didn't know if he'd have a chance to accept Magda. A hospital was often a frightening place to those of her time. How much more frightening would it be for Magda? If she woke up and admitted that she wasn't whom they thought she was, she could easily earn herself a trip to the psych ward. Maggie was suddenly more frightened for Magda than she was for herself. "We need to get her back."

Davy nodded. "And ye as well, but how?"

Maggie dropped her head in her hands. "I dinna ken."

# Chapter 4

Magda woke up to brightness. She was unbelievably sleepy, cold, and sleeping on her back, something she didn't normally do. She tried to roll over and reach for the covers Davy had probably kicked off during the night before the storm had brought the cold, but she was prevented from doing so by hands that tucked warmed blankets around her.

"Everything went well. Your husband is waiting for you in your room. We'll take you there in just a minute."

Magda struggled to open her eyes to see who was in her cottage talking to her, but she only managed to open one a slit. She thought she saw a black face with a green hat and shirt before her eyes closed again. She had the sensation of motion as if her bed were on wheels. She struggled to put her mind around it, to decide what it meant, but sleep claimed her again.

Even before she opened her eyes the second time, Magda knew she was no longer home in her cozy cottage in Kirkinwall, snuggled in bed with Davy. Even with her eyes closed, she could tell that everything was wrong. Gone was the pleasant, warm, sleep scent mixed with the lavender in their mattress. A sharper scent that she couldn't identify permeated the air and linen. The feel of the sheet against her skin was different as well, smoother and stiffer than the coarse softness of their linen sheets. The mattress was firm and solid, not slightly molded to her body, and it was slick beneath the sheet as if it had been oiled. Gone were the sounds of home, the sigh of wind, the patter of rain, the songs of birds greeting the day. Whirring and beeping and the sound of clicking heels against floors replaced them.

Magda knew she was alone in the bed, but not alone in the room. She lay on the bed afraid, but unmolested for the moment. Something was stuck to her arm in several places, and her belly hurt in two distinct spots high on either side of her navel. Inching her hands to investigate the source of the pain, she encountered a flat belly.

All plans of sneaking a peek at her surroundings through barely opened eyes fled.

"My baby, where's my baby?" she demanded, sitting up in a strange blue room.

"Hopefully bouncing down your fallopian tubes to your uterus," a deep, pleasant voice that was at once both strange and familiar answered her.

"Davy?" she gasped, turning toward the voice.

A strange man with sandy-colored hair was seated in the chair across the room. He wore long, tan trousers and a white, short-sleeved shirt with a fanciful drawing of a rodent person with gloved hands, shoes and trousers.

"Davy, huh?" David grinned, rising and walking to Magda's bedside. "Dr. Angelo said everything went perfectly. How do you feel?"

Magda clutched the bedding to her chest and stared at the man with widening eyes as he approached. He was bigger than he'd looked seated—bigger and, despite the smile on his face, more threatening. He wasn't as tall as Davy or as heavily muscled, but she had no doubt that he could hold his own with just about anyone else. "Who are you? What have you done with my baby?"

David's smile froze on his face. "Maggie? What's wrong? Are you all right?" He reached for her.

Magda flinched away, avoiding his touch as she repeated her questions, adding, "Where's Davy?" for good measure.

Before he had a chance to answer, a nurse came in, pushing a machine to take Magda's vitals. "Well, Mrs. McDonald, awake at last, I see. That's good. You slept the afternoon away. That's perfectly normal, but I think it worried your husband a little. We'll just take your blood pressure and check your incisions. They'll bring you supper in a few minutes."

Soon Magda would be trapped on the bed between the woman with the cart and the man. She slid from the bed, keeping the cart between herself and the woman. She felt a breeze on her backside and realized the short, sleeveless gown she wore was open in the back, providing the man on the other side of the bed a view no man but Davy had ever seen. It couldn't be helped. Ignoring the woman's protests, Magda used the strange cart to clear a path to the door. Tubes attached to her arm pulled on a bag of liquid hanging from a stand, causing it to crash to the ground and tug irritatingly at the back of her left hand. Intent on getting away, she ignored both the final sharp pain as the tube pulled free from her hand and the shouts to stop as she slipped through the door.

The hallway was unnaturally bright and strangely devoid of windows or torches. She turned right and ran, her gown flapping open behind her. Disembodied voices sounded overhead, and a rush of men and women wearing baggy coats and trousers appeared in doorways to give chase. She made it to an anteroom that connected several other corridors before she was caught—grabbed from behind by a man with hairy arms. She fought, struggling against strong arms, calling frantically for Davy. A large woman with a resolute face stabbed her in the arm with a pin, and the world went dark.

When Magda regained consciousness, she was in a dimly lit room. No light filtered in through the drawn drapes on the window. Two men held a conversation in hushed tones. She needed to find a chamber pot, but she was strapped to the bed.

"I need to make water," she said.

The voices stopped. The men approached.

"Maggie?" She recognized the handsome sandy-haired man from before.

She looked at his worried face and was confused. She didn't know this man, and yet some look in his green eyes was familiar. Was he someone she'd met at the castle or a distant relative of Davy's? She didn't know. And she needed to relieve herself.

"I need to make water," she repeated.

He exchanged looks with the older man dressed in a white coat and pants and an oddly shaped silver necklace. "Can she?"

"Do you know what your name is?" the old man asked.

"Of course." She hesitated, trying to remember what they'd called her. "Maggie." They'd called her Maggie, Magda remembered.

"And who is this?" he asked, pointing to David.

Magda swallowed nervously. "'er ... husband."

The doctor paused a moment. Had she said, "Her husband"?

"I really need to make water," she said, feeling the painful need increasing as the moments passed.

The gray-haired man appeared to be in charge. He eyed her speculatively for a moment.

"Please," she repeated, directing her plea to him, though he seemed the less sympathetic of the two.

"What is your husband's name?" the man asked.

"Can't this wait until she's gone to the bathroom?" David asked.

Magda looked from David to the doctor. "Please." She wiggled under the soft restraints that held her to the bed. The need to relieve herself had supplanted all other thoughts.

"Just there and back," the man said, waiting for her nod before releasing the belts that held her to the bed.

She was still wearing the less-than-modest shift with the rent up the back and the tubes attached to her arm. The younger man grabbed hold of the tall silver pole with bags of fluid hanging from them and brought it near her as she sat up.

"I'll help you with this," he said.

She nodded, held her shift closed in back, and slid carefully from the bed. She followed him to a small room behind a partially opened door. He paused at the doorway, reaching inside to touch the wall. Instantly, the tiny room was ablaze with light that came, not from the sun, candles, or lanterns, but from the ceiling. Magda nearly wet herself in surprise and fear. Instead, steeling herself with a ragged breath, she bravely entered the gleaming white, tiled room.

Shining white basins of various sizes adorned with sparkling silver handles crowded the walls. Fear, disorientation, and confusion warred with need. The man pushed the door closed.

Alone inside the silver and white room, instinct took over. She relieved herself into the water in the odd chamber pot. The number of fixtures in the room befuddled her mind, but her body seemed to know just what to do. She reached for and used the toilet paper before it occurred to her to think about it. Her hand reflexively reached for the silver lever on the toilet and flushed, before she thought to question how she knew how to use these things. The noise startled her, causing her to jump away from the pot. She watched the water swirl down the hole at the bottom on the pot and then, just as mysteriously, begin refilling. How had she known what to do?

Another cold white basin stood waist high. A sign above it admonished her to wash her hands. It showed a picture of water running from a silver hose like that just below it. She closed her eyes. It was too confusing. She knew and yet didn't know how to work the sink.

Her hands automatically turned the knobs to make the water come, something she'd never thought of doing. Her hands pushed another lever and received a drop of pleasantly scented soap—liquid soap—while her brain marveled in stunned amazement over indoor plumbing. She looked up for a towel and froze at the face that looked at her over the sink. What she had at first thought was a window she soon realized was a mirror.

The thin, pale, shorthaired blonde with the bright blue eyes was her reflection, not some intruder. She touched the mirror and then her own face. She watched her reflection as she felt the high cheekbones and tapered chin. The girl they called Maggie McDonald was taller and more willowy than Magda had been. And she wasn't pregnant. The flat stomach with the two small bandages had never been stretched with child. No one had taken a baby from this woman. But someone had taken a baby and more from Magda.

Auld Annie.

Bile rose in her throat. Somehow Auld Annie had done this, but how and why?

"Maggie? Are you all right?" the man she'd called Davy asked.

Magda swallowed tears. No. She wasn't all right. Her surroundings were passing strange, yet her body seemed to know instinctively how to deal with them. She seemed to see everything twice, once through her eyes where everything was new and frightening, and then through another set of eyes that saw through the strangeness into the ordinary.

She needed to get out of this place and figure out some things. But she couldn't fight her way out nor run. That much was clear. They tied the runners and the fighters to beds. Magda needed freedom to discover what had happened.

"Maggie?" The man's voice came again.

"I'm fine," she lied, opening the door. She held her gown closed in back and looked into the concerned eyes of Maggie's husband's for a moment before her attention skittered back to the other man.

"Why don't you climb back into bed, and we'll talk," the older man said.

She reentered the room, forgetting the IV tree behind her. David caught it before it crashed to the ground. "Careful."

It was good advice. She planned on taking it, if only she knew how.

"Maggie, you gave us quite a scare before," the middle-aged man said once she was settled back in the bed. "Why did you run off like that?"

"I was confused." Magda answered as simply and as honestly as she could, hoping that the men would give her clues about how to answer the questions correctly without raising suspicion.

"What did you think was happening?"

"I didn't know." She looked at the other man, wishing she knew his name. They were connected. He was Maggie's husband, but she felt she knew him as well. It was probably just more of that strange duality she was experiencing—knowing and not knowing, seeing everything twice.

He stared at her with such care and concern that she wanted to comfort him. He'd lost his wife just as she'd lost her world. She pushed that thought aside for later. Now she had to figure out where she was.

"Maggie?" David prompted.

"I was just confused." She still was. She didn't know either man, and yet she did. The young one was Maggie's husband and the older one was a doctor. It said so on the tag he wore pinned to his white coat—Dr. Jorgenson. She knew what the letters spelled just as she'd known what the sign said. She hadn't been taught to read—no girls were, but she knew what reading was. It amazed her that she knew how and that she also knew that "Dr." was short for "doctor" and that the business of doctors was healing, though she'd never seen nor heard of one before. But there was no sense of familiarity around the doctor.

"Have we met?" she asked Dr. Jorgenson, taking the risk that she might appear foolish.

Dr. Jorgenson smiled as if she'd passed a test.

"No, Maggie. Dr. Angelo asked me to check in on you after your little episode. Do you know where you are? Or why you're here?"

She didn't, but she could guess. She looked at Maggie's husband for clues. "I'm in a sickroom," she said. "But I'm not sick." What had he said when she woke up and asked about her baby? "Dr. Angelo said the procedure went well."

David smiled. She could see the profound relief in his grin. "See, doctor, she's fine. It was a strange reaction to the anesthetic. She came out of it in the middle of a dream or something, but it's over with. She's fine. Waking up in a hospital is a scary thing. I'm surprised more people don't have adverse reactions."

Dr. Jorgenson nodded. "It's not that uncommon."

Hospital. That's where she was. She knew what the word meant now that she'd heard it.

"We'll still keep her overnight for observation," the doctor said.

She had to stay here overnight? She swallowed the rising panic. She wanted to go home to Davy. She desperately needed some time to think, to figure out where she was and how she'd gotten here. She was torn by the need to be alone, yet she feared being alone. Maggie's husband was her only connection.

Sleep called to her as a solution. Sleep had brought her there; maybe sleep would bring her back home. She closed her eyes, blocking out Maggie's husband and the doctor. She let the sound of their voices wash over her like waves as darkness overtook her.

Magda woke hours later, alone in the dark room. She wanted Davy.

She sat up in bed and looked around. Light filtered from the hall through the glass panel on the door, making a rectangle of light on the floor near the foot of her bed. Plagued by fears in the middle of the darkened room, she sought the smaller confines of the lavatory. Scrambling over the foot of the bed, she knocked the chart to the floor with a crash. Without thinking, she grabbed it from the floor as she fled. Once safely inside the bathroom, she pulled the door closed and flipped the lock. The faint glow of parking lot lights shining through the small window and reflecting in the mirror eased the darkness of the room.

A switch glowed red against the wall. Magda flicked it up and was again startled by the suddenness of light. She squinted her eyes until she could see. The weird duality of perception continued. The standard fixtures of a bathroom, even an extremely cramped one like this, were initially comforting. Maggie's body recognized this room as a place of relief and comfort even if Magda's mind didn't. Magda caught a glimpse of the pale face she now wore reflected in the mirror. The blue eyes were haunted with Magda's loss and confusion. She turned away so she wouldn't see the tears she felt forming there. She was lost.

Pressing her back against the locked door, Magda cradled the chart to her chest as she gave into the tears. She slid down the door until her forehead rested on her knees. Sobs wracked her body.

A knock on the door interrupted her grief.

"Maggie?" A woman's voice came through the door. "Are you all right?"

Magda swallowed back the tears, smearing them as she drew a bare arm across her face. "I'm fine," she croaked in a voice that betrayed her.

"Open the door, and I'll help you."

"No!" she said blurted out before softening her response. "Uh, no, thank you." She scrambled to her feet. "I'm fine. I just need a bit more time to …"

Her thoughts trailed off with her voice. To what? To hide? To mourn? To delay facing the unbelievable situation she found herself in?

"You go ahead and take a few more minutes. I'll be right here."

Magda knew she didn't have long before the woman would insist she come out. She needed to get control of herself or they'd tie her to the bed again. She sat on the toilet, chart in lap. She scanned the top sheet. Her husband's name was David. She blinked back the tears that blurred the page before her. The date caught her eye. May 10, 2002. Her heart skipped a beat. It wasn't possible.

The edges of her sight turned dark, and once again she crashed to the floor.

She woke up in bed surrounded by people with machines. While she'd been unconscious, someone had put a mask over her face. She could hear the hiss of air filling it. There was a black band around her arm squeezing it in irritating rhythmic pumps. A woman was plugging a needle into the tube that entered the back of her hand. The bag and its silver tree were back now, joined by another bag.

Hands pulled aside the front of her indecent shift to expose her.

"No!" Magda tried to cover herself only to find herself held.

"It's okay," a woman answered. "We're just putting a heart monitor on. It won't hurt. You passed out in the bathroom, and we want to find out why."

*Oh, God! Please don't let them find out why.* She wondered what they did to witches in this time. She wasn't one, but knew if she were accused that it wouldn't matter. She was not of this time—different. When they found that out, they'd kill her.

Her body was slick with sweat. The cardio-monitor went wild graphing her racing heart. They slid an oxygen monitor on her index finger.

The buzzing and chattering of machines added to the anxious chatter of voices above her.

"Her blood pressure is 170 over 95. Respiration shallow and fast."

Magda knew she was panicking, but she couldn't seem to help it. By the time she thought to close her eyes and calm her breath, it was too late. Once again the room closed in on her, and she passed out.

Several hours passed before she woke again. Dim light seeped around the drawn curtain and glowed from the light fixture at the head of her bed. The man she knew was David sat in a chair near the bed, watching images on a box suspended near the ceiling on the opposite wall. She felt unnaturally calm as if she'd been drugged, but she couldn't work herself up enough to care.

"David," she said, softly.

"Maggie." He turned to her, watching her carefully. "How do you feel?"

"Sluggish," she said.

"Do you know what happened last night?" he asked. He'd been told to ring for the nurse as soon as she woke so they could ask her if she knew who and where she was, what day it was, who was president, and such. He did none of that. Instead he took her hand in his and squeezed it.

"I fainted. When I woke up, there were people everywhere poking and prodding. They frightened me, and I fainted again."

"You frightened them." David squeezed her hand. "They were running tests to see why you fainted, and you had a panic attack. They gave you a mild sedative, and you fainted again."

Magda grabbed David's hand with her free hand. "I want to go home."

"I know. They want to keep you here another day to make sure you're okay."

"I won't be okay here. There's no privacy. They poke at me and ask me if I know where I am." She stared pleadingly into David's eyes. "I know where I am, and I don't want to be here. I want to go home." She clung to his hands. He couldn't send her home, but he could take her from here and bring her to somewhere that she might think. "Please."

"I'll call the nurse. We'll talk to her, and she'll see you're fine. Then we'll go home."

"Bless you."

David looked closely at her again. Maggie may be more religious than he was, but still it wasn't normal for her to use that phrase.

Dr. Jorgenson stopped by during rounds.

"I hear you had a rough night."

"I don't like it here very well." Magda held David's hand as she answered.

"Well, I see here that you're doing better." He looked up from the chart. "Do you remember what you were thinking when you woke up the first time from the anesthetic?

Magda looked at David. She'd been following his lead since she'd waken. He'd gotten her through the nurse's questions about date, time and president. She trusted him to get her through this as well.

He nodded encouragingly.

She took a deep breath and decided to answer as clearly as she could while omitting that she wasn't who they thought she was. "When I woke up, I thought I'd been pregnant and that someone had stolen my baby, but now I know that didn't happen." Tears filled her eyes as she both lied and told the truth. "I was never pregnant."

"Oh, Maggie," David said, pulling her into his arms. She went willingly, not because she wanted to be there, but because she knew he'd take her out of there. He was her savior.

The doctor regarded her more critically. She buried her face in David's chest, hiding from the doctor's prying eyes.

"Sometimes people have reported odd dreams when they wake from anesthesia."

"I'm sure that's all this was," David said, sounding more hopeful than he felt.

"How are you feeling now, Maggie?" the doctor asked.

"Embarrassed, hungry." Confused, afraid, and guilty because she was finding comfort in David's arms.

"Don't worry, Maggie." David kissed her hair, squeezing her tight. "It was the anesthesia. Everything will be all right. This happens all the time, right, Doctor?"

"Not all the time. Post-operative disorientation varies from patient to patient, but it is rare that it is this severe. Still, reactions to anesthesia are common enough that we routinely keep patients overnight for evaluation. Your disorientation appears to have ended. I'd thought so yesterday, but then you passed out twice last night and had a panic attack."

"She hadn't eaten in twenty-four hours." David went on the defensive. Maggie had been through more than enough. "She got up too fast from the toilet and passed out. The anxiety attack came from waking up in bed surrounded by people and every kind of machine this hospital owns. That's enough to give anyone an anxiety attack. I know they were doing what they thought was right, but I think it was overkill. Maggie is obviously fine."

"I'd have to agree," the doctor said, signing the chart. "We'll have the IV taken out and the monitors removed, and you can go home."

Magda waited until the doctor left the room before slowly disentangling herself from David. She'd felt safe in his arms, but guilty. He wasn't Davy. For now she needed David, but she wanted Davy.

"I'm leaving this place … I'm leaving this place." Magda repeated the words over and over in her mind as the nurse wheeled her in and out of an elevator and through the hospital corridors on the way to David and the waiting taxi.

She was learning things about this new world. She knew that the body she wore knew things—how to put on the underclothing that had been in the pile of items David claimed were hers and how to fasten the trousers. If she didn't fight it, her mind came up with the correct words for things like bra, jeans and elevators. If she relaxed, things came almost naturally.

Still, there was the part of her that was her. The part that made her Magda and not Maggie, that reacted with shock and fear at the multitude of never-imagined things that confronted her. It was the part that was shocked by the skimpy undergarments and the idea of wearing men's clothing. It wanted to flee and hide as she did in the forest. But the threats of this world were so different from the ones in her world that she wasn't sure which ones warranted flight and which didn't.

She tried to take clues from the Maggie part of herself as well as the people around her. Rooms that went up and down and doors that slid open by themselves were apparently of no consequence. The stench and the noise that filled the air outside the hospital door were apparently normal. Sirens and the roar of passing vehicles caused no one alarm. The lack of earth beneath her feet and the encroachment of buildings that blocked the sky seemed to bother no one else.

Forcing a smile, Magda thanked the woman who'd pushed her wheelchair to this spot. David opened the taxi door, and she climbed in without comment or visible pause. She automatically slid over to the far side, leaving room for David.

"You'll be glad to get home," David commented, taking Magda's hand. "Your hands are freezing!" He grabbed the other one as well and held them in his warm ones.

Magda let him bring her hands to his mouth and blow on them. Her heart clenched. Davy did that too.

"I called Brian and told him you wouldn't be in today or tomorrow. He was okay with it, said they'd work around your solos."

Solos? Magda grinned at the ridiculousness of the situation. She knew what the word meant. Or Maggie did. How could she do Maggie's solos when she didn't know what instrument she played? Who knows? Maybe she sang. What else could one have a solo in? Magda had no idea, but apparently Maggie was good enough at whatever it was to have solos. Her memory as Maggie seemed limited to touch and sound. If it remembered language, would it remember music, or would she have to feign illness to avoid her solos? She could only guess who Brian was. Would she remember him when she saw him, or would she stumble through that as well?

Oblivious to her turmoil, David smiled as if sharing a joke.

"Okay," he said. "Maybe 'okay with it' was a bit much. He made me swear that you'd be better in time for opening night next Friday. Once I told him you would be, he calmed down."

Magda's smile dimmed. She knew it was Wednesday. David had clued her in to that earlier in the day. That gave her nine days to figure things out. Sweat broke out on her brow. Nine days. Maybe she could do it if she heard the music a few times. She had not been without talent in her own time, but she worried about Maggie. She told the McClellan she'd play the flute for the Festival of First Harvests this Sunday. That was only four days away, or was it? The days didn't seem to match up. The thought added to her worries, but she pushed it aside. There were more important concerns. How would she get back? Did Davy even know she and Maggie had changed places?

The trouble Maggie could get into while wearing her body worried Magda. She tried to see her world through Maggie's eyes. It would seem as strange, in its way, as this one did. Magda worried about how Maggie would act. Would people notice anything different about her? There was great danger in appearing strange. She'd been too close to Auld Annie. Any strangeness would be suspect. If Maggie was accused of witchcraft and killed, she would never get home and neither would Magda.

"Are you all right?" David asked, calling her back to the present.

"I'm fine," Magda lied, swallowing panic. "I'm a bit tired."

They stopped in front of a stone house squeezed between two larger buildings. A lone maple tree was rooted in a small patch of ground surrounded by concrete. A single chain looped its way through metal uprights, creating a fence to protect the tree and its accompaniment of blown tulips from errant footfalls. She'd known it was earlier in the year here than it had been when she left Kirkinwall, but seeing the flowers brought it home. Here the Festival of First Fruits would be more than a month away—if they had it at all.

Magda followed David into the house. Beautiful bronze sculptures of people greeted her eyes.

"Oh," she gasped despite herself. She knew she was supposed to behave as if everything were ordinary, but she couldn't. Her attention darted from one statue to the next. It was all she could do to keep herself from rushing about to examine each more closely. She supposed she should have guessed that David would be an artist as Davy was.

"You act like you've never seen them before," David said, noticing her reaction.

"I keep forgetting how gifted you are," she said.

Davy shook his head in bemusement. "You've always been my greatest fan."

How could she not be? Magda wondered. As she looked around the room, the statue of one particular little girl playing a flute in a calf-length dress called to her. There was something familiar about the long curly hair and fine features. Forgetting her resolution to stay put, she went to it, staring intently at the pixie face with its smiling eyes and turned-up nose. It took her a moment to realize why it was so familiar. It was a sculpture of her, Magda, as a child.

David watched as she caressed the statue's head as if it were real. She always greeted that statue that way, as if it were a real child, and it never failed to tug at his heart. He hoped the GIFT had worked. More than anything, he wanted to give her a real child.

Magda looked at David and smiled. She wanted to ask David the statue's name, but she didn't dare. There was something in his eyes that told her she, or rather Maggie, had done this before. Maggie would know what the statue was called even if Magda didn't.

"See, I didn't sell her while you were gone," Davy said, picking up Maggie's overnight bag and purse.

"You couldn't sell her," Madga protested. "She's—" *Me?* She couldn't say that, not hardly "—my favorite."

David chuckling, walked to her side. "Give me a kiss and she's yours."

Magda cocked one brow at Maggie's husband. The situation was so familiar—like the games she and Davy would play. David had no intention of ever selling that bronze girl. He had almost certainly promised it to Maggie many times before, but he was not above seeing how many kisses he could get out of it.

"Isn't she already mine?" Magda asked, her tone light and teasing. "Haven't we done this before?"

David shrugged, taking her in his arms. "I don't remember. Maybe a kiss will remind me."

She should kiss him, Magda knew. Maggie would laugh and kiss him. If he were Davy, *she* would laugh and give him the kind of kiss that would lead to something else.

She stiffened and pulled back. She wasn't Maggie—and he wasn't Davy.

"A faulty memory is a worrisome thing," she said, trying to keep the situation light as she stepped out of his embrace. "Do you know what day it is?" she teased, repeating the question she'd been asked so many times over the past couple days.

David laughed. "I know date and place." His stomach rumbled. "And even time. Let's get some lunch." He preceded her through the back door of the gallery into their house. "What do you want to eat?"

"Are you cooking?" Davy could hardly heat up cold stew.

David smiled. "Don't worry, Magpie. I'm just making sandwiches. You want ham or roast beef?"

"Whatever you're having." She followed him into the kitchen. It was huge with a built-in table in the middle of the room like an island. She sat on one of the high stools lining one side of it and looked around. Her kitchen would have fit tucked in one corner of this room, leaving space for table and chairs, fireplace chairs, and her entire bedroom. And yet, in this kitchen, there was no fireplace to cook at. Instead, there were cupboards, closets, and drawers faced in wood, black glass, and a white metal. As odd as it all was to her, though, she knew that if she were the one to make lunch, her hands would know just what to do and where to find things.

"Do you want some tea?" he asked, filling the kettle at the sink against one wall.

"Please." She remembered running water at the hospital, but she hadn't considered that it would be in their house. It was a marvel, yet her body recognized it as normal. She watched intently as David put the kettle on a circle on the island and knew, as he turned the knob and brought fire, that she could have done the same.

"You're quiet," David said as he made the sandwiches.

She paid close attention to where he got the bread and meat. There were only a few pieces of bread left. A soft white bread—finer than she'd seen on the castle table—and already sliced. What would she do when they ran out? Had Maggie baked it? She didn't know where to get more.

"We're almost out of bread."

David shrugged. "I'll add it to the list. Are you going to go to the grocery store after practice tomorrow?"

"Possibly." If she figured out where she needed to go for practice, what she needed to practice, where the grocery store was, and what she'd use as coin.

David put the sandwiches on plates, handed her one, and poured the tea.

"Are you feeling all right?" It wasn't like Maggie to sit and let him mess up her kitchen like this.

Magda took a bite of the sandwich, not tasting it as she pondered the question. Should she tell him the truth? Could she find her way home without his help? Could she even survive? Would he judge her insane and send her back to the hospital? She was too newly loosed from that place to risk being returned there. And what if she were judged a witch? What hell would she face then? In the end, it was her fears that made her lie.

"I'm fine. A little tired, maybe. I think I'll take a nap this afternoon."

"Good idea," David said with a grin. "Maybe I'll join you."

"No!" It was out of her mouth before she could stop it. "I mean, you've taken two days off work, maybe you should spend the day carving—I mean sculpting." Sweet Brigid, she had stuck her foot in it. She dropped her head in her hands. She had to get a grip on herself or he'd send her away for sure. "I really need a nap."

"Okay," David said softly, puzzled. Working bronze wasn't a silent pursuit. "I'll work on some sketches in the studio so you can sleep."

Magda lifted her head and gave a weak smile. "Thank you." She stood.

"Eat first," David directed. "You'll sleep better."

Magda grimaced. "Right." She ate the sandwich, but it didn't fill the hole she felt in her stomach.

Magda lay in bed, waiting until she was certain David had gone to his studio before rising. She needed to find out about Maggie. She'd seen framed images of her and David in the hallway as she'd passed. Now she tiptoed back to stare at them. One was a wedding picture, no new information there. The others contained other people, probably Maggie and David's families. Judging from the pictures, David seemed to be an only child like Davy had been, and Maggie had a younger brother.

She needed more information. Where should she look? Surely there would be papers or something in the desk she'd seen as she'd walked past the library. Stifling the urge to sneak, she concentrated on walking normally down the hall. Once inside the library, she closed the door and sighed.

The desk, a cluttered roll top with the roll partially down, was the most obvious place to look. She pawed through papers, reading as she went. Reading. She smiled at the concept. A wonder is what it was. Her smile faded as she read the pages and found that they were bills. They owed money for gas and electricity, insurance, and a variety of other things. One drawer was filled with programs and newspaper clippings about Maggie and David. Magda pulled out the chair, sat down and began to read.

*"Margaret McDonald Plays The Met"*
   *Manhattan's most famous flutist will open at The Metropolitan Opera House in The Lincoln Center of the Performing Arts this Friday accompanied by the New York Orchestra under the conduction of Brian Williams.*

Maggie played the flute. Magda nearly moaned in relief. She let go a breath she hadn't realized she'd been holding. She'd be fine. She had a fabulous memory for music. Once she heard a song, she could play it. She'd be all right even if Maggie's fingers didn't remember the song. She'd be fine at least in this aspect of Maggie's life.

Another newspaper clipping revealed that David was a highly respected, successful artist. She'd only had to see his sculptures to know that, but it did calm her heart a bit about the money they seemed to owe everyone. The clipping said he was highly paid and his works greatly sought after. It seemed as if they could pay their bills. Another thing not to worry about.

She looked at publicity photos of herself and the conductor, Brian Williams, and rifled through the pile for photos of them with the orchestra. She wondered who amongst the group were Maggie's friends.

Friends, family, and David were Magda's biggest worries. If she were trapped in this time, how would she fit in with people she didn't know? How could she keep it from everyone who she really was? The impossibility of the task overwhelmed her. Tears came unbidden to her eyes. She didn't even know Maggie's brother's name or if their parents still lived. She didn't know how to get food or how to get to The Metropolitan Opera House or the Lincoln Center. She didn't know the music she was supposed to play or even where her flute was.

And she missed Davy.

Sorrow clawed at her heart and emptied her soul. She collapsed into herself, sobbing quietly. "Why?" repeated in her head like a chant. "Why me? Why am I here? Why did Maggie take my life and leave me hers? And how will I get home to Davy?"

She cried herself to sleep, knocking the forgotten clippings to the floor.

David found her there and nearly cried in relief. He hadn't been able to sketch, hadn't been able to concentrate. Something wasn't right with Maggie. He'd left the studio and gone to the bedroom to check on her. Panicking when he'd seen the empty bed, he rushed around the house calling her name. He'd thought she was gone.

"Maggie." He whispered her name like a prayer of thanksgiving. "Maggie."

She didn't stir.

He stood next to her, puzzled by the mess and her tear-streaked face. What had she been looking for? And what had made her cry?

He picked up papers from the floor. They were the mementos she'd been saving for their scrapbook—happy things. He frowned in concern. What had caused the tears?

He wanted to shake her awake and ask her, but he didn't. The dark rings under her eyes spoke too clearly of exhaustion. He'd leave her be for the time being and check back later. A short nap at the desk might be just what she needed.

Magda awakened an hour later feeling stiff, but better—not so raw. She collected the memorabilia, putting everything back in the drawer she'd found them in. She still needed more information about Maggie. She finished searching the desk before looking around the rest of the room.

There were so many books on the shelves—more than lined the laird's shelves. Everything around her screamed wealth beyond imagining. She was foolish to worry about the bills in the drawer while surrounded by such obvious riches. Or was their wealth in things? She could only guess.

She examined the books. Most of the books on the bookshelves seemed to be stories, though not the ones she'd heard around the fire. There was a section filled with books and binders of sheet music. Written music! Her worries about paying the bills fled. They had only to sell a bit of music, and their financial worries would be over. Still, there were more books. A shelf behind the desk contained oversized books with dates written on the spine, spanning the 27 years of Maggie's life. Magda pulled the oldest one off the shelf and opened it.

It was a book about Maggie as a baby with pictures and captions. This was what Magda needed. She took the book to the couch and paged through Maggie's past. There were pictures of Maggie's christening. The baby, dressed in a trailing white gown trimmed with eyelets, cried herself red as the priest poured water on her head. There were pictures of the baby Maggie in a variety of relatives' arms—both sets of Maggie's grandparents were alive and spry at the time of her birth. If it hadn't been for the captions beneath the pictures, Magda would never have guessed that the smooth smiling faces were Maggie's grandparents.

There were photos of family outings to the circus, to the zoo, to the beach. In the pictures, Magda saw black-and-white striped horses and a beast with an unbelievably long neck. Maggie had been a healthy baby, fat and dimpled with rosy cheeks and a wide smile. Magda especially liked a picture of Maggie standing up, holding on to the edge of a small table, her face alight with glee.

Magda turned the page. Baby Maggie sat in a high chair with her face puckered up, blowing out candles on top of a frosted cake. The next shot showed Maggie covered with frosting, elbow deep in that same cake. Magda had to smile despite her confusion.

A picture showed that Maggie, with her fine, pale hair captured in a pigtails, had gotten her first flute at the age of three and played in something called Suzuki. Maggie's baby brother, Todd, was born that year. Pictures and captions claimed that Maggie and Todd were best friends despite their age difference. The grins on their faces as they played in a miniature kitchen or, in another shot, rolled cars and trucks along a pale blue carpet bore witness to that fact.

Magda went back to the shelf for the next couple of books. She was midway through the third book when she heard David in the hall. She slouched onto the couch, closing her eyes to feign sleep.

"Maggie?" David whispered, seeing her sprawled on the couch once again surrounded by memorabilia. This time it was the scrapbooks her mother had made for her in some class. He lifted one off her stomach and set it on the coffee table. "Maggie, honey." He touched her arm to wake her.

When she flinched, but kept her eyes closed, David realized that she wasn't really asleep. Stunned, he watched her breathe. Her breaths were deep and even—the picture of studied relaxation. The jump of the pulse in her throat told a different story. She was frightened. The realization tightened his chest. She was pretending to be asleep because she was afraid of him.

Why?

He wanted to gently shake her until she could no longer fake sleep and ask her, but he didn't. He loved her, and something wasn't quite right. He looked at her face. She looked tired. Hoping the feigned sleep would change to real sleep and that the rest would clear her mind, he grabbed the afghan off the back of the couch and draped it over her.

"I love you, Maggie," he whispered, giving her a kiss on the cheek.

She didn't move, but he felt the muscles tighten and saw her pulse jump.

Oh, God. What was wrong? What had he done? He stared at her a moment, knowing the torture he was probably inflicting but unable to stop himself.

What had gone wrong? Was it the GIFT? Was it the anesthetic? Two days ago she wouldn't have pretended to be asleep. She'd knock the books on the floor and pull him onto the couch with her. Two days ago she wouldn't have spent the afternoon sifting through newspaper clippings or pouring over old scrapbooks. She had a concert in a few days. She should have been in the studio serenading him as he worked. They were each other's muse. The hours they spent together in the studio were nearly as wonderful as the hours they spent together in bed. And, even after seven years of marriage, they did a lot of both.

But now. Now she flinched at his touch. She feigned sleep to hide from him.

Telling himself that she needed a little more time to recover from the procedure and that tomorrow everything would be fine, he left the room, closing the door behind him.

Alone again, Magda breathed a sigh of relief and unfolded herself from the couch. She took the scrapbook from the coffee table and paged through it until she found where she'd been. Forcing herself to focus, she made her way to the end. She knew more about Maggie now, but it wasn't enough. Knowing pieces of Maggie's history didn't help her *be* Maggie, and it didn't help her get home. Actually, it didn't help with much. It didn't tell her what music to play at rehearsal tomorrow, how to get there, or even if she should try. It didn't tell her how she should deal with David until she could figure out how to get home.

She'd already decided she couldn't tell him the truth, yet she seemed to scream it at him every time he came near. He loved Maggie. She'd loved him. Magda had seen how they were in the scrapbook pictures. She'd felt the chemistry when they touched. Maggie's body wanted to be in David's arms. And yet, she wasn't Maggie. She was Magda. She loved Davy. And, chemistry and artistic ability aside, David wasn't Davy. He didn't share her past or her heart. She couldn't be with him as she was with Davy, as Maggie had been with David. She couldn't do that to Davy. She couldn't do that to herself.

So … how did she pose as Maggie yet keep David at bay?

She didn't know. Hated tears crowded her eyes again. There was too much fear, too much uncertainty. She was hopeless and helpless, alone in a strange world with no idea how to get home again. She hated it. She prayed and cried until an exhausted sleep overcame her.

Magda woke in the pale grayness of morning. She was still on the library couch. It was tempting to roll over and take refuge in the oblivion of sleep, to forget the list of problems she couldn't solve, but she resisted. In order to find her way home, she had to figure out why she was here.

Auld Annie.

She pictured the old woman and shivered. Never be nice to witches. It would be her new credo. Of course, she hadn't thought Annie was a witch. She hadn't believed in witches. It just went to show that it didn't matter what you believed; what was, was. And, as impossible at it still seemed, she was Maggie for the time being. And Maggie had practice today.

She was frying eggs and toasting bread when David came into the kitchen. He stopped walking to stare at her.

"What are you doing?"

"Making breakfast." Magda didn't bother looking up. The bread was almost toasted and, since it was the last piece of bread in the house, she especially didn't want to burn it. Once the bread was done, she slid it from the fork onto the stack warming on a plate over a pot of oatmeal.

"Is the toaster broken?"

She pictured the long toasting fork she had at home. She'd only been able to find this short one with the knives. It would have been too short to have managed over the cooking fire in her cottage kitchen without getting burned once or twice, but it was plenty long with the small gas fire out in the open as it was.

"I couldn't find it."

David wrinkled his brow. "It's right there on the counter."

She looked where he pointed and shrugged. The name of the silver box seemed right, but this was the way she always made toast. She'd turned the knob and lit the fire to make the oatmeal and fry the eggs. There was no need to start another fire just to make toast. Some folks did it in the oven. She might have done so had she been baking today, but since she wasn't, there was no reason to fire the oven.

"Are you ready to eat then?"

David sat down at the table. "How are you this morning?"

She didn't meet his eye; just looking at him was painful enough. Why did he have to be so handsome? "Fine."

"I missed you last night."

She swallowed hard. "Uh, sorry about that. I must have been really tired."

He said nothing.

The silence lengthened until she realized that he knew she'd been faking. "I …" she stumbled for something to say. "I didn't realize how comfortable our couch was. I'll have to sleep there more often."

He looked at her, brows pinched with worry. "I'd rather you slept with me."

"Oh." Anything but that. She couldn't sleep with him. They wouldn't sleep.

"Is there something wrong?" he asked, covering her hand with his.

The warmth of his hand reverberated through her like lightning. She jumped at his touch and pulled away, shaking her head. She was drawn to him. It was like those days before she'd wed Davy. It had been nearly beyond their power to wait for her Uncle Father to give his blessing. Each touch had led to more until they couldn't touch for fear they'd go too far. She held her hands against her chest to avoid future touching while she said, "No, nothing."

Such a blatant lie left him speechless for several moments.

She divided the eggs and toast between two plates and ladled thick oatmeal into bowls. She got the butter and syrup out of the refrigerator, automatically preparing the bowls as she would in Kirkinwall—a pat of butter for hers and dollop of syrup for Davy's.

He blinked at her. He didn't know how she remembered the way he liked his oatmeal but she couldn't remember how to make toast. He couldn't let her loose on the streets of New York: she'd never make it back home.

"I was thinking of going to rehearsal with you to listen, if that's okay with you," he told her. "I've really missed your music." He knew that Brian would hate it. Brian hated visitors at rehearsals. He said they distracted his musicians. Actually, they distracted Brian by making him feel he needed to watch his normally acerbic tongue.

She smiled in relief. If he went with, he could help get her there. "That would be great."

David hid his worried frown. Maggie should have reminded him that Brian liked closed rehearsals. On a normal day, he'd have expected her to laugh at his suggestion and promise to play to him tonight while he sculpted. Normally, she wouldn't have accepted his suggestion nor looked so pleased about it. Maybe that's where the problem lay. He was grasping at straws and knew it, but he continued to grasp anyway. Maybe she was nervous about something at work, and she didn't want to worry him about it. Maybe that's why she seemed so different.

"Is something wrong at rehearsal?" he asked.

"Uh … no, not that I know of."

"So it's okay if I come later?"

Her smile faded. "Later? I thought you'd go with me; make sure I didn't get lost on the way there." She hadn't meant to say it aloud. Maggie would certainly know how to get to practice, but Magda didn't; the thought of traveling about in the bustling city terrified her.

David was torn between a smile and a frown. Was she joking? He didn't know. It should have been a joke. The words were a joke. Despite his concerns, she shouldn't need his help getting there. Maggie could probably get to Lincoln Center in her sleep, but her facial expressions were totally wrong. She looked worried, not teasing, as if she were truly concerned about getting lost. What was going on? Had the anesthesia permanently affected her memory?

"Sure, I'll come with you," he told her, and he was instantly rewarded with a relieved smile.

Magda was grateful beyond words that David had taken her to Lincoln Center. She hadn't known where she was going. She'd turned left outside of the brownstone and walked down the street. That had been correct. She could have managed to get down the stairs into the underground tunnel without any help, but once there she would have been lost. Her new body could take her where she needed to go as far as walking was concerned, but it held no recognition of subway lines.

Without David, she'd have panicked as the huge vehicles pulled to a stop in front of her. She'd have watched the people go in and out, but she would have had no idea which carriage she should take. She'd have stood there, lost, not daring to board. There was no telling where she'd have ended up had she gotten on the wrong one by mistake.

She followed David's lead, paying close attention to every step, every detail—feed the coin into the slot, walk through the moving gate, get on to the Number 9 train to Lincoln Center.

Even with David to guide her, Magda's stomach was in knots by the time she pulled open the stage door and entered Lincoln Center. "Get through this practice, and you'll never have to leave the house again," she silently promised herself.

"I'll say hello to Brian and sit in the auditorium," David told her at the door.

Magda wanted to scream "no" and cling to his arm. How would she find her flute and the stage without him? "You could come with me and say hello to everyone," she suggested desperately.

"No," he said, extracting his hand from hers and flexing it to restore the circulation. She'd held his hand in a vice grip since they'd entered the subway station. "You know how to get to your locker. It's in the practice room straight down this hall, first door on the right. You have your key on your key chain, don't you?" He waited while she fumbled through her purse for her keys, and then he took them from her hand and separated out the smallest one. "See. You have your key. It has your lock number on it and everything. You've done this a million times before. You'll be just fine."

She nodded. Even in her jangled state she knew that he realized something wasn't quite right. She took a deep breath and forced a laugh. "I know that." It sounded false to her ears and certainly didn't fool David, but she couldn't deal with that right now. She closed her eyes, rallied her courage, and walked down the hallway.

She found her performance flute under lock and key, exactly where David had told her it would be. She nearly cried when she saw its polished silver sparkle in the artificial lights. It wasn't like her flute. She picked it up, examining it cautiously. It felt heavy and cold in her hands. Her wooden flutes were warmer and lighter; they had holes, not levers. The image of Davy's face as he gave her his hand-carved flute flickered through her mind's eye. She pushed it away. The next few hours would be hard enough without missing Davy. She was about to play music she didn't know on an instrument so unlike hers that she wondered if she could even play it.

"We missed you the past couple of days." A tawny-haired woman uncasing a cello interrupted her thoughts. "You should have seen Brian. The man was a nervous wreck."

Brian was the conductor, Magda reminded herself. "Really? How could you tell?" The newspaper clippings she'd read about Brian had led her to believe that he was a gruff, strong-willed dictator with a baton. He ruled the symphony with an iron fist. She couldn't imagine the man she'd seen in the publicity photos acting like a nervous wreck.

The cellist laughed. "He yelled more."

Magda smiled weakly. She followed the other musicians onto stage and froze. *Good Lord.* The place was huge. The photos hadn't done it justice. The stage itself was far bigger than most of the cottages in Kirkinwall, but it opened into a gigantic room. The Met was so huge it dwarfed the great hall at the castle. The space was covered in row after row of chairs. There were balconies, several balconies—she was too stunned to count exactly how many—full of chairs. The walls of the auditorium were gilded and ornate and acoustically designed so that the sound of chattering voices and tuning instruments filled the auditorium.

"Finally." Brian's booming voice wrenched Magda's attention back to her immediate surroundings. "The prodigal flutist has returned." He smiled and crossed the stage to give Maggie a hug. She recognized him from the pictures. "How are you, Maggie? You had me worried."

The desire to cling to him rivaled the urge to run and hide. She compromised with a brief but intense hug. It surprised her when he didn't let go.

This man was more than Maggie's conductor, but less than her lover. He was obviously her good friend. A friend she would disappoint greatly if her fingers didn't remember the music. She shoved down the thought and answered the question. "I'm a bit worried. I haven't played in a couple of days now. Maybe I've forgotten the music." Forgotten the music, huh! That wasn't the worst of it. She didn't know where to put her fingers or what notes she should play.

Brian laughed too brightly. "Not a chance, Magpie. You've played it so often that it's a part of your body. Relax and your flute could almost do it alone."

"Maybe we should try it and see," Magda said.

Brian chuckled. "You'll be fabulous. Now get to your chair and warm up."

She swallowed her fear as she walked to the chair he indicated set in front of the others, near the conductor's podium. She stood, scanning the seats for David. She caught the movement as he waved from the middle of the ground floor. She sat, relieved that he was still there, and then placed her cold fingers on the keys of the flute. Her hands seemed to know where to go despite her mind's confusion. She looked at the flute. It shone more brilliantly under the bright lights. She closed her eyes and let music fill her head. She'd always been able to play the notes in her head. Bringing the foreign flute to her lips, she prayed she'd be able to now. She played *Song for First Fruits* as a warm up.

She was doing it! She could do it! A silent cheer lifted her heart. She was going to be all right.

As the last note faded from the air, she noticed that the hall had gone silent.

"Sorry," she told Brian who stood on the podium staring at her. Everyone was staring at her. She swallowed hard. It was clear to her, though she wasn't sure how, that when the conductor mounted the podium musicians became silent out of respect, awaiting his direction. She'd been so wrapped up in the music that she'd broken that cardinal rule. "Sorry." She blushed.

He frowned. "No. Play that again, Maggie."

"Again?" She stared at him questioningly until he nodded.

Putting the flute to her lips, she played again. *Song for First Fruits* held the joy of warm days and new abundance. Originally a thank you to the old gods, its words had been changed to give glory to the one God. The song was a proclamation of love that gave thanks for gifts given and received. Its tune was sweet, yet haunting, the type of tune that stuck in your mind once you heard it. A song that was infinitely memorable, yet somehow had been lost to the modern world.

"God, Maggie. That's gorgeous," Brian said when the last note faded. "What is it? Did you write it?"

Magda froze for a second, stumbling over her words. "Write it? Uh … n … no. It's an old, old song." It had been old when she'd played it—old when her grandmother was a child.

"How old?"

Magda shrugged. "I don't know. It's old. Before Christianity came to Scotland."

"Who wrote it? Do you have music for it?"

Magda shook her head. She knew he meant written music. She hadn't even seen any until a few days ago. In her time songs were just passed down, not attributed. Like as not, some old bard or bored shepherd had composed it. Music was for everyone, but for a long time writing had been for only the wealthy or the church. "I don't know if there is any. I learned in from my grandmother."

"Ask your mom if she knows who wrote it."

That's right, Magda remembered. Maggie's mother was still alive. "I don't think she'll know. My grandma would have told me had she known."

"We need to find the composer," Brian insisted.

"Why?" Magda asked.

"I think we found your encore number. If it's that old, I doubt if anyone holds the rights to it, but I'll check. What did you say it was called?"

"*The Song for First Fruits.*"

He wrote down the title. "Okay." He faced the orchestra, lifted his baton, and looked pointedly at Maggie. "Are you planning on playing without music today?"

She laughed nervously. Music. *Oh, God. I don't know how to read music.* Sweat sprang to her brow. What was she going to do? Maybe she'd faint and not have to play. She looked at the podium in front of her. A thick black folder full of music sat there. She shakily opened it, grabbed the song on the top, praying that it would be the correct song, and placed the music on the stand in front of her.

Brian nodded, raised the baton again, and marked the beat.

When he cued Magda, she played. Her fingers did, indeed, know the music. Mozart's *Magic Flute* filled the air. She didn't dare pause to think for fear that her brain would interfere with Maggie's fingers and that the music would stop. She just played.

# Chapter 5

Davy got up from the breakfast table. "We'll work on how to get the two of ye back where ye belong when we've an idea how it can be wrought," he said as he helped Maggie with the dishes. He had no idea where Auld Annie had gotten to, which was probably just as well since he'd most likely have throttled the witch and earned another curse. "Right now, ye needs learn about where ye are so as to fit in."

"Good idea." Maggie understood the problem. She needed to learn to be Magda so someone didn't think Annie had bewitched her. She followed Davy out of the cottage for a tour of the outbuildings. There were a chicken coop where the hens slept at night, Davy's workshop, and the barn where Magda's cow and Davy's draft horses lived.

"Magda feeds, I mean fed, the chickens twice a day and gathered eggs in the morning. I do not suppose ye live on a farm in New York?" he asked.

She shook her head. "Not in New York, but I was raised on one in Wisconsin. My parents still live there. David and I go back every fall to help with the harvest. They dinna really need us, but we like to."

Davy kept his face carefully blank. "Then ye'll know about chickens, kine and such. We've not much of a farm here, not like some, just a few animals so we'll have fresh milk and eggs. I'm the wood smith around here, and Magda plays a bit of music come festival time." He opened the door to the hen house, and the chickens bobbed out. Opening a bin just outside the hen house door, he took out two handfuls of grain and scattered it to the waiting chickens.

"What does she play?" Maggie asked, watching the chickens peck at the grain.

"Flute." Davy frowned, remembering. "She's to play at First Fruits in four days." He shook his head. "Heaven help us. I'll tell the McClellan yer sick or the babe is threatening to come early."

"I play the flute," Maggie said. "Perhaps I can learn the song in time."

She smiled at him, and his heart caught in his throat. He reached for her hand, but he stopped himself in time, covering the motion by scratching his arm. She was so like his Magda that it was hard to remember that she wasn't. It was hard to remember not to touch her. Davy frowned, turning away. "Barn's this way," he said, as if she couldn't see the building ten yards away.

"When is the bairn due?" she asked, as much to break the silence as to find out. It was clear that the pregnancy was well advanced. Magda's body was fully rounded, and her belly button protruded inside out.

He didn't look at her. "Four to six weeks, give or take."

"Oh." Maggie swallowed. They didn't have much time to figure out how to get her and Magda back where they belonged. Somehow she didn't think Annie meant to give her Magda's baby, but judging from Davy's tight voice and stiff back, she didn't think he'd agree.

When the silence between them grew uncomfortable, Magda laid a hand on Davy's arm. It was the normal thing to do. She and David were always touching each other, always reconnecting physically. Touching him calmed her, reassured her that everything was all right, but it was more than that. Their touching sparked recognition on a deeper level. It was as if it awakened memories of past intimacies—spiritual as well as sexual. As if by touching, they reestablished a claim. Each touch proclaimed the other, "Mine." And the same rightness was there between her and Davy until he jerked away.

He swore, staring at her with narrowed eyes. He'd felt it too.

"Sorry," Maggie said, her eyes wide with ill-concealed hurt.

Davy shook his head, willing both of them to forget the last minute. "Did yer David farm?"

Maggie understood his need to ignore the chemistry between them, but she didn't agree. It would be better if they talked about the switch, but she recognized the stubborn set of Davy's jaw. He'd no more talk about it than David would. She'd leave it alone—for now. "Uh, no. He's an artist—a sculptor. He's verra talented. His sculptures are life-sized people and animals that look so real that ye half expect them to move except they're cast in bronze."

Davy watched Maggie's emotions play across his wife's face. Magda looked that way when she talked about his work. They were so alike, this Maggie and his Magda. So alike, and yet … God, he missed his woman.

"I'd like to see yer workshop," Maggie said, watching Davy.

Davy led the way to the barn.

The clean scent of wood greeted them at the door. Davy pushed past her to open the shutters. Light filled the barn, illuminating workbenches lined with tools, a soot-blackened fireplace, and furniture in different levels of completion.

She looked around briefly, noting how similar woodworking and sculpting tools were. Or maybe it was the layouts of Davy's shop and David's studio. She only knew that they felt the same to her. She felt comfortable here. She could come in here and play her flute as she did in David's studio at home. Her focus skipped around the room until she saw the rocking chair and the cradle. She crossed the room without thought as if the chair and cradle had called to her, compelling her to touch them.

"Oh," she gasped, running her hands over the carvings on the silky wood. Davy was an artist. His work was not simply beautiful; it had been crafted with love, and that love showed in the work. David did that too.

But it wasn't just the beauty of the carvings that struck Maggie—it was the subject matter. Davy carved acorns and oak leaves to express growth and strength just as David did.

Maggie blinked, swallowing hard as she brought herself back to the present. It was clear that oaks and acorns were important to Davy and Magda as well. She tipped the cradle over and looked at its plain bottom. She'd expected his signature or at least his initials and date. Work this good should be signed.

"Dinna ye sign yer work?" she asked when she didn't see his initials anywhere on either piece. When he didn't answer right away, she glanced up at him.

He was watching her with a haunted look in his eye. He'd been trying to separate Maggie from Magda, trying to pick out differences, but Maggie had caressed the carvings as Magda did. Most people looked and commented, but Magda touched. It was as if she could see better with her fingers than with her eyes.

She'll pass as Magda well enough, Davy thought, purposely ignoring the fissure of fear that was forming in his heart. Would he have known she wasn't Magda if she hadn't told him?

"Dinna ye sign yer work?" she asked again.

He shook his head to clear it. "Aye. I make me mark." He went to her, pointed to the curved oak leaf that was his sign.

"You sign with an oak leaf?" she asked, feeling a bit dizzy.

"Aye," he answered, watching her in that intense way of his. "How does yer man sign his work?"

Maggie turned away from him. The answer caught in her throat. "He marks them all with an acorn."

Davy narrowed his eyes. "An acorn? Why?"

"It was my idea, really."

"Oh?" He crossed his arms in front of his chest.

"Well, yes. I named the first sculpture he made while we were together 'Acorn' because acorns grow into oaks."

"Yes," he said, looking at her as if she were touched. "They do."

"I know it's silly," she said. There was something in the intensity in which he watched her that made her nervous. She dipped her head, hiding her face in her hair. Long hair definitely had its uses. Maybe she'd grow hers long when she got back.

"How so?"

Maggie shrugged and gave Davy the same explanation she'd given David then. "David and I were under an oak tree, and I was thinking about babies. Neither one of us is small. David is about yer size, but not as broad. Anyway, I was thinking that our children would start little like acorns and grow big and strong like oaks. It's stupid, I know."

"Not so stupid." Davy frowned, remembering a similar conversation with Magda.

# Chapter 6

Holding tightly to David's hand for fear of becoming lost, Magda entered the grocery store. This was where food came from. She'd paid special attention to how they'd gotten from the theater to the store, which subway line, which exit—everything.

Magda looked around the store. Shelves full of food plentiful enough to feed all of Kirkinwall for a month-long gathering lined walls and made hallways. She wondered what she and David would buy.

"We need bread and what else?" he asked her.

She shrugged, but she supposed that it was her job to say even if she didn't know what they needed or if they had coin enough to pay.

Maggie's life was far more complicated than her own. Her own world wasn't full of this overabundance of decisions or mazes with moving parts, flashing lights, loud noises, and crowds of people. She longed for the open sky, silence, and solitude. But mostly, she longed for Davy and the babe she'd carried. Even as she stuck close to David's side and held tightly to his hand, she longed for Davy.

David's touch worried her. The clasp of his hand was a necessity to prevent becoming lost, but it was more than that as well. It was a connection that she was tapping into. A physical and spiritual connection between Maggie and her husband that Magda felt a part of and wanted nothing to do with. It tugged at her. It promised an intimacy that she planned to avoid at all costs. The touching had to stop. Once they were back in their house—his and Maggie's house. Once they were back at the house, she wouldn't touch him any more.

Later, in Maggie's kitchen, they worked together putting away the groceries. David made a big deal about announcing where he was putting everything.

"I'm putting the pancake mix in this cupboard beside the cold cereal, all right?"

Magda would have found that annoying had she not been so grateful to hear what kind of food they already had and where it was. When she had an item in hand, she could automatically put it where it went, but her hands couldn't find objects her mind didn't know existed.

"Thank you for your help," Magda said, watching David fold the paper bags and put them away.

"No problem." He reached for her, but she stepped out of his grasp.

"Would you like some tea?" she asked, busying herself by filling the kettle.

"Not really," David said. "I'd like to know how you are, really."

"Really?" He was giving her an opening to confess all. Could she chance it?

"Really," he said, sitting on a stool.

She took a deep breath and fought the fear. She needed help living in this world. She needed help being Maggie. She needed help to get home. "I'm not myself, and it scares me," she said, trying to be both honest and cautious.

He watched her carefully. "What does that mean?"

Magda turned from him to get the tea from the cupboard. "I'm different. I don't remember things."

David frowned. "Different how? What things don't you remember?"

Magda avoided his eyes while she thought about what to tell him.

"Maggie?" He slid off the stool and started around the island to her.

"No." She shook her head at him. "Just stay there. I can't think when you are so close."

He stopped and regarded her quizzically. "How are you different? What don't you remember?"

She swallowed hard. "Promise you won't take me back to the hospital."

"Oh, Maggie," he sighed, looking at her with worry and disappointment.

The look of disappointment wounded Magda. Still, she insisted. "Promise, David. Promise or I won't say another word."

David frowned at her. "I'd never take you back there if you didn't want to go."

"Promise?"

"I promise."

She nearly sagged in relief.

The kettle whistled, startling her. She grabbed the kettle from the flame and set about making the tea.

He sat on the stool and watched as she stalled, focusing her attention on pouring steaming water into a mug. When she'd added milk to her tea as she always did, he frowned. There were so many things that were the same, yet there was enough that was different for him to wonder. "Are you ready to talk yet?" he asked, trying to keep the confused frustration from his voice.

She smiled nervously, putting down her spoon. "I don't know where to begin."

"Tell me how you are different."

She nodded. "Ever since I woke up in the hospital, I haven't been the Maggie you know. I'm ... it's like I'm someone else."

"How so?"

"I don't remember things."

"Like how to get to Lincoln Center?"

She nodded. "Or what to play once I'm there."

"You did fine, more than fine. You were spectacular as always."

She smiled. "Thank you. But the thing is, I didn't think I would be. I couldn't remember where my flute was or what the music sounded like."

"And then you did."

She shook her head. "Not quite. My body did. My body remembers things it's accustomed to, like playing music I've practiced or knowing where things belong, but it doesn't remember things like subway lines or who people are."

"Do you remember me?"

Magda looked at her untouched tea. "I know who you are."

"But you don't remember me." The words burned through both of them.

She raised her gaze to David's face. She didn't know David well, and yet strangely she felt as if she did. It hurt her to hurt him. "Not as a husband, no."

"What do you remember me as?" He was hurt, and his words were angry.

Magda shook her head.

"What do you remember?" he demanded.

Magda shrugged. What could she say? *I remember my life, who I used to be?*

"So you did some research last night, going through the scrapbooks, trying to find out who you are."

It wasn't a question, but she nodded anyway.

"Did it help you remember?" The vulnerability in his words clawed at Magda's heart, making her want to lie.

She shook her head sadly and gave him the truth. "I know who Maggie was, but I'm not her."

"Of course, you are," David insisted, reaching across the island to grab Magda's hand.

She pulled her hand away, shaking her head sadly as unbidden tears filled her eyes. "I'm not your Maggie, David. I'm someone else."

"Who?" he demanded, shaken. "If you aren't Maggie, who are you?"

She took a deep breath, fearful that he'd think her mad and send her away, but she was unable to go on any longer pretending to be someone she was not. She had to tell him.

"I'm Magda McClellan."

David forced a laugh, trying to make a joke of it, but he didn't succeed.

"You believe this? That you're someone else, a woman named Magda?" he asked. Tears welled up in his eyes.

Magda nodded.

"Dammit, Maggie." He dashed the tears from his eyes with his sleeve. "Don't do this. Don't play with me."

She shook her head, and tears streamed down her face. "I'm not. Do you think I'd pretend this? Do you think Maggie would? She loves you. I don't know much else, but I know that she loves you."

"*She* loves me?" he repeated incredulously. "*She* does? If *you* don't remember anything, how do *you* know?" he yelled.

"I …" How did she know? Because in Maggie's body she felt the pull between them? Because in Maggie's body she almost loved him? "I just do."

"Shit." He pushed himself off the stool. "I can't handle this Maggie, Magda, whoever the hell you think you are." He shook his head. "I can't believe we're having this conversation." He rounded the island, reaching for her arm. "Come on. Get your coat. We're going to the hospital. They gave you the drug that did this, and they'd better have the drugs to undo it."

"No!" She backed away, sobbing. "You promised. David, you promised."

"Shit." He stopped mid-reach and looked at his wife's panicked, tear-streaked face. She was pressed in the far corner of the kitchen, arched slightly back over the counter, hugging herself and shaking. "Shit."

"You p … p … p … promised."

"Oh, Maggie," he said sadly, reaching for her to hold her, to comfort her.

She arched farther back, staring at him with wide, frightened eyes. She looked like she was about to climb onto the counter to escape.

"Shit." Lowering his hands, David stepped back. He was scaring her, making it worse. "Shit."

Magda didn't relax.

"Come on, Mag—" Had she said Magda? Who would name their kid Magda?

She shook her head.

He swore again, closed his eyes and lifted his face to the ceiling. "I can't do this now." Lowering his head, he looked at Magda. "I can't do this now."

She made no response.

He turned on his heel and left the kitchen, pausing just long enough to grab his coat on the way out of the house.

Magda was alone in the silent brownstone.

Slowly the tension that held her stiff in the corner drained away, leaving her empty and frightened. Why had she told him?

As the hours passed, the streetlights came on, but inside the brownstone Magda sat in the dark. She'd moved to a chair in the gallery where she huddled in the sculptures' silent company. She couldn't think. Nothing made sense, least of all why she'd told David. Maybe she'd told him because she needed help, because she couldn't handle it alone. Now she *was* alone.

She closed her eyes and, squeezing out tears that slid down damp cheeks, she tried to pray.

In the dark, the clock on the wall ticked in an unnaturally loud rhythm. Even God didn't seem to hear her desperate prayers.

David didn't come home that night. Magda didn't know where he'd gone, only that when she awakened with a sunbeam hitting her eyes she was still alone in the house.

Maggie had practice at ten.

Magda wandered around the house getting ready. She wasn't certain why, other than it was something to do—something that didn't require thought. She tried not to worry about David, about where he might be or what plans he was making for her. At home, this kind of fear would have sent her to Davy's arms or to the woods, but here that wasn't an option. This world offered more peril than the occasional wild animal, English soldier, or wanderer she might meet in the forests around Kirkinwall. She would gladly have skipped practice, concentrating on getting back to Davy and Kirkinwall, but she couldn't begin to think how.

She let Maggie's body take her through the motions of getting ready for work. She took the keys from Maggie's purse and locked the door on the way out.

He was there when she returned.

"I made supper," he told her as she hung up her coat. The air was redolent with smells that tempted her palate and made her stomach rumble, though she didn't recognize the ingredients they came from.

"It smells good. What is it?" she asked.

"Lasagna, your favorite." He opened the oven to let her look in.

Lasagna was Maggie's favorite food then. A wave of richly scented air washed over her as she peered into the oven. A spicy red sauce bubbled around noodles and cheese. She wondered what might make the sauce red.

She changed clothes while David served dinner and poured wine. Focusing on getting their relationship back to normal, he never considered that she might be pregnant and probably shouldn't be drinking wine.

They ate in the dining room by candlelight. She expected a confrontation or at least a discussion, but she got neither. David seemed to have decided to ignore yesterday's conversation and pretend that all was well between them. Magda suspected he thought she was really Maggie suffering from some sort of memory loss and was hoping to spur her memories with the romantic dinner.

She watched David take a bite of the lasagna before she tried it. It was delicious. She could easily believe that it was Maggie's favorite meal.

"What makes the sauce red?" she asked as she mopped the last bit from her plate with a piece of garlic bread.

"Tomato sauce."

She froze with the piece of bread halfway to her mouth.

"What?" David asked.

"Are you sure it's safe?"

He looked at the shocked expression on her pale face and tried not to laugh. "Tomato sauce? I hope so. We've eaten it enough. I think tomato sauce was the only vegetable I ate while growing up."

"Really." They must do something to the tomatoes to counteract the poison. "Why?"

She forced a smile. "No reason. It's just … aren't tomatoes poisonous?"

He laughed. "No. If you ask for catsup in certain restaurants, they may look at you like it is, but I'm sure it's not."

"Oh." She blushed, wondering what catsup was. "Good. I mean, this was really good, thank you."

"And now that you're sure it isn't poison, would you like another piece?" David teased.

Magda felt her face grow hot but smiled at him anyway, grateful that he hadn't taken offense. "Uh … no. I'm full."

"Me too. What do you say we take our wine to the living room?"

"After I do the dishes," Magda said.

"All right. After we do the dishes." He took the salad bowls and plates, leaving her to follow with water glasses and breadbasket. A few minutes later, the rinsed dishes sat in the dishwasher, and David was filling both glasses of wine.

As he started the dishwasher, Magda carried both glasses into the living room. She set his on the coffee table in front of the couch before sitting in a chair with hers. She didn't want to sit on the couch for fear that he'd join her, but the chair was more like a chair and a half, nearly big enough for two. She sat in the middle of it, slipping off her shoes and pulling her feet up to take up more space.

David came into the room, carrying a newly opened bottle of wine. His lips formed a wry smile when he saw how she'd positioned herself so he could not sit with her.

"May I join you?" he asked, putting down the wine bottle and picking up his glass.

Did he mean in the living room, in a drink, or in the chair? Since she wasn't sure what he was asking, she didn't know how to respond. So she changed the subject. "You make very good lasagna." There were so many things she wanted to ask him, like where he had gone last night, but she was afraid to bring up the subject of her displacement.

"Yours is better," he said, turning on soft instrumental music before sitting on the couch. "I can cook, but you're such a good cook that I hardly ever do. Besides, you like it."

"Do I?" She smiled. "I think I could get used to having someone else do the cooking."

It was precisely the answer he expected from Maggie. David grinned. "Can't blame a guy for trying."

Magda watched him over the rim of her glass, relieved that they could laugh together. She took another sip of wine. It was good, not like the vinegar-tasting brew they drank at the Hall.

They talked of small things, laughing often. Magda didn't notice how David kept her glass filled until she stood to make her way to the bathroom. On the way back, feeling very relaxed and maybe a bit wobbly, she stopped just inside the living room door to listen to the music.

"Maggie?" He crossed the room to her side.

She smiled at him.

"Would you like to dance?"

"I don't know how. I don't know the steps."

"Your body will remember. We've danced before."

She knew she should say no. He wasn't Davy, no matter how he made her smile and laugh. But she loved to dance. At festival everyone danced with everyone. This would be no more than that. She nodded, holding out her hands.

She nearly bolted when he pulled her into his arms. This was not the sort of dancing she'd done before.

"Relax," he said, holding her close. "It's just a dance."

"Is this the way it's done, then?" she asked.

"Yes," he said, taking her right hand in his and moving to the music.

He was right. Her feet remembered the steps. The problem was the rest of her body remembered things too. He held her too close for comfort, yet not close enough. Her breasts felt good pressed against the warmth of his chest. And their legs seemed more tangled than they should be despite their synchronized movements. Maybe it was the wine—the tip of her nose felt numb. But before she could comment on their proximity, the dance had ended.

"See? You remembered how perfectly." The next song wasn't as slow. He hesitated, and she drew away. "I'll find another slow one," he said, reaching for the remote.

"No," she said, a bit breathlessly. "I think that's enough for one night. It's getting late."

David glanced at the clock. It was almost time for the eleven o'clock news. "Sit with me and watch the news."

"Maybe I should just go to bed," she said, not trusting herself to be near him. It was the wine, she told herself—the wine that made his smile so sweet and his arms so inviting.

He took her hands in his and looked into her eyes. "Stay."

She swallowed visibly, hesitating.

"Please."

She nodded once.

He flicked on the television and pulled her into the chair with him. She tried to get up.

"Shh," he whispered. "It's okay."

She shook her head. Her body ached to settle next to his, to feel the strength of his arms around her. Had he been Davy, there would be no question.

It was the thought of Davy that had her on her feet. It was one thing to dance with another man, but it was something else to snuggle in his arms. And that had been what she'd been about to do.

"I think I'll read in the library for a while," she said, walking to the door.

"Maggie."

She stopped, turning to look at him.

"You don't have to sleep on the couch. If the thought of sleeping with me makes you uncomfortable, I'll sleep in the guest room."

Filled with equal parts of relief and guilt, Magda nodded and left the room.

Three weeks passed, filled with rehearsals and performances. Magda navigated around Maggie's life as best she could, but it wasn't easy. Her stomach was a constant ache. She used it as an excuse to avoid David's touch. She used every excuse she could think of to avoid David's touch. She said she was afraid it would risk the pregnancy, even though she knew she wasn't pregnant. Even before her courses started, she'd known. Even though it technically wasn't her body, she knew its rhythms just as well as she had known her own. She'd immediately known when she'd conceived with Davy. She'd been so certain, she'd told him so. And he'd believed her.

Now she was lying to David.

Every day, every hour: "My head hurts."

"My stomach hurts."

"It will risk the baby."

"I'm too tired."

Lies and more lies. Lies that he knew were lies.

He didn't press her, however; he didn't argue the obvious. He brought her flowers and chocolates, and he ran her baths. He didn't ask for the truth, and she didn't give it to him.

The only time she was happy was when she was playing the flute—when she lost herself in the music. She loved performing, and the audiences loved her.

She woke up the morning after her latest concert with a stiff neck. She was rubbing it as she entered the kitchen.

"I thought we'd take the day off," David said, pouring a cup of coffee for her. He looked up and handed it to her. "What's the matter? Stiff neck?"

She tried to nod and winced.

"Poor baby," he said sympathetically, setting down the cup and walking around her.

She groaned without meaning to when he began massaging her neck and shoulders.

"Come on." He stopped rubbing her back and took her hand. "Let's do this right." Before she even thought to protest, he led her back to her bed. "Lie down, face down."

His hands were warm and gentle on her sore muscles.

"This would be better if you weren't wearing this shirt," he said. "Why don't you undress and crawl under the sheet, and I'll get some massage oil."

She knew he was right about the shirt, and it hurt too much to question his motives or argue. When he left the room, she undressed, involuntarily whimpering in pain as she raised her arms to tug the shirt over her head. She kicked off her trousers and took off her undergarments as well before climbing under the sheet. Face down on the bed, she silently prayed for relief.

He arrived, laden with supplies. Soon soft music played and scented candles were lit. He pulled the sheet down to her waist and drizzled warm oil over her back. She lurched when he touched her.

"Relax," he whispered.

She gave herself over to his skillful hands, nearly sobbing in relief when he kneaded the knots from her neck and back. He worked her body like clay, manipulating the muscles until they were soft. As the pain eased away, it was replaced by something nearly as painful—desire. She yearned for his hands—not just on her neck and back, nor just on her arms or legs. She wanted to turn over and offer her breasts—and the rest of herself as well.

If he had touched her in more intimate places, he would have found her pliable to his every desire. And knowing that, he didn't.

Touching her was exquisite torture. He'd been hard from the first, from the anticipation of touching her. Her body was ready for him. He could catch the faint scent of her musk, and it made him bite his tongue to keep from licking down her spine, from tasting the contours of her round bottom, from easing in between her thighs.

He wanted her. His body was ready. Her body was ready. But her mind … her mind was not. To take her now would be wrong. She loved him. He could see it in her eyes even as she made excuses to avoid his touch. And God knew he loved her, but …

It was the "but" that stopped him. Something had changed three weeks ago when she'd been in the hospital. Maggie was still Maggie with her talents and preferences, with her interests and sense of humor, but something was different. It wasn't the chemistry between them, that connection that had had him proposing to her a week after they'd met. That was still there. It was something else. Something in her eyes beyond the drug-induced lack of memory. Something she wasn't telling him. It fascinated and frightened him in turn. He felt as if he were falling in love with his wife all over again. It made the wooing fun. When she gave herself to him whole-heartedly, he knew he'd find it worth the wait. And so, instead of joining her in the bed, he kept his hands away from certain areas and continued to work on her muscles until she drifted off to sleep.

Magda awakened alone, naked and smiling. David had covered her up and left her. He'd had her for the taking, yet he hadn't taken. She lay in bed feeling glorious, more glorious than a mere massage could make her. David loved her. And she loved David.

Davy's face filled her mind. Davy.

It's funny how feeling so good could lead to feeling so bad. She'd betrayed Davy. Not physically, thanks to David's willpower. She'd betrayed Davy in her mind and in her heart. How could she? It had only been three weeks.

Three weeks. In her world she would have played for First Fruits already and be nearly ready to deliver her first child.

How could she forget that even for a moment? How could her heart let her? And what was she doing to get back?

Nothing. She was doing nothing. She had done nothing. She'd sat here in Maggie's life and fallen in love with Maggie's husband. Self-loathing curled around Magda, threatening to choke her. Her oil-slick body felt dirty. She'd let him run his hands up and down her naked body, and she'd wanted more. Never mind that it wasn't really her body. It had been *her* mind that wanted him.

She ran to the bathroom and showered, viciously scrubbing her body, wiping out the memory of his touch with pain. She scrubbed her breasts—the breasts that had ached for his touch.

Tears of self-recrimination scoured her face. She was in a winless situation. There seemed no way home and no way to live with herself here. She had to keep out of David's arms, but the sexual tension between them had grown and with it her guilt—guilt over denying him his rights as husband and guilt over not wanting to deny him.

She truly felt ill. How could she live like this? The lie of her existence threatened to swamp every attempt to stay afloat in Maggie's world. She needed to get back to Davy. But how?

# Chapter 7

Maggie puttered around the kitchen, making supper. Cooking in Magda's kitchen was a lot like cooking in the rough cabin she'd camped in as a child. Davy had sent her from his workroom shortly after their acorn/oak leaf conversation. She'd gotten the feeling that the eerie similarities between herself and Magda and himself and David had bothered him as much as they had her. She'd have liked to talk about it, but Davy had clammed up. "Go figure out the kitchen. Willna be long before Magda's uncle, Father Toddy, will be showing his face. He visits about dinnertime two or three times a week."

She'd left without telling Davy that she had a brother, Father Todd. There were just too many similarities for it to be coincidence. She had a theory, that she and Magda were the same person in different time frames, but she didn't know what she thought about it at present. It would be easier if she could believe that this was just a long, involved dream.

Maggie was nearly ready to call Davy into dinner when the door opened to admit a portly cleric.

"Magda, lass, do ye have enough for yer wee uncle to join ye?"

Even without Davy's warning, Maggie would have instantly known who the man was. It was her brother, Todd, or rather a shorter, fatter version of her brother. She laughed at the sight of him.

Her brother's one vice was vanity. He was a handsome, fit man whose hobby had always been weightlifting. This man, though he wore her brother's face, was easily twice as heavy. And, by the way he bee-lined to the cook pot and lifted the lid, he wasn't bothered by his weight.

"Ah, lass, yer Davy's a lucky man, and tell him I said so."

"Tell me yerself, Father," Davy said, coming in through the open door. He shot an assessing glance at Maggie.

She smiled at him and his heart clenched. Was Magda back?

"Well, and ye best know yer lucky," Father Toddy said, dipping a spoon in the pot and giving the contents a quick stir before raising a steaming spoonful to his lips.

"And here I thought ye were all about God's gifts and not about luck."

Father Toddy blew on the stew and laughed. "And what did ye think luck was? 'Course it be one of God's gifts. Ye must be getting that man of yers to the kirk, Magda. He's gone pagan, he has."

"That'll be Davy's cross and not mine," Maggie laughed. The familiarity of the scene was both reassuring and unsettling. David didn't attend Mass with her either, and this was a common joke between them in her time as well.

Father Toddy sipped at the stew's broth. "Mmm. A gift from God is what ye are, Magda." He blew on the chunks of vegetables and meat on the spoon once more before eating those as well. "Dinna ken why He'd waste ye on a base woodman like yon cub, but His ways are not for us to ken," he said while he chewed.

Davy smiled as he poured ale into two cups. "I think ye should thank Him that He made Magda yer niece," he said, handing Magda's uncle a cup. "Ye'd naught get round my table else."

"Thank ye." Father Toddy accepted the cup and raised it to his lips. "Don't think I dinna ken that."

Davy sat at the table, and Father Toddy joined him without invitation.

Maggie shook her head. It was just like at home with David and Todd sparring back and forth as if they weren't the best of friends. Todd worked at a mission in New York and played handball every Wednesday with David.

This had to be a dream. It was like the *Wizard of Oz* without the evil witch and the ruby slippers. All the people of Oz were people Dorothy knew in Kansas. So, too, it was with Maggie. She could hardly wait to wake up and tell David all about it. He'd have a laugh over Todd as the obese Father Toddy.

But it wasn't a dream.

She ladled stew into wooden bowls and set them in front of the men along with massive hunks of bread. She'd been unable to find the bread knife and made do with ripping the loaf into chunks. She expected the men to comment on it, but they didn't seem to notice anything amiss.

She sat down with her own bowl and looked at Magda's uncle expectantly.

"Tis yer man's job to ask the blessing," Toddy said, as if this too were a part of their normal pattern.

"What's the good of having a priest to table if it still falls to me to ask the blessing?" Davy grumbled.

"It's likely the only time he gets to hear ye pray," Maggie said, following the familiar script.

"Magda!" Davy said, beaming at her. She was back! His wife was back! It took every ounce of his will power not to leap from the bench, pull her into his arms, and kiss her soundly. His Acorn was back.

Maggie blinked at him.

Father Toddy looked at Davy, surprised. "Dinna scold her, lad. She's got the right of it. Ye doona darken the kirk's door, now do ye? Where else am I to hear ye pray?"

Smiling widely and ignoring the priest, Davy stared at Maggie.

Father Toddy and Maggie exchanged puzzled looks.

Davy reached across the table to grab Maggie's hands, his expression one of joy and relief.

Watching Davy closely, Father Toddy cleared his throat. "All right, then, Davy, we're waiting on ye for the blessing."

"Oh, aye," Davy said distractedly, squeezing Maggie's hand. It was clear that his mind was on his wife and not on dinner.

"The blessing," Father Toddy prompted.

"Aye," Davy said, shaking his head to clear it. "Bless this food and them that eats it. Bless me wife, who I couldna live without. And pray that the cursed witch n'er returns."

"Quite the prayer, that," Father Toddy said, staring at Davy, not noticing how pale Maggie had gotten. "Though I'll give me amen to it." He ripped a chunk of bread from his portion and used it to scoop up a mouthful of stew.

Maggie squeezed Davy's hand before freeing hers.

Davy turned to his dinner, still grinning ear to ear.

"Are ye ready to play for First Fruits, Magda?" Father Toddy asked between mouthfuls.

"Maybe," Maggie answered, trying to be honest. She wasn't ready now, but if she could hear the song, she could probably play it with a bit of practice. "What is that tune again?"

Father Toddy laughed. "I'll bet ye hear the song in yer dreams."

"Not really. Ye've such a nice voice. I'd love to hear ye sing it."

Father Toddy laughed, clearly pleased by the flattery. "Sweet of ye to say so, Magda, but as yer pastor I must council ye against telling lies. Endangers yer immortal soul, ye ken." He winked at her. "Why dinna ye fetch yer flute and play it, so as to practice?"

"Am I not to eat?" Maggie asked. She was worried, but she tried to keep her voice light and teasing so that no one would know.

Davy wasn't fooled. He had been watching her closely, his confidence that she was his Magda rising and falling with the conversation. She looked a bit pale, but that wasn't uncommon. As her pregnancy advanced, she frequently looked tired and wan at the end the day. Playing music would prove for sure who she was. Magda would know the music while Maggie claimed she didn't.

"Of course, I'll let ye eat. I'm just wanting to hear the song. What does it sound like, Davy?" He winked at his nephew-in-law. "I canna recall."

Davy obligingly hummed the chorus.

"That was beautiful." Maggie smiled at Davy in appreciation.

Father Toddy laughed. His niece adored her husband so, that even his out-of-tune humming seemed to please her. "It's much prettier with the flute," Father Toddy said.

Maggie frowned at him.

"Well, it is." Father Toddy defended himself, looking to Davy for support.

Davy shook his head and resumed eating.

Father Toddy shrugged, before turning his concentration to mopping up the last of his stew with a chunk of bread.

Davy grinned. "Best dish him out a bit more, Magda, else he's like to wear through the bowl."

Maggie was busy running the song through her head to imprint it there and praying that her fingers would know the rest of the song.

"Can ye spare another mouthful?" her uncle asked when she didn't offer to refill his bowl.

"Oh, I'm sorry," she said. "Would ye care for a bit more?"

"Always." Davy frowned, looking at Maggie. "Here, lass, let me get it for him. Ye look done in." He rose from the table with his and Father Toddy's bowls in hand.

"If yer that tired, lass, I'll not make ye play."

Maggie watched Davy, wondering what was going on in his head. "That's all right. It will do me good to run through it once or twice." Now that she'd heard the tune, it *was* best if she implanted it firmly in her brain. There was no better way to do that than play it.

"Really?" Davy paused mid-ladle, looking unaccountably relieved.

She nodded, watching him carefully, trying to read his thoughts.

"Good," he said, finishing filling the bowls and bringing them to the table. "I'll get yer flute, and ye can play while yer uncle Father and I finish."

Davy retrieved Magda's flute from a drawer and brought it to her.

Maggie stared at it in disbelief. *A wooden flute?* It took her a moment to remember that metal flutes hadn't been invented until Boehm developed them in the early 1800s. Davy had told her that the year was 1718. All flutes would be wooden, and more people would play recorders than flutes for a few more years.

She ran her hands over the beautifully carved instrument. She knew in a flash that Davy had made this. He'd made it for Magda.

The thought brought tears to her eyes.

"What's wrong, Magda?" Father Toddy asked.

She shook her head, not trusting her voice.

"It's just the bairn," Davy explained, knowing that giving his wife a hug would only bring more tears. "Tears come easy. She'll be fine in a minute."

Maggie was surprised to find that he was right. She was over the heart-clenching that had brought the tears, but she was worried about her fingering. It had six holes—three on the left and three on the right—but no keys. How was she to play it?

She brought the instrument to her lips, closed her eyes, and ran through the scale. When she watched her hands, she faltered, but her fingers knew what to do to produce the notes in her head. The fingering seemed more like that of a tin whistle than the modern flute, but if her hands knew what to do, she wasn't going to let her mind interfere and ruin it.

She mentally replayed the tune Davy had hummed before trying it on the flute.

It was, indeed, prettier on the flute—and longer too. Her hands, once they started the song, seemed to remember it—verses and all. It was amazing … and moving. Tears filled her eyes and spilled down her cheeks. She couldn't have said what the tears were for—gratitude, relief, the beauty of the piece? Honestly, it didn't seem to matter.

When she finished the song and lowered the flute, Davy swept her into his arms and kissed her soundly.

"Magda," he pronounced, now sure beyond a doubt that she was indeed his own sweet wife.

Maggie was too stunned to do anything, not that he had given her a chance to so much as shake her head in negation before kissing her again.

Father Toddy cleared his throat loudly.

"Magda," Davy murmured into her hair, squeezing Maggie tightly before slowly lowering her to the ground.

Father Toddy shook his head, regarding the couple with a bemused smile. "It was lovely, indeed, Magda. But, Davy, ye must remember yerself. It willna do to be sweeping her up for a kiss at the festival no matter how pleased ye are with her or how ripe she is with yer first fruits. It's not seemly."

Davy bent down to place a kiss on the top of Maggie's head. "Not seemly," he repeated with laughter in his voice.

When he released her, Maggie clutched the flute to her chest. Davy's kisses had stunned her. It wasn't just the fact that he'd kissed her; it was how she felt about the kisses. She felt … stimulated.

She stumbled to the cabinet to put the flute away.

Smiling, Davy watched her go, once again assured that his world was not upside down.

Having wrapped the flute in its cloth, Maggie closed the drawer and leaned against the cabinet. She vaguely heard Davy and Father Toddy conversing beyond the clutter of her own thoughts.

Davy's kisses.

She touched her lips in memory. She'd kissed other men before David. Truth be told, she'd gotten physical with other men before David. She'd been in college, in the music program, and … well, it had been a different time. But once she'd seen David, there had been no one else. There had been an instant connection—love at first sight, savage desire at first touch. David's kisses had moved her from the first, leaving her feeling special … loved … heated. No one else's kisses had ever done that. Despite what went on between them, no one else had been able to capture her heart with a look. No one but David.

Until now.

Davy's kiss had contained David's heat, his arms David's comfort, and his mouth David's taste. It scared her.

Flushed and bemuddled, she worked on automatic pilot, clearing the table, washing the dishes, and making dough for the morning's bread using starter from a jar in the buttery. She'd just covered the bowl of dough with a damp cloth when Davy called to her.

"Come sit a while, Magda. Yer uncle and I are going to play a game or two."

She looked across the room at the men and the chess set. For a moment it seemed as if David and Todd were superimposed on Davy and Father Toddy. She shook her head to clear it.

It was too much to handle, too much to think about. The long day and her unaccustomed bulk weighed down on her. She was suddenly exhausted beyond all telling.

"No. I'm more tired than I'd realized. I think I'll make an early night of it."

"Shall I go, lass? Leave ye with yer husband?" Magda's uncle asked.

"No." She couldn't handle being alone with Davy, not now when her mind was foggy and her defenses were down. "No, play yer game. I'll just finish here. Then I'm for bed." Stifling the urge to dash from the room, she struggled to appear normal. "How's the ale lasting? Shall I fill the pitcher?"

Davy smiled at her. "We're fine, Acorn. Get some sleep."

*Acorn.* The name hung in her mind as she gave the cabinet top a last swipe with the washrag before hanging it on a rod near the fire to dry and escaping into the relative privacy of the bedroom. She managed to get the door closed behind her before breaking down. She leaned against the door and let the tears come.

*I'm Margaret Mary McDonald. I'm tall and blond and a concert flutist. I live in New York with my husband David.* She repeated the litany over and over, standing with her back pressed to the door, her eyes shut tight, crying quietly into her hands.

It didn't help. Her feet ached. Her back ached. Her skin was pulled so tightly over her belly that a spot to the left of her navel burned. She lowered a hand to rub away the pain. There was a hard bump where the burning was. An elbow or knee or some other part of the stranger in her womb was pressed firmly against her side.

Maggie pressed back to move the child and ease the pain. She was surprised when the lump disappeared for a moment and then returned with a jarring bump.

Wonder and love replaced the tears of sadness and loss.

No matter how confusing everything else was, this one fact was clear—a baby grew in her womb. Her heart swelled with love for the child.

This was what she'd longed for and feared she'd never have. She didn't know how it had come to pass that she'd been given this gift, but she knew for certain that it *was* a gift.

Leaving the door, Maggie walked to the wardrobe. She pulled off her dress and hung it on the peg before stripping naked. This body, which hadn't been hers yesterday, was hers today. She caressed her huge belly possessively. The baby that filled it and the man that helped create it were hers as well.

Maggie kissed her fingertips and transferred that kiss to her belly before pulling the nightgown from its peg and sliding it over her head.

A confusion of intense feelings of love and loss, longing and possessiveness filled her. She wanted this child, her child, Davy, David. It was too much to unravel and she was too tired.

She crawled into bed, pulling the sheet to her chin before closing her eyes.

She was drifting to sleep listening to Davy and Toddy talk, when their conversation turned to Auld Annie.

Instantly, all thoughts of sleep fled as she listened.

"Have they found the body?" Davy asked. There was no need for him to say whose body. There was no doubt whom he meant. Still, it wouldn't do to say Auld Annie's name aloud—not if she truly was a witch. Prudent people didn't call the attention of witches and demons by mentioning their names.

Father Toddy shook his head. "No, and I dinna think it's likely that they will. Seems she's truly gone."

"Was she a witch then?"

Father shrugged, picking up his cup. "It seems likely, though I'd naught believed in them afore."

"Nor I," Davy said. "But I agree that it seems likely. There'd be a body else."

"That's what worries me most," the priest confessed. "I canna help wondering how she disappeared, where she went, and if she'll return to take her vengeance. I believe the laird, as well as Rob and Sanna, are worried. I've been to the castle to say extra Masses for the safety of the clan and the continued health of Sanna and her babe. Sanna has been vindicated, but she doesna appear verra comfortable with her innocence."

Davy snorted. "Comes from lying and making false accusations. It was because of her that the guard sought out the old witch."

"Hard to say that she was lying now that there is no body."

Davy frowned. "Do ye think it's true then, that Sanna and Rob were bewitched?"

Father Toddy spread his hands, palms up. "I'd not thought so before. Now, I dinna ken."

Silence fell while both men contemplated the contents of their cups.

"How's Magda taking it?" Father Toddy asked. "She wasna quite herself at dinner."

"Not herself?" Davy asked, worried anew. "How so?"

"Oh, it's probably nothing. Tired from the babe most likely, though she did seem nervous about playing, for all it sounded like teasing. Do ye think she's worried about the witch?"

Davy drained his cup before answering. "Aye. She's mentioned her once or twice. Ye kent she offered Magda a wish?"

Toddy's eyes grew large. "No, I dinna. What did Magda do?"

"Told her thank ye kindly, but she was happy with her life as it was." Davy grabbed the pitcher and splashed ale into his cup.

Toddy nodded, reaching out his own empty cup to be filled. "That's good. Tell me niece I think she's naught to fear. Magda did the witch a good turn, feeding her and such. Good isn't rewarded by evil."

"What do ye mean by that?" Davy asked. "That evil people dinna reward good deeds, or that good deeds aren't rewarded with bad things?"

"What I meant was that I dinna believe the witch would do anything to harm Magda."

"What about the saying, 'No good deed goes unpunished'?" Davy asked.

"I think yer irreverence has reached a new high, or is it a new low?" Father Toddy wrinkled his brow at Davy. "Still," he continued, lifting his cup, "I think good is always rewarded. Sometimes it's its own reward—warms the soul so to say. Sometimes ye get rewarded in this world. Might be ye recognize it or mayhap ye dinna. Might be someone does ye a good turn or yer crops thrive despite the frost. Might be yer babe is born lusty and yer wife's milk plentiful and rich when else it wouldn't have been. It's not for us to know. Sometimes, like in our Lord Jesus's case, the rewards dinna come in this world, but the next. But no matter what, God sees the good we do and blesses us for it."

"I wish I agreed," Davy said sadly. "Seems all too often those that do good are rewarded with pain."

"God's ways are not always clear," Father Toddy said, nodding. "But He does take care of his own."

"I've been blessed and well I know it," Davy said, "but not all have been. Fat Jenny takes care of the sick, and still she's lost every bairn she ever birthed—that's nine if I remember right. And Dougal, nicest man that ever breathed, but he canna seem to keep his wee ones fed. And what of Job in the Bible? What about Jesus himself? He talked about turning the other cheek, not getting rewarded for good behavior. Jesus did good, and still he suffered for it in this world."

"Aye, he suffered," Father admitted. "But he opened Heaven's gate, and now he's sitting at his Father's right hand. Fat Jenny will be rewarded for her faith as will Dougal, dinna ye fret. I hold with my belief that good is always rewarded. And dinna ye worry about Magda none. She'll be having that bairn before long and be herself again. The witch willna return. She kens well what kind of reception she'd get. There wouldna be a trial, just a burning."

In the darkness of the bedroom, an idea dawned on Maggie.

Suddenly, it all became clear to her. She and Magda were one. David and Davy were one. And Todd and Father Toddy were one also. Time and place had changed, but not the players. She hadn't lost David, and he hadn't lost her. They were just seeing each other in different incarnations.

The thought stopped her and brought a smile to her face. David would love the concept. If he were reading this in a novel, he'd stop and call her from another room to share it with her. The concept that love is eternal—that *their* love was eternal—would thrill him as much as it did her.

She didn't understand the reason for the switch, though, and tried to remember everything Annie had told them.

What was it Annie had said? Something about not being able to have children every lifetime? Something about needing to be apart for a time to get their baby? If Annie was behind this strange switch, then maybe ... just maybe ...

Maggie's eyes popped open with anticipation. Maybe she and Magda would return to their original times once Magda got Maggie's body pregnant. A grin split Maggie's face. What an opportunity for both of them. Or for her twice.

The concept of reincarnations trading places temporarily confused her. Still, there was no jealousy in the thought of Magda and David making love. She wasn't sharing David with Magda; she was Magda. It was a gift beyond telling to love and be loved by David now and in the future. She hoped Magda realized this gift soon in her incarnation. It wasn't just so that Magda could get Maggie pregnant. It was so that Magda would realize the joy and love of being with Davy/David in both times, in both bodies.

Maggie caressed her belly, at peace for the first time since exchanging times and bodies. She gloried in the baby that rolled in her womb and listened to Davy and Father Toddy talk philosophy in the other room. It was wonderful how their relationships hadn't changed. She and David were still deeply in love, and Todd was still joyful in his calling.

Smiling, Maggie drifted off to sleep.

It was nearly an hour before Father Toddy took his leave.

Davy turned out the lamp and opened the bedroom door. Moonlight streamed through the open window. He walked to the bed and looked at his wife asleep on her side—a small, round lump in the bed with brown waves of hair fanned on her pillow and her hands folded beneath her cheek. God, he loved her. A wave of fierce tenderness constricted his throat and made tears prick his eyes.

He stood in the dark looking at her, wondering what had happened this past day. Had Maggie come and gone again? Or had this day been just a long, confusing dream? He hesitated to undress and get into bed. What would tomorrow bring? Would Magda greet the dawn with him, or would it be the changeling Maggie?

The ale he'd drank added to his introspective mood, but it didn't help him formulate any answers. He climbed onto the bed without undressing. It would be far easier to explain to Magda why he was sleeping fully clothed on top of the covers than to explain to Maggie why he wasn't.

Promising himself that he wouldn't touch her tonight, just in case, he settled on his side with his back toward his wife and gave in to sleep.

Maggie woke, as she had nearly every day of her married life, wrapped in her husband's arms. Layers of bedding kept their legs from tangling casually together in the normal early morning intimacy that sometimes led to other intimacies. In the moments before she opened her eyes, she had no doubt who and where she was or who was beside her. The memories of the previous day hadn't begun to register, like a dream dreamt in the night and all but forgotten. She snuggled closer to her husband despite the mounded pillow in front of her stomach, pressing a leg gently into his crotch. She was rewarded by a muffled snort as he woke to the pressure. She smiled, letting herself drift on the remnants of sleep while he decided whether or not to accept the invitation.

"Mmmm," he sighed appreciatively, still mostly asleep himself as he sought her breast through the layers.

When he couldn't readily breach the barrier, he opened one eye. It took him several seconds to realize that he was on top rather than beneath the covers, and several more seconds to remember why. His other eye sprang open, and sleep fled in a rush.

"Magda?" he asked, and then, to head off the inevitable question of whom he thought it would be, rushed on. "I had the weirdest dream."

Maggie froze for a second before jerking her body away from his. It was Davy.

He jerked away as well, leaving her with more space to remember what had happened yesterday.

She took a deep breath, willing herself to relax. She'd figured it out yesterday, she reminded herself. *Davy is David. Toddy is Todd. I am both Maggie and Magda.* She repeated it a half-dozen times before her heart rate slowed.

"I'm sorry, Maggie, so sorry," Davy said, getting off the bed. His face was pale and his expression contrite. "I thought ye were Magda is all. I'm …"

"It's all right, Davy," Maggie said, interrupting. "It's all right."

Davy stared at her. "I thought ye were my Magda."

"I know. It's all right."

Davy shook his head. "No, it is not. I canna tell ye apart. I know I should, but I canna. God, help me, I canna."

They looked at each other desperately.

"I dinna think yer supposed to know," Maggie said. "I think Magda and I are supposed to take each other's place for a little while. I think that I'm supposed to be Magda; that somehow I *am* Magda, and she is me."

He snorted derisively.

"I'm not certain, but it's the only thing I can come up with that makes any sense."

"Ye think that makes sense?" he asked incredulously.

"Aye, in a way."

He crossed his arms in front of his chest. "In what way?" he demanded.

"Ye've told me that Madga was offered a wish, but she wouldna take it. And ye told me that on the night before the switch, Magda dreamed that Annie—"

Davy interrupted. "Dinna say her name!"

"Fine," Maggie grumbled, "the witch then. Magda dreamed that the witch came to her and said she'd found a way to grant Magda's wish. But it wasna Magda's wish. It was my wish—mine and David's. We wanted a child, but we couldna have one. The witch told us that not everyone is meant to have children every lifetime or something like that. She told David and me that if we were willing to be apart for a while, I'd get pregnant. So she switched Magda and me. I think she could do it because we're the same person in different times."

"Yer not making any sense."

Maggie sighed. "I dinna know if I can explain it any better."

Davy perched on the edge of the bed. "Try."

Maggie frowned. "Do ye believe in reincarnation?"

"I'm not sure what ye mean by that."

"Being born again in a different time."

Davy shook his head. "I dinna know. Christians believe in heaven and hell, not coming again. I'd have said 'no' a few days ago, but then I dinna believe in witches a few days ago either."

"And now ye do?"

Davy shrugged and then nodded. "I dinna ken. I guess if ye truly are Maggie, then I must, mustn't I?" He looked at her expectantly, part of him hoping that she'd deny being Maggie so that he didn't have to deal with this.

Maggie looked Davy in the eye and slowly nodded.

Davy frowned at her, saying nothing for several long moments as he let the concept sink in.

Maggie looked away first.

"Is that what ye think happened?" Davy asked. "That Magda was born again in the future as ye?"

Maggie nodded.

Davy sat silently for a long time, trying to get his mind around Maggie's words. Finally looking up at her, he shook his head sadly. "I dinna believe it. I've tried, but I canna do it. I'd more easily believe ye've bumped yer head and gone daft." He stood and stalked around the room. "I'd more easily believe that ye've been bewitched." He shook his head, muttering, "Being born again as someone else and then switched back here. It's impossible. It's crazy." He looked at Maggie. "And I suppose next ye'll be wanting me to believe that I will become reincarnated with Magda as yer David?"

Hesitantly, Maggie nodded. Davy's patience had reached its end. She recognized the signs. He was holding his breath longer and longer before exhaling, and he was alternately opening and clenching his fists. The David she knew didn't often get angry with her or anyone else, but when he did, it wasn't pretty. At home, he'd go for a long walk or lock himself in the studio and throw clay around until he felt under control again. She didn't know how Davy handled his frustrations, but she knew she was about to find out.

Davy's face was red with emotion. "By Brigid and the Bride, woman, are ye mad? Ye want me to believe the impossible."

"Not really," she said, perhaps recklessly. "I'm asking ye to consider that love transcends time and place."

Davy stared at her, shaking his head. "I canna," he exploded, heading out the door. "God help me, I canna."

Maggie heard the front door open and slam shut again. She heard him muttering in Gaelic as he stomped across the yard. The slam of the woodshop door was like a gunshot.

# Chapter 8

David lost miserably at his weekly handball game the following Wednesday.

"What's going on?" Todd asked. "Your game's been off for a month now, and you haven't even mentioned whether Maggie's pregnant or not."

"She's not." David grabbed his towel out of his bag and wiped the sweat from his face before leaving the handball court.

"That's it?" Todd asked incredulously, grabbing up his own bag and rushing to catch up. "No, 'And-we've-an-appointment-to-do-it-again?'"

David kept walking. "No. We aren't doing it again."

Todd caught up. "Are you trying something else?"

"No."

Todd stopped, mid-stride. "No?"

David opened the locker room door and went in, leaving Todd standing stunned in the hallway.

David was nearly finished with his shower before Todd recovered enough to strip down. "What the hell is going on, David? You and Maggie aren't having problems are you?"

David ignored him, turning off the water and grabbing his towel.

Todd turned off his shower without getting in. He followed David to the lockers.

"Are you and Maggie all right?"

"Not taking a shower today?" David asked. "They'll think you're one of the customers at the mission."

Todd frowned. "You're fighting?" he asked, stunned.

David shook his head. "Not fighting."

"You're not fighting, but something's not right," Todd said, thinking aloud. "Is it the not-getting-pregnant thing? Is she depressed about that?"

"No. Forget the pregnancy thing. It's best that we aren't expecting."

"Holy Father," Todd said. It sounded like a prayer. "What's going on, David?"

David shrugged, pulling on his jeans.

"Don't give me that," Todd said. "I know you too well. Heck, I'm Maggie's brother. If you don't tell me, I'll ask her."

"Maybe that would be a good idea."

Todd froze. Something was seriously wrong if David felt he needed help with Maggie. "Shit."

David nodded.

"Call her," Todd directed. "Tell her you asked me to dinner."

David looked at his brother-in-law, considering the suggestion. "Shower first."

Magda knew she wasn't ready to meet Maggie's brother. She told David not to bring him, but they were coming anyway.

She frowned over the photo album. Todd looked too much like a younger, thinner version of her uncle for her to feel comfortable seeing him. Too many things were almost, but not quite, as they should be. David was almost, but not quite, Davy. She was almost, but not quite, Maggie. Their relationship was almost, but not quite …

It was too much. She couldn't handle it anymore. She needed help, but she didn't know where to turn. Resisting David was almost more than she could do; she couldn't handle anything else. She couldn't make small talk with someone else she was supposedly close to. She either had to avoid Todd or talk to him. Really talk to him. She slammed the album shut and returned it to its shelf. What was she supposed to do?

She longed to curl up in a ball and fade away—anything not to face the guilt of betraying Davy by loving David. Prayer hadn't helped. It hadn't taken her home, erased her memory of Kirkinwall, eliminated her growing feelings for David, or made Auld Annie appear. God had deserted her here without a way to get home. All-too-frequent tears burned their way down her cheeks.

She was walking to the bathroom to wash her face when the sound of David's key in the lock sent her dashing down the hallway.

Todd was shocked when he saw his sister. Maggie had never been vain or overly conscious of her looks, but she had always managed to look put-together—to look as if everything she wore had been made for her. He'd seen her wear the clothes she had on now before, but somehow she didn't appear comfortable in the jeans, rose-colored tee, and floral vest. It wasn't the weight she'd lost. It was something else. It had something to do with the haunted look in her eyes and the forced smile. Something to do with the way she wouldn't look him in the eye. One look at his sister made him want to grab David, shake him until his teeth rattled, and demand to know what the hell he'd done to her. And he would have, had David's eyes not held the same lost look.

"Todd," Magda said with forced brightness. "It's been too long." She didn't rush forward to hug him.

"Maggie." It was all he could manage for the moment. He wanted to grab her and hold her close until her eyes cleared and the smile on her face was real.

"Come on in, Todd," David said, stepping further into the entryway.

Magda skittered out of the way to avoid his touch.

Todd frowned. The way his sister normally greeted her husband was just this side of embarrassing. Nothing in their seven years of marriage had dimmed the spark. Nothing until now.

Todd stared searchingly at his sister and then at his brother-in-law. "What is going on?" he demanded, forgetting the years of counselor training he'd had both in and out of the seminary.

Neither answered or returned his look. David looked longingly at Magda, while Magda stared at the floor clearly fighting back tears.

Todd shook his head sadly. "David, why don't you order some pizza? Sausage and mushroom okay with everyone?"

No one commented. Maggie didn't insist on green olives or onions as she should have. David didn't insist on pepperoni or ask Todd if he got a clergyman's discount. David just nodded and left to call the pizza place.

"Come on, Maggie. Let's go sit in the library," Todd said, purposefully not reaching for her arm.

She nodded and then preceded him down the hall. She sat in at black leather chair while he closed the door.

"All right, Maggie. What's going on here?"

Magda watched him cautiously. She still didn't know what to do, what to tell him. Small talk seemed the best solution. "How have you been?"

"Don't play games with me, Maggie. Something's going on here, and I want to know what it is."

Magda looked away.

"Have you talked to Mom?" Todd asked.

"Once." It had been a strange experience. The disembodied voice of someone she didn't know but had to pretend to know had come through the receiver, asking questions and expecting answers. It was too much. She could handle television and radio, but the telephone rattled her. She answered it when David wasn't home because he insisted that he be able to reach her, but she didn't make any calls.

"Did you talk to her about what is going on with you and David?"

"No." They'd talked about the only thing about Maggie's life that Magda had known something about—the concert series.

"Did you tell her that the GIFT didn't work?"

Magda blushed, uncomfortable with the direction Maggie's brother's questions were taking. "No."

"Did you tell her it had?" he asked, wondering if she'd lied to their mother.

She shook her head. "No. We didn't discuss it one way or the other. She was much more tactful than you are."

"Tactful? Our mother?" Their mother was as outspoken as they came. If she hadn't asked about the GIFT, it was because it had been too early.

Magda shrugged.

Todd watched his sister play with the folds in her jeans.

"Maggie," he said softly. "What's wrong?"

She shook her head in mute response as unwanted tears filled her eyes. It had been easier dealing with his frustration and anger than his pity. She closed her eyes and fought the tears. She was so intent on battling her emotion that she didn't notice his approach until he crouched on the floor in front of her and placed his hand gently on her knees.

His touch had her jerking back as if scalded.

"Don't!" She batted at his hands.

He held on. "Maggie, talk to me."

"Why?" she demanded, glaring at him. "What can you do?"

"Nothing if you don't tell me the problem." His professionally calm, counselor voice contrasted with her agitated one.

"And likely nothing even if I do," she snapped at him.

"Why don't you try me, and we'll see."

She stared at him.

"Come on, Mag. We've always told each other everything."

Magda looked into his eyes. Maybe Maggie had told him things, maybe not. "Not everything."

He frowned. "Okay, not everything, but most things."

"Like what?" she asked, trying desperately to distract him.

"Like everything: all the childhood secrets—who you liked and who I liked, where we should bury the spaghetti squash so Mom couldn't serve it anymore. I knew that you were sleeping with David almost from the start. And you knew about my calling long before I figured it out."

Naturally, Magda didn't remember any of the things he said, but she could imagine Maggie would have. Maggie had probably trusted Todd. The question was—could Magda?

"Are you really a priest?" she asked, looking at Maggie's jean-clad brother and wondering if she could tell him the truth—if he'd believe her.

Todd nodded, trying to keep the concern off his face. "Even without the collar, Mag. You know that."

She nodded. "Then I invoke the privacy of the confessional."

"O … kay," he said hesitatingly, sitting back on his heels. "What have you done?"

"You can't tell anything that I tell you during confession, can you?"

"Uh … no. You know that. But I can counsel you to tell others."

Magda nodded. "And you know that I would not lie in confession. Not ever."

"I know."

"Okay." She suddenly decided to talk. She swallowed heavily and took several calming breaths. "Shouldn't I kneel?" she asked, looking him in the eye.

Todd shrugged. "If it would make you feel better, but it's not necessary."

"I'd feel better," she said, cueing him to back up.

It took him several seconds before he caught on and went back to the couch. "Oh, sorry."

She flashed him a weak smile before dropping to her knees beside her chair. "Bless me, Father, for I have sinned. It's been nearly three hundred years since my last confession."

"What?" Todd interrupted.

Magda looked at him. "Father, are you not to let the penitent confess before speaking?"

"Not when it's nonsense."

Magda stared at him for several long seconds before getting off her knees. "Fine then. I won't tell you."

Todd groaned. "All right, Maggie. This had better be good."

She said nothing.

He sighed extravagantly, closing his eyes. "All right. It's been nearly three hundred years since your last confession." He opened his eyes and smiled. "You really need to get to church more often."

Magda got on her knees, ignoring his attempted joke. Staring at her clasped hands, she continued softly. "I was born Magda McDougal in Kirkinwall, Scotland, in 1700."

Todd watched her closely, but he said nothing.

"I married Davy McClellan in 1717. In early June of 1718, round with our first child, I gave food and comfort to a witch." For a moment, she looked at Todd for condemnation, but, seeing nothing on his studiously blank face, she continued. "The witch, Auld Annie by name, gave me a wish in return. I told her I was happy in my life and wanted nothing. A few days later, she went before the ecclesiastic examiners who decided to test her by water. She sank, which should have proved her innocent, but when the men tried to pull her up, they found she'd slipped her ropes and was gone. They looked, but they could find no sign of her in water or on land.

"Davy thought that was the end of it, but that night I had a dream. In it, Auld Annie was underwater being tested. She vanished for a moment, and then she came back to tell me she knew what wish to grant me. Then she disappeared again. I told Davy of the dream, and he told me not to worry, that it was just a dream. I went back to bed and had a hard time getting to sleep. When I woke in the morning, I found myself in this time, in a hospital, wed to another man." Somewhere during her confession she'd started crying. She turned her tearful face to Todd. "Father, I can't find my way home. I'm falling in love with your sister's husband and ruining their relationship."

Todd stared at his sister, stunned. He didn't know what had happened to cause this identity crisis, but it was clear that she was in crisis. No matter what the truth was, Maggie clearly thought she was Magda. He needed to talk to her as if she were Magda.

"How are you ruining their relationship?" Todd asked.

"He didn't believe me when I told him who I am. He thinks I'm Maggie." More tears swelled in her eyes and spilled down her cheeks. "He believes that he's my husband and belongs in my bed."

"And how do you feel about David?"

She swiped away the tears with the back of her arm, but they kept falling. "It doesn't matter. I'm married to Davy. I love Davy."

"I've no doubt of that," he soothed. "But you said you were falling in love with David. You *do* love him too, don't you?"

She closed her eyes, nodding sadly. "Heaven help me."

The doorbell rang while Todd was trying to figure out what to do or say next. His training told him to counsel Maggie to get professional help. He had the card of a good psychologist in his wallet. Dr. Maxwell would be able to prescribe medication to help Maggie if she could be convinced to go.

"You've talked to David about this?" he asked, knowing that David would be there in a moment. "Could I talk to David about this?"

Magda narrowed her eyes in suspicion. "Why? He didn't believe me."

"We might need his help to figure out what to do next." Maybe David could convince her to see someone about her delusions.

"How? He promised me there'd be no doctors and no hospital."

David knocked on the door. "Pizza boy," he said, announcing himself with forced brightness as he pushed the door open with his elbow. "What does everyone want to drink? There's soda, beer, and cider."

"I'll get it," Magda said quickly, rising from her knees and cutting a wide swath around David as she went to the door. "What will you have?"

"Beer," David told her.

"I'll have the same," Todd answered.

As soon as she was out of the room, David turned to Todd. "So did she tell you?"

"Everything she told me she said in confession."

David turned a sickly shade of green. "I knew it. There's someone else."

"I didn't say that!"

David shrugged. "She won't let me touch her. What else could it be?"

"Maybe it's something she's already told you," Todd said, stretching the edge of confidentiality as far as he could.

"She told you about Magda, didn't she?" David's voice was bitter and angry. "How could she be someone else? I don't believe it. She's found someone else—someone who can give her a baby. What I don't know is why she won't just come out and say so."

"Maybe it's because it isn't true," Magda said, carrying two beers and a can of apple juice in her hands. She handed a beer to Maggie's brother and glared at him. "I should have known you weren't a real priest."

"I didn't tell him anything," Todd protested, feeling guilty about how close he'd come to telling David.

Magda turned from him and handed David his beer. "It doesn't matter. Times have changed. It used to be a person's word was their bond, and priests held the confessional sacred. Now …" She shrugged, looking at David. "I told the false priest who I really am. Now you two can eat your poisoned pie and make plans to lock me up somewhere." She held on to her apple juice and pivoted toward the door. "I'll leave you to it."

David went after her, touching her arm to stop her.

She turned to him with a potent blend of fear, pain, and confusion in her eyes.

"No, Maggie. I promised. There'll be no doctors or hospitals unless you say."

She nodded, blinking back tears.

He opened his arms to her, knowing she needed his touch almost as much as he needed hers. There was hesitation and desire in her eyes mixed with the pain. She shook her head, choked back a sob, and fled.

David slammed the doorframe with an open hand, covered his eyes with the other, and stood shaking in the doorway.

Todd watched helplessly.

Eventually, David wiped his streaming face with his sleeve and retrieved his beer. Popping the top, he guzzled half of it before facing his brother-in-law. "Have some pizza. We don't need to save any for Maggie. Now that she claims to be Magda, she thinks tomatoes are poisonous."

"What?" Todd frowned.

"That's why she called the pizza a poison pie. She thinks tomatoes are poisonous. Isn't that a hoot?" David didn't laugh.

"When was it she said she was from?" Todd said, trying to remember the exact date.

David shrugged. "She claims she was born in 1700 and that it was 1718 when she came here."

Todd frowned. "Did she tell you why she thinks they're poisonous?"

David shook his head, playing with the slice of pizza he'd put on his plate.

Todd picked up a piece of pizza and looked at it. "They used to think tomatoes were poisonous. And they were, kind of. Back when peasants ate from pewter plates and the aristocracy ate from silver, tomatoes were considered toxic. And they were. The acid in the tomatoes leached the mercury out of the pewter or silver and made them deadly."

"How do you know that?" David asked.

"It was in some research I did for a history class."

"Would Maggie know it? I mean, did you tell her or anything?"

Todd shrugged. "I don't remember telling her, but I could have." He looked away puzzled. "It's just such an obscure piece of history." He turned back to his brother-in-law. "Don't you find it weird that she knows?"

# Chapter 9

After Davy stormed out, Maggie tried to focus on other things in order to give him time to think. She milked the cow, fed the chickens, collected the eggs, and did other domestic chores before hunger prompted her to fry bacon and oatcakes. When breakfast was on the table, though, she hesitated to call Davy.

The fact that he hadn't come back on his own worried her. David hadn't been one to miss a meal. His size and metabolism combined to make him frequently hungry. She imagined Davy would be the same and somehow doubted that he kept a food stash in the workroom. He would need to eat, and hunger wouldn't help his temper.

Resolved to go get him but still hesitant, she meandered slowly across the yard, purposely comparing this farm to her parents' in Wisconsin. Both were tidy and well cared for. Both farms were obviously at least second generation. The house and outbuildings were kept up, but not new. She was unaware, however, how progressive a spread this was—that the stone foundations were a modern idea that had allowed the house and barn to resist rot long enough to be handed down a generation.

She passed the well and thought of the old hand-pump her parents had replaced. Times and technology changed, but the feel of rural life didn't. On a farm things were run by nature's rhythms, not by the clock. There was a sense of peace here. She hadn't realized how much she'd missed it. New York—and especially the entertainment industry—had a frenetic pace—everyone rushing around, but not necessarily getting anywhere. And the noise ... the city was never silent. Even the rhythmic thump and crack of Davy splitting wood seemed peaceful in comparison. She'd missed silence.

The chickens were still pecking the ground, looking for seeds they'd missed earlier. Maggie's stomach growled, telling her it was late for breakfast.

She headed toward the side of the barn, silently vowing to visit her parents at the farm when she got back to her world. And she would get back. She had to get back. She knew she could live in this world, adjust to the tempo, adjust to David as Davy. She could do it, but could Magda? New York was like nothing she would have ever known. Could Magda survive New York? Could Magda survive the loss of her unborn child?

Maggie wished she knew for certain what Annie had meant to do and how she'd planned on switching them back. Annie hadn't been angry with Magda; she'd been grateful. The wish was meant as a gift, not a punishment. Surely she hadn't meant to switch them permanently.

Maggie shook her head. There was no way to find out what Annie had meant. Coming back to Kirkinwall meant certain death for her. A shiver ran up Maggie's spine. She needed to talk to Davy. If he thought she was a witch or even bewitched, it could mean trouble. Not from him, of course. She trusted Davy to do everything in his power to protect her. He loved Magda too much to report her. It was the other people in this time she had to worry about.

The thought stopped her in her tracks. How many days did she have until First Fruits? Could she do it? Could she fool the town folk into thinking she was Magda? And what would happen if she couldn't? She had to talk to Davy. He had to help her. If he acted normal around her, everyone else would. But if he didn't …

The thought didn't bear delving into. Magda couldn't return to a body burned to ash.

She ran the rest of the way to the chopping block.

"Davy!" she gasped. "We need to talk."

He didn't look up, didn't seem to hear her.

Staying well outside the circle of woodchips, she had to nearly yell his name before he stopped chopping. "We need to talk."

He wouldn't look at her. "Not now, Maggie."

"Please," she begged.

"Not now, Maggie." His voice was cold and distant.

"But breakfast is ready," she said, desperately.

"I'm not hungry," he said, wiping the sweat off his brow with his sleeve.

Maggie frowned. David never willingly missed a meal, and she doubted that Davy did either. "But it's all made."

"Go ahead and eat. I'll be in later for something."

She wanted to argue the issue, to insist that he eat with her, that he talk to her, but she didn't. Davy wore David's stubborn look. The pigheaded look he'd had when she'd suggested they elope in the face of her parents' initial opposition to their engagement. He'd insisted that they spend the summer at the farm and win them over. She'd given in to him. He'd won over her family in a matter of days, and they'd been married in her parents' living room two weeks later. It had been a magical summer. And she'd learned that David wasn't casually stubborn. He only got his back up when something was important to him. Maggie knew that eating breakfast together wasn't the issue, and it frightened her beyond words.

She needed Davy, but he was obviously too bothered by what she'd said this morning to deal with her now. And as much as she needed to talk to him, she knew that now wasn't the time. Maggie blinked hard to keep at bay the tears that threatened to fill her eyes. Davy was David. When he wore that look, it wasn't worth the breath it took to argue.

"I'll wrap up some bannocks and cheese for ye to have later then," she managed to say around the lump in her throat.

Davy still didn't look at her. Positioning another log, he swung his axe, effectively dismissing her.

# Chapter 10

David went looking for Maggie as he'd started to do every morning after his shower. Trying to avoid him, she never wittingly entered a room he was in. He discovered early on in the six weeks since the failed GIFT that if he wanted to see his wife, he had to seek her out.

Today he found her in the library, wrapped in an afghan, sobbing quietly.

"Maggie," he gasped, rushing to her side. "What's wrong?" It was a stupid question. Everything was wrong, and they both knew it. They'd been living together like strangers.

"I mean, why are you crying?" he amended. His arms ached to hold her. It had become a familiar feeling. He clenched his fists to keep from reaching for her. How could he comfort her when she wouldn't let him?

When she didn't answer, he tentatively touched her arm. "Maggie?"

She raised her tear-streaked face.

"Tell me what's wrong, why you're crying. Maybe I can help."

She shook her head. "You can't help. No one can."

"I can't help if you won't talk to me."

She closed her eyes. "You wouldn't understand."

"Try me," he begged, desperate for her to open up to him. As much as he hated to see her upset like this, part of him rejoiced—this was the most she'd said to him in days.

What could she say to him that he'd believe? "I should be pregnant." She'd been round with child when she'd left her world. She should be giving birth soon, if she hadn't already. She hugged her skinny abdomen, pressing her arms against her flat belly. The weight she'd lost in the past six weeks made it nearly concave. "But now there's no baby." She'd lost that too.

"I know," he said, thinking she meant the failed procedure. "We both want a child."

She blinked at him.

"When you're feeling better, we can try again. Not GIFT," he rushed to reassure her. "We can try the natural way again."

She stared at him incredulously.

"Or maybe adoption."

Later, in the privacy of her room, Magda curled under the bed's comforter. What had David meant with his comments about making a baby? Had he forgotten who she was?

She held herself tightly, shivering despite the warmth of the comforter and the room. David's confusing remarks didn't bother her half as much as her own jumbled thoughts.

Thoughts of Davy and the baby she'd lost made her ache. That was good. It was only natural that she mourned their loss. She should feel that pain. But why did she feel as if she were somehow forcing her mourning? She hurt, true, but it wasn't as intense as she felt it should have been. The loss of husband and child should have paralyzed her, but it didn't. It was almost as if part of her said that everything was okay, told her that she hadn't really lost anything. It was ridiculous, she knew. A quick look around the room proved the point—smooth yellow walls, factory-made furniture, photos she was in but didn't remember. She'd lost everything. How could she feel as if she hadn't? Why did she feel differently from what she knew she ought to feel? Why wasn't she mourning as she should?

Tears filled her eyes, but even they felt wrong. They weren't sorrowful tears; they were guilty ones.

She should be mourning Davy, but when she closed her eyes, it was David's face she saw. When she dreamed of making love, it was David who covered her. No matter how much she avoided him during her waking hours, she couldn't escape him or the growing attraction she felt for him when she slept.

She should have found his comments about making a baby repulsive. But she didn't. And it was that acknowledgement which had her huddled under the covers crying softly.

She climbed off the bed, dragging the comforter with her. Wrapped against the chill of her guilt, she fell on her knees and asked God to take away the attraction and cleanse her from impure thoughts. She begged. In the six weeks she'd been in New York, she'd done more praying than in all of her previous eighteen years.

She didn't understand herself. How could she love Davy and yet yearn for David? She didn't know. She loved Davy. She knew that. It was a fact and never in doubt. She would love Davy all her life with all her heart.

And yet, she felt things about David. It was more than attraction. There was some kind of connection. Maybe it was because of the body she wore. Magda didn't know; all she knew was that somehow in her mind the two men were blending, becoming one. It was all so confusing.

Her knees ached against the hardness of the floor, but she ignored the pain. She prayed and tried not to think of Maggie in her world, in her body, with her husband and child. But those thoughts were impossible to avoid. She knew she should hate Maggie. She should hate the woman who inadvertently had stolen her life, but somehow she didn't. She felt her own loss, admittedly not as much as she felt she should, but didn't feel the jealousy or hate that she felt she should.

Prayer wasn't helping.

*Oh, God, please.*

Nothing.

Minutes passed and still there was nothing. No answers. No relief.

Her conscience was just as heavy when she got up from the floor as when she had knelt down. All she had to show from her prayers were aching, red knees. She needed more than that. She needed to talk to someone, to get another perspective. But from whom? David?

Her heart leapt at the thought. That was reason enough to pick someone else. Who then? Maggie's brother? The false priest came over every few days, but she'd managed to avoid him too.

Perhaps she shouldn't avoid him anymore.

# Chapter 11

It was still fairly early when Maggie finished wrapping the bannocks and cheese for Davy and tidying the small cottage. Restless and faced with a day of being ignored by Davy, Maggie turned to music. She had a festival to play for and a flute to learn.

She went into the yard, finding a sunny spot that pleased her near the edge of woods. Then, closing her eyes and putting the flute to her lips, she played.

It wasn't as hard as she'd imagined. With her eyes closed, she couldn't see the flute and be distracted by its strangeness. She concentrated on the way the sun felt on her face and let go. Still, it surprised her how her hands knew which notes to play and how to play them.

In college, she'd played the recorder and the fife and other flute-like instruments on occasion, but the fingering for this flute wasn't like those other instruments. If she opened her eyes and concentrated on what her hands were doing, she couldn't play. Or rather, she could play about as well as she'd originally thought she'd be able to play on it. But if she listened to the music in her head or thought of other things, her fingers found their places automatically.

She practiced the First Fruits song until she knew it as well in her head as in her fingers—until she could play it with her eyes open. Satisfied, she let her fingers have free reign and smiled to find they knew other tunes as well. Hours slipped by as she played.

The sun halfway up the sky, its warmth beating on the top of her head and bringing sweat to her brow, cued her to the passing time. She'd wasted the morning at play.

It wasn't a thought she'd have had in her time. In her time, playing was working. Here, there were other chores to be done. Here, everyday jobs took more time. Chicken didn't come from a grocery store, and the laundry wasn't delivered. Here both dinner and laundry were complicated chores that took time, time that she'd wasted practicing the flute.

She hurried to the kitchen.

She wasn't sure why she decided to do the laundry. She'd been here only a few days, and she was less than sure how to do it. Yes, it needed to get done, but even in her own time, it was not something she cared to do. Besides which, it was Friday. And according to nursery rhymes, wasn't doing the wash a Monday thing rather than a Friday thing?

Still, she found herself dipping a small amount of semi-solid lye soap from a jar in the kitchen and stirring it into a kettle of dirty clothes and hot water. She'd read enough books about pioneer days to have some idea how they washed clothes, but an hour into the process, she couldn't believe how difficult it actually was. It was one thing to know that everything had to be hand washed, and quite another thing to do it. And the clothes she needed to wash were truly dirty. These clothes hadn't been worn once; they'd been worn several times and smelled like it. A quick dip in the washtub wasn't going to do it, especially since she doubted the quality of the soap. She seemed to remember reading something about boiling the whites to get them clean.

She was wet and cross, standing over a pot of stinking, boiling clothes when Davy popped in long enough to grab the bannocks and cheese she'd set aside. She purposely didn't say anything to him, though she couldn't keep herself from mumbling nasty things under her breath. What had made her think this world was more restful than her own?

Maggie scrubbed stains and wrung the water out of the clothes by hand, wishing she'd had the old wringer washer from the farm. To say that laundry was a much bigger chore now than it was in modern times was a complete understatement. Never again would she complain about how much time it took to fold clothes. The only consolation Maggie had, and it was small, was that there were fewer clothes now.

While the clothes dripped on the line, Maggie turned to the kitchen. There was water everywhere.

"Probably should have washed the clothes outside," she mumbled, noticing how the wash water had soaked the rushes on the dirt floor.

One job led to another. Mumbling invectives, she flung open the shutters to let in the breeze and began lugging out buckets of water to toss in the side yard.

She didn't dump the wash water on the garden since she wasn't certain what lye would do to the plants. It wouldn't do to kill her garden.

By the time she'd dragged out the washtub, hauled out the sodden rushes, located some fresh ones in a bin by the barn, lugged them back to the cottage, and spread them out, it was time to make supper. *No,* she thought as she stripped off her wet dress, tugging on a clean one before putting the soiled one in the empty washtub. *I'm not going to cater to Davy.*

She sniffed in frustration when she remembered that she'd tossed out the wash water. Cold water would have to do, she decided, lugging a final bucket of water from the well. She took her frustrations out scrubbing the dress. *I'm not making dinner. If Davy wants to eat, he can get something himself.* She'd eaten a late lunch of leftover breakfast between loads of wash and was more tired than hungry.

She wrung out the dress and stomped back to the well, carrying the wet dress and getting angrier with every step. She was the one who should be catered to. She was the pregnant one, the one in the wrong time. And there she was dragging around buckets of water. How many had she carried today? Nine for washing, nine for rinsing, and two more for this stupid dress. That was eighteen, nineteen, twenty—twenty buckets of water that she carried in and out without a single offer of help from Davy. She was the one with the right to pout.

She dipped a final bucket of water from the well to rinse the dress, muttering about ungrateful, pigheaded men.

Davy came out of the workshop as she slapped the sodden dress onto the line.

"And if ye think I'm making ye dinner, ye've another thought coming," she snarled at him across the yard.

He looked at her, trying to figure out who she was. "I'd have carried the water for ye," he said. "Ye ken that."

"And just how would I ken that?" Maggie snarled at him. "Ye havena said a word to me since I made the mistake of calling ye to breakfast."

"Maggie," he said the name aloud as if merely confirming her identity.

Maggie threw her hands in the air. "What difference does it make what my name is? Ye still treat me like a slave. Yer just like David. What am I saying? Ye are David, just as lazy and self centered and unappreciative as ye've always been."

Davy smiled despite himself. Washday always put Magda in a rare mood. She worked like a mad woman all morning, yelled at him at lunch, and congratulated herself on the fine state of the clothes and house in the evening. Maggie was doing the same thing. She was a few hours late, but the day was fine and the clothes would be dry before dark. There was naught to worry about. She'd even picked the right day of the week for it. Magda dinna hold with doing the Monday wash. She did it on Friday if the weather was fair so she could iron and cook Saturday and rest on Sunday. Maggie seemed to be following the pattern. It was comforting and disconcerting at the same time.

Maggie crossed her arms in front of her chest and glared at him. "What are you smiling at?"

His grin faded. She was so like Magda. How would he ever be able to tell the difference?

Maggie narrowed her eyes at him, but she didn't push the issue, turning instead to the dripping dress on the line. She wrung in out in sections before straightening it on the line and pinning it with several hand-carved clothespins.

Davy emptied the bucket of rinse water and carried the bucket back into the house. He up-ended the pot that contained what remained of the cold, coagulated oatmeal onto a plate. It came out it one unappetizing glob. He sliced the mass into five pieces before sliding two onto another plate.

"Honey or molasses?" he asked Maggie as she came through the door.

"Vinegar," she said.

"Ye want vinegar on your oatmeal?"

"No," she said, smiling at her own expense. "I thought ye were asking me if I was honey or molasses."

"Vinegar, is it?" He smiled. "I'd have said good Scottish whiskey. Fiery and tasty with the perfect kick."

Maggie blushed.

"But dinna ye mind, lass. It's washday. Yer always a bit feisty on washday."

"Am I?" She wasn't sure what she thought about that. Part of her was relieved that her mood was normal, that she was indeed Magda, but part of her was made more irritated by his comments. No one wants to be predictable and told that she is. She narrowed her eyes. "So yer this helpful every week? Hasn't it ever occurred to ye that my mood might be yer fault? Ye could be a little more helpful. Maybe drag the washtub outside so that I dinna drown the kitchen. Maybe haul a few buckets of water or build an outdoor fire pit so that I dinna have to heat the water inside."

"Vinegar it is."

"Oooo," she growled at him in frustration, closing the distance between them to punch him in the shoulder.

He grabbed her hand and pulled her into his arms. "Hush, lass." He held her gently, but not closely. "I'm sorry I poked fun at ye. I'd have pointed out the fire pit and hauled the water if I'd known ye'd be doing the wash."

"I thought you said it was the normal washday." She wanted to fight, to burn out the tension she'd felt in some degree or another since she'd arrived, but being in Davy's arms had the same calming effect on her that being in David's arms did.

He felt her body soften as the anger evaporated. She felt as if she belonged in his arms, and he had to remind himself that she didn't. He should let her go and step away.

"That it is, but I'd not expected ye to do it." He gave her a gentle squeeze before releasing her. "Truth told, I wasna thinking about the day nor the wash this morning."

"What were ye thinking about?"

She hadn't stepped away, so he had to. "About what ye said and who ye are."

"Ye still dinna believe me." She sounded hurt and small, even to herself.

He shook his head. "No, Maggie. I believe ye. I wish it weren't true, that Magda and I had never met the witch, but I believe ye are who ye say ye are."

She smiled, relieved. "Ye believe that Magda and I are one?"

He shook his head. "No. I believe ye are Maggie, and that Magda is living in yer world."

After a dinner of cold oatmeal and honey, Davy followed Maggie into the yard. The stiff breeze tugged at her hair, pulling strands loose. She tucked the errant locks behind her ears and waddled to the clothesline.

"Here," Davy said, as she reached for a sheet that snapped out of her grasp. "Let me help ye. We wouldna want the wind to undo yer work."

They cleared the line together, folding items before putting them into the basket.

Maggie's irritation eased as they worked. What had seemed an impossible task earlier in the day was nearly complete. It helped that Davy worked with her on the larger items, keeping them from touching the ground. It also helped that the breeze had eliminated the biggest wrinkles.

"I'm not ironing tonight," she told Davy as he carried the basket of clothes.

"Of course not," he said. "Ye've done enough for the day, Maggie. Ye've need of yer rest."

She nearly stumbled as she thought of the sleeping arrangements. There was only one bed in the cottage. She had no doubt that Davy would give it to her. But would he sleep with her? Did she want him to?

She was faintly surprised to find that she expected him to sleep with her. It wasn't the sexual aspects of sleeping together that she wanted—though she found to her surprise that she wasn't as adverse to the thought as she figured she should be—it was an issue of comfort. She'd slept with David nearly every night for seven years. It was normal to sleep nestled in his arms. And if Davy truly were David, then it would be normal to sleep with him. And that was without factoring in the pregnancy and location. Being pregnant made her joyful and yet very vulnerable. Being out of time just made her vulnerable. She needed the comfort of Davy's arms and the reassurance of his touch. She needed Davy as much as her counterpart would need David. Now was not the time to deal with marital rejection.

"I'll sleep by the fire," Davy said, nudging the cottage door open.

"There's no need," Maggie told him, taking the kitchen linens from him. "Ye dinna last night."

Davy frowned. "I'm sorry about that. Last night I thought ye were me Magda."

"And ye were right."

He shook his head, making certain to look her in the eye. "No, Maggie, I was wrong. Yer not Magda, and I shouldna have slept beside ye. I shall not be making the mistake again."

"But it wasna a mistake. I am Magda, and she is me."

"Stop. I dinna believe that, and neither do ye." Davy turned his back on her, carrying the clothes and bedding into the bedroom.

That did it. The irritation came back with a vengeance. She followed him. "Dinna tell me what I believe. I'm the one walking around in this body. I think I'm in a better position to ken who I am than ye are."

"Looking like Magda doesn't make ye her," he said, dropping the sheets on the bed.

"And carrying yer child doesn't make me yer wife?"

That stopped him midway to the chest, his arms still laden with clothes.

When he didn't say anything, Maggie continued in a softer tone. "I'm scared, Davy. Even if ye dinna believe that I'm Magda, aren't I still yer wife?" She caressed her round belly. "Isna this still yer child?"

Davy looked her over, again. "It's me child," he said, placing the clothes on the dresser. "But yer not me wife, Maggie."

"Are ye sure?" she challenged him softly. "I've been doing a lot of thinking. If this isna all a weird dream, and part of me definitely thinks I'll wake up in the morning and find that it is, then there have to be some kind of rules. Annie canna just stick someone in someone else's body. It doesna make sense. And our names are so close—Maggie and Magda, Davy and David, Father Toddy and Father Todd. There are too many similarities for this to be random. So I think that while I am here, I'm Magda."

Davy shook his head.

She touched his arm. "Think about it, Davy. What if we never switch back? What if I'm here for good? What if I give birth to this baby and stay to raise it? Then I'm its mother, right? And yer its father. And aren't I also yer wife?"

Davy paled.

"It's too much, Maggie," he said, getting a blanket from the trunk. "I canna get my head around it. If ye hadna said ye weren't Magda, I'd have kent what to do. If I hadna believed what ye said about being Maggie, I might not know. But ye did. And I do." He held the blanket close to his chest like a shield as he backed out the bedroom door. "And I'll not be sleeping with ye tonight." He pulled the door closed behind him.

She ran to the door and pulled it open. "Davy?" she said in a choked whisper.

"Go to bed, Maggie," he told her without turning back. "I've cattle to feed."

Feeling panicked, she spoke when she knew she should remain silent. "But … I'm frightened."

He turned back to her, regarding her coldly. "Ye'll be fine, Maggie," he told her evenly, not relenting at all. "I'll be close. I just willna be in yer bed."

# Chapter 12

"What makes a person who they are?" Magda asked Todd the following Wednesday when he accompanied David home from the club for dinner. "What makes you Todd and not, say, David here?"

The men blinked at her. It was shocking enough that she was actually eating with them much less talking.

"Uh …" Todd stumbled, scrambling to organize his thoughts. "A lot of things, I guess." He looked at David for help.

David shrugged.

"Uh …" Todd turned back to Magda. "Well, I'm not certain what you're asking," he said, though it wasn't totally true. He suspected she was going to try to prove that she wasn't Maggie. "There are the obvious physical differences."

Magda nodded. "Okay, forget about physical differences—pretend you're identical twins. You're exactly the same down to the last freckle. What makes you, you, and David, David?"

Todd squelched the desire to answer automatically that a person's soul was what made them an individual. Even though he believed that God made everyone individually with unique souls, it wouldn't help in this discussion. No one could prove a soul. It was a faith issue and not the question here. The question was how to prove to Maggie that she was herself when she didn't believe it. He didn't know. Despite his training, he couldn't come up with anything.

He looked at David and picked the most easily chartable differences besides looks. "We like different things, have different tastes and talents. I like sausage pizza. He likes pepperoni. He's an artist. I couldn't draw my way out of a paper bag."

David shook his head. "I think what she's after is memories and experiences. Am I right, Maggie? You think that it's a person's experiences and memories that make them who they are?"

Magda nodded.

"Then what about amnesia victims and people with Alzheimer's? Are they not who they are because they've forgotten who they were?" David asked, turning to Todd when Magda didn't answer.

"I'd say you could make a case either way. Legally, I think they are still whoever their physical body says they are. They have the same fingerprints and stuff, but essentially—that is, what makes them really who they are—their heart and their soul—I guess are their memories."

"So," Magda said. "If I don't remember growing up with you ..." she pointed at Todd, "... or marrying you ..." her finger turned to David, "... then I'm not really your sister or your wife."

"Yes, you are," David insisted.

"Relax, David."

"Butt out, Todd. This isn't philosophy 101 we're talking here. This is my life. This is my wife."

Todd tried again. "I don't think she really means it that way. Do you, Maggie?"

Magda shrugged not knowing really what she meant. Did she want to disown David and Todd and lose their protection? No, not really. "I think I want for both of you to acknowledge that I'm not the Maggie you know, that something happened at the hospital that took her and left me." She looked at them one at a time. "I want you to acknowledge that I'm not just a crazy Maggie, that I am really Magda."

Both men watched her intently in silence.

"I don't know why I'm here. I don't how long I'm here for. I just know that I can't be Maggie. I've tried, but I'm not her."

David swallowed heavily before speaking. "If you're Magda, where does that leave me? Where does that leave us? I won't divorce you. We've too much of a past."

"*We* have no past," Magda said, emphatically. "That's what I've been trying to tell you. I don't have a past with you. My memories of you started that morning in the hospital."

"Then you *do* want a divorce," he accused.

"No one is talking divorce but you," Todd rushed to interject before Magda could say anything different. "Maggie, I mean, Magda, just wants to be treated like herself and not Maggie."

David protested, "But I don't know how to treat her as Magda." He looked at the woman he knew to be his wife. "I don't know how to not love you."

Magda nodded as her eyes filled with tears. "I know, David. And I don't know how to treat you either. I feel so many things about you, about us—confusion, attraction, guilt, fear … love. I don't know how to behave. I don't know what to think. I just know that I'm not Maggie, that six weeks ago I was married to the only man I've ever loved and that I was near to bursting with his child. I know that I mourn his loss and that of the child, but I can't reconcile those things, those feelings, with how I feel about you. Maybe this body remembers things I don't. I don't know. I'm confused and afraid. I need help to figure out how to get back or to figure out how to live here. I don't know which, and I don't know what kind of help. I do know that sitting in this house, nice as it is, and playing music isn't resolving anything. I don't know what will." She shook her head sadly. "I just don't know."

"What about seeing a psychiatrist?" Todd asked.

"No!" Magda and David answered in unison.

"I understand why Magda would say no, but I don't get why you would, David."

David only had eyes for his wife. "When I give my word, I keep it. I promised you no doctors and there will be no doctors unless you want them. And I promise you this right now—that I love you no matter what your name is. That I will do everything in my power to make you mine again—or for the first time, whichever way you want to look at it. I will work day and night to win you. I'll never abandon you. I'll never give up on you, on what we had or will have. I won't let you go … Magda. Do you hear me?"

Magda nodded.

"I won't let you go."

# Chapter 13

Maggie woke alone in the pale predawn light on a tear-dampened pillow wondering where Davy was. Loneliness assailed her—loneliness and helplessness. Feeling abandoned and vulnerable, she'd spent the night tormented by dreams. She was alone in a strange world, denied by the one person who knew her. Her dreams were too close to reality to dismiss. Davy was rejecting her. She'd made a fool of herself the night before, begging that he stay with her.

"I'm scared," she'd told him.

"You'll be fine, Maggie," he'd told her in a voice that said he didn't care if she would be or not. Then he'd left with the parting shot—"I'll be close. I just willna be in yer bed."

She had gaped at him, feeling like a trollop. But it was comfort, not sex, she wanted. She needed to be held, to be reassured that despite everything, Davy was there for her. But clearly he wasn't. The conversation had ended then. She hadn't been able to think of anything that didn't sound like a condemnation, nothing that wouldn't push him farther away. He'd left, and she hadn't heard him return. It was better, wasn't it, to say nothing than to scream at him in anger and pain?

Maybe not, but she simply hadn't the energy to fight last night. She hadn't had the energy to do much more than sob herself into a restless sleep, alone in the strange bed.

Now it was morning, or almost morning, and they still hadn't talked about the festival tomorrow or how he needed to behave normally around her.

Tears trickled down her cheeks. She didn't feel any less tired.

Davy opened the bedroom door.

"Maggie?" he whispered.

She stared at him, not bothering to wipe her eyes or hide the fact that she was crying again.

"Can I come in?" He looked rumpled and tired as if he'd gotten no more sleep than she had.

She shrugged and turned purposely to the wall so that her back was to him. He wasn't there to see her anyway. He probably only needed a change of clothes.

He walked to the side of the bed.

"I'm sorry, Maggie."

She said nothing, keeping her back to him, wondering if he'd gone to town last night to betray her to the rest of the populace. It was a foolish thought, she reassured herself. He wouldn't endanger his wife, would he? She gave a mental shrug. What did she know? She hadn't thought he'd reject her either.

"You've been crying." He didn't know how to comfort her without taking her in his arms. Even as children, he'd held her when she'd cried.

She said nothing, not willing to comment on the obvious.

"Magda had dreams," he began. "Nightmares really. That she was round with my child, and I left her. English soldiers had come, and I was fighting or some such, and she was alone and frightened, having my baby. And I swore to her that I wouldna leave her. That if the English came, we'd flee together and be together. I swore I would always be at her side." He looked away from Maggie's back, ashamed. "And last night, I left ye. Ye said ye were afraid, and I left ye on yer own. Ye were crying, and I couldna stand the tears. I'd meant to guard yer door, but I couldna trust myself to act as guard. I knew ye'd be safe enough, so I went to the workshop. All night I sat there face-to-face with the cradle I'd carved for the bairn ye carry, face-to-face with the knowledge that I was abandoning ye, that I was abandoning Magda."

Maggie turned to face him.

He saw the motion, and slowly raised his eyes to meet hers. "I looked long and hard at myself, and I dinna much like what I saw. I saw a man who'd broken faith. A man who'd promised to stay, but fled. Magda or not, ye carry my child within ye. Magda or not, I'm pledged to ye as husband and protector. Dry yer eyes, Maggie. I'll abide by my pledge, and I'll not let ye down again."

Maggie sniffled. This is what she wanted, wasn't it? Davy's support? She closed her eyes, squeezing more tears loose. No. Despite his promise, he let her down again without knowing it. It wasn't that she didn't want his support. Of course, she did. But that wasn't the issue. She didn't want him to be with her out of obligation. She wanted him with her out of love. She was herself—as much Maggie as Magda. What had Juliet said to Romeo? "What's in a name? That which we call a rose by any other word would smell as sweet." What difference did it make what they were called in this lifetime? They were still Maggie and David. She didn't want Davy with her if he didn't love her.

"That's okay," she said, angrily dashing her tears with the sleeve of her nightgown. "I wouldna want ye to put yerself out."

"What?" His eyes narrowed in confusion.

"I mean that ye needn't feel obligated. Sure I'm yer wife and this is yer baby, but what of it? I willna be yer penance."

"What?" Davy stared at her in disbelief. "Are ye daft, lass? What are ye saying?"

"I'll not take yer charity, Davy McClellan, no matter how noble it would make ye feel. I'll do just fine by meself." She pulled the covers more firmly around her. "Now, if ye'll kindly take yerself out of the room, I'd like to get up."

"Maggie?" he asked, stunned.

She stared at him coldly. "Yes?"

"I'll let ye be to dress," he said. "But this conversation is not over. Ye canna dismiss me. Yer my wife, and ye belong to me—"

"Dinna push it, Davy," Maggie interrupted. "Ye may be my husband, but no one owns me no matter what lifetime I'm in."

# Chapter 14

After a night spent ruminating over David's promise to never give up on her, Magda was tired but more relaxed than she'd been since before Auld Annie had entered her life. His words had freed her. He wanted her and would pursue her until she was his. Now, finally, she could think without worrying. She wouldn't lose him. She wouldn't be left alone in a strange world. She had David as she'd always had Davy.

Knowing she was loved and desired unconditionally granted her the ultimate freedom. She could *be*, knowing that who and what she was was cherished. She didn't have to be perfect. She wasn't meant to be perfect.

It may have taken her most of the night to realize that David had given her a marvelous gift instead of a frightening threat, but she now knew it for what it was. She remembered Davy telling her the same thing in thousands of ways as she grew from child to woman. The knowledge of their connection made everything easier.

David's promise shouldn't have made anything easy. It should have conflicted with Davy's, but it didn't. It was a gift. She'd done nothing to deserve it, nothing to encourage it. There was nothing she *could* do to earn it. And because of that, she was free. She hadn't betrayed Davy or his love—and she wouldn't. This was a different life. What she had here couldn't affect what she'd had there. What had come before would always be within her. Even the dimming of memory wouldn't erase it. Not that she'd ever forget Davy. She couldn't. It wasn't possible. Even if she forgot his face, she wouldn't forget his love. Davy would always be with her.

And if she never got back …?

That was the hardest thought.

If she never got back, Davy would want her to have a life just as surely as he would cradle the child they'd made and hopefully love the woman who bore it.

*Oh, God.* Why did it have to hurt so much? She didn't hate Maggie, didn't wish her ill. She just missed her life. It had been everything she'd ever wanted, and now it was gone. Moving on meant leaving it behind, but, ready or not, time moved on. Here and now wasn't there and then. She hadn't the power to recapture the past. It wasn't her fault.

It had taken her most of the night to come to this conclusion, and she considered it a night well spent.

She showered and dressed before heading down the darkened hall to the kitchen. It was early. The streetlights had faded, but traffic was still slow. She would make a pot of coffee and take a cup to the gallery with her.

The gallery had become her sanctuary, the place where, surrounded by her silent audience, she escaped into her music. At Brian's insistence, she practiced the old songs. It was a bittersweet chore since each note carried memories. The CD they'd record over the next few months would both resurrect and bury the past. The music would live again, but the woman who'd once played the songs by the ruined circle on the hill had been replaced.

She sighed and pushed open the kitchen door.

"Why don't you play in the studio today?" David asked.

She jumped at the sound of his voice. "You scared me."

"Sorry." He flicked on the overhead light. He'd gotten up early and had waited in the darkened kitchen to talk to Magda. "Why don't you practice in the studio? The acoustics are much better there than in the gallery."

He knew the answer. They both knew the answer, but he hoped that she'd be unwilling to admit it and that maybe, just maybe, in the wake of last night's conversation, he could convince her to play in the studio as she used to.

To say he missed her was too gross an understatement. For two months they'd lived separate lives in the same house. Now that would end. He'd given her notice last night, and she hadn't fought it. He wouldn't let her go. It was time to start acting on his words.

Usually, Magda avoided eye contact with David. It was simply too much to see the pain and love in his eyes and not run to him. Her body hurt with the need to be held. Her heart ached with it. All these weeks her mind had plagued her. Her guilt over love lost and love not accepted had made sleep elusive. Last night, for the first night in what seemed like forever, dreams of her and Davy or those of her and David hadn't plagued her. It might have been because she had hardly slept, but she hoped it was because she'd been freed.

"Magda?" David's voice pulled her from her thoughts. "Why don't you play in the studio just for today? At least try it."

She looked him in the eye. "You called me Magda."

"Isn't that who you are?" he asked, silently rejoicing over the eye contact.

Her face lit in a smile. "Yes, it is."

*She's so beautiful,* he thought, fighting the desire to pull her close as he smiled back.

She fought the need to fall into his embrace.

They stood grinning at each other as the coffee maker sputtered its finale.

Drawn to her, he moved closer without meaning to. He didn't even realize he had until he'd reached out and touched her arm. "So, Magda, will you play your flute in the studio today while I sculpt?" He took the fact that she didn't immediately step away from his touch as a very good sign.

"O … kay."

"Good." He squeezed and then released her arm, not wanting to push her too far and lose the ground he'd gained. "I'll put your flute in the studio." He left before she could argue. With her flute in the studio, she couldn't back out.

# Chapter 15

Maggie didn't so much as glance at Davy as she strode into the kitchen.

"What's all that?" he asked, pointing to the bundle of clothes she had in her arms.

She refused to answer, intent on collecting what little already-made food there was.

"Maggie, what are ye doing?" Davy's clipped tones clearly showed his uneasiness.

Maggie looked at the pitifully small pile she'd collected, two hard bannocks, a small lump of cheese, and a joint of beef meant for the soup pot. There wasn't enough cooked food to last the day. If she wanted to eat, she'd have to cook before she left. She set down her bundle with a disgusted sigh.

"Are ye planning on going somewhere?" Davy asked cautiously.

"Well, not right now," Maggie snapped at him. "I'm obviously going to have to make provisions to take with me or starve."

"And where, exactly, did ye think ye'd be going?" Davy carefully asked.

Maggie glared at him. "To find the witch, of course."

"Of course."

"I canna stay here," she insisted.

Davy crossed his arms in front of his chest. "And why is that?"

Maggie rolled her eyes and shook her head, refusing to answer so obvious a question. Getting a bowl from the cupboard, she turned her focus to making bread for her trip.

He watched her get provisions out of the pantry. "I've told ye that I was wrong and that I'm sorry."

When she said nothing, pouring a scoop of rolled oats into a pan to toast, he continued. "It should be worth something. There's not many a man will do as much."

She snorted her disdain for men in general and Davy in particular.

"I dinna even ken what yer angry about," Davy said, exasperated. "The least ye could do is tell me that."

Maggie repeated her snort of disgust.

"Now stop that, lass." Davy grabbed Maggie by the upper arms and turned her to face him.

She gave him a surly stare. "Did ye want breakfast?"

"Of course, I want breakfast. But first, I want ye to tell me why yer so angry of a sudden."

"If ye dinna let go of me arms, the oats will burn."

He growled his frustration and released her. "Talk while ye cook then."

"Fine," she snapped, giving him her back while she turned the toasting oats. "I need to find Annie so that she can send me home."

"And just where did ye intend to look?"

She shrugged. "Around."

"Oh, yes, of course. Around would be best," he said softly just before he exploded. "Are ye daft, woman? A lass gone round with child out searching the heath and heather for a witch. And not just any lass, no ... me own wife. I say it again, are ye daft?"

She spooned the toasted oats into her bowl and added flour, water, and a pinch of salt. "No," she said, stirring the mixture. "I'm practical. I'll not stay where I'm not wanted, and that clearly means that I willna stay here."

"Ye are daft. Dinna I just tell ye in the bedroom that I'll care for ye?"

She turned on him. "No, what ye just told me was that even though ye don't care for me, you're determined to be burdened by me."

Davy slammed both hands on the table. "I said nothing of the sort! I told ye that I was wrong to leave ye and that I wouldna do it again."

"Ye said ye'd abide by yer oath," she accused.

"And I will," he argued back. "What I dinna understand is why that makes ye so angry that ye want to leave."

She put the bowl down with a sob.

"What is it?" he asked irritably.

She shook her head, lowering it to hide behind a wall of hair. Needing to be held, she wrapped her arms around herself.

Cursing, he opened his arms. "Come here, Maggie."

She shook her head. She didn't want his charity.

"Come on, Maggie-girl," he said, gathering her in.

She stiffened in his arms.

"Hush," he whispered, holding her close as one would hold a fretful child. "Relax." He smoothed her hair, whispering to her in Gaelic. "Dinna fight it, lass." He guided her to the rocking chair by the fireplace and, sitting, pulled her into his lap. "Hush." He rocked her. "This is what we need, the both of us."

She let go, resting her head on his shoulder. Tension and tears leaked from her body. Being in his arms felt like heaven.

"It's all right, lass. We'll make it all right."

"But ye dinna believe it," she protested soggily.

He paled. She had him there. "I admit I've not had an easy time of it. Neither of us have, but dinna worry. We'll figure out something."

"You'll help me find Annie?"

Davy shook his head. "I canna let ye wander about seeking a witch."

"Why not? It's clear ye dinna want me here, and there's no other way to get things back the way they were before."

He rocked her in silence for several moments.

The memory of the smoldering heap that had been Magda's parents' croft came unbidden.

Davy had been coming back from the castle later than usual that night. He'd delivered a cedar-lined chest hours earlier, but he had lingered to eat the evening meal with Magda before heading home. It was full-dark with a sliver of moon on the rise, but neither he nor his team needed light to negotiate the familiar path. Davy's mind was divided between Magda's parting kiss and their plans for the future. He smiled, breathing deep. The air was crisp with the coming winter, and the sky was full of stars. As his empty wagon rattled along the rutted path, he caught a whiff of something. Frowning, he sniffed the air, puzzling over the scent. It wasn't the homey smell of a hearth fire, but stronger and strange. A fickle breeze blew a blast of smoke his way. He urged his team faster as his nose began to burn with the stench of pitch, burnt feathers, and charred flesh. Fear whipped him forward. He didn't remember the rest of the journey, rounding the copse of trees, climbing the hill, or crossing the burn.

There were a dozen crofts in this stretch outside of Kirkinwall. Where a dozen families had made their lives, a dozen fires lit the sky, and a dozen columns of smoke rose to obscure the stars. Davy arrived too late to be of any help. The English soldiers had divided, attacking as many cottages as they could at one time to kill as many families as possible before the alarm was raised. The whoresons had barred the croft doors from the outside before firing the roofs. They'd left their victims to die, pounding on doors and screaming for help.

The roof of the last building collapsed as Davy leapt from the wagon. He knew each family—the name of each body he pulled free of the smoking ruins. His hands burned and blistered as he worked, but he wasn't mindful of that pain. At Magda's cottage, he paused to vomit in the dirt. Her da had been caught outside and cut down in the yard. The bloody English had slashed his belly and left him for dead as they blocked Magda's ma and young sister inside to burn. Trailing innards, Magda's father had dragged himself through the dirt to the door, but hadn't been able to move the log that wedged the door closed. His clothes had caught on fire when the wall collapsed.

All Davy could think of as he buried her family was Magda safe at the castle.

And now he had to do all in his power to keep Maggie safe as well. Once a thing happened there never seemed a way to get life back to the way it had been before.

"I dinna ken that it's in our power to do anything but live with things the way we find them," he admitted.

"That's why I'm going to look for her," Maggie said.

Davy shook his head. "That's not the answer."

"How do ye ken that?" Maggie demanded, looking into his eyes. She didn't really want to go wandering about an unfamiliar country in an unfamiliar time, but she couldn't stay here either. She'd lived too long in a loving marriage to settle for anything else.

He shrugged. "I just know that having you wander about alone is foolhardy, and I'll not allow it."

Maggie narrowed her eyes at him. "Dinna go down that road, Davy. I may be pregnant and alone, but I'm not helpless."

He pressed her head back to his chest. "Hush, now. Yer not alone," he whispered into her hair.

Pulling away to sit up straight on his lap, she snarled, "What would ye call it? Ye dinna want me."

"Dinna be daft. Of course, I want ye."

"Dinna ye be daft." She threw his words back in his face. "Ye've told me I'm a burden, but that ye'll care for me because of the oath ye made."

"Yer twisting my words around, and well ye know it," he said, holding her firmly in his lap as she struggled to get up.

"Let me go," she snapped, pushing at his arms.

"No," he said, not slackening his grip. "Best ye settle, Maggie. I can hold ye all day if I've a mind, will ye or not."

"Fine." She sat stiff and still in the confines of his arms. She knew she couldn't escape his grasp. She simply wasn't strong enough.

"I'll not make ye rest yer head, though I wish ye would," he said, pretty much guaranteeing that she'd sit up straight out of pure stubbornness.

When she didn't relax her stance, he sighed. "All right then, Maggie. I dinna say I dinna want ye. It's just that yer not me Magda."

Maggie stared him in the eyes. "How do ye know? If I hadna told ye, how would ye know?"

He blinked at her.

"If I walked out of this room and back into it and claimed I was Magda, how would ye know if I was or wasna?"

The color leached from Davy's face.

"If I hadn't said anything yesterday morning, and I almost didn't, ye'd have thought I was Magda and loved me as Magda. If I hadn't said anything that first morning, though that would have been nearly impossible considering the incredible strangeness of the whole thing, but if I hadn't, ye'd have never known I wasna Magda." She stared boldly into his eyes. "Even now, there's nothing about me other than my admission that would let ye know that I'm not Magda. And yet, ye dinna love me. If my confusion were caused by a bump on the head instead of a witch's curse, would ye love me or would ye care for me because ye felt ye had to?" She watched Davy's face grow red as she continued. "If I grew old and forgot everything that had happened in our whole life together, would ye love me for who I'd been or reject me as yer doing now?"

"I'm not rejecting ye."

"But ye dinna love me."

His face blanched. "Dinna say that."

"Well, ye dinna," she accused.

She allowed him to pull her against his chest. His arms nearly crushed her with the power of his hug. "Dinna ever say that."

She felt his chest vibrate with his unshed tears, and her heart ached. His warmth radiated up through the coarse linen shirt and sparked an answering warmth in her heart. Something tight inside her loosened, and she realized how much she loved him. Not as her protector or the father of the baby she carried. Not because of the body she was in. It was more than that. She loved him. Not just as Magda, but as Maggie. And she realized, for the first time that he was her husband. Not Magda's husband. Her husband. She'd already known it in her head; still, it struck her hard. She was Magda without Magda's memories. And he was David without David's memories. But they were the same—she and Magda and he and David. And she was his wife, now and then. And she loved him, then and now.

Loving him was as natural as breathing. A shift in position brought their faces together. Their lips met blindly, desperately. The spark that always existed between them roared into flame. He cupped her face in his hands and kissed her with well-remembered passion. The taste and texture of their loving was different only in its desperation. Clothing disappeared beneath frantic hands.

He carried her to their bed, whispering of his love for her.

She gave him her words in return.

Their joining was the blending of souls it had been from the first time.

Davy didn't doubt. It was his wife who met his thrusts with such abandon, her voice that called his name in fulfillment, and his babe that kicked at him from her womb as they held each other afterward and drifted off to sleep.

# Chapter 16

The studio resonated with the haunting sound of the flute. David's hands molded the clay automatically, his mind on Maggie, no … Magda. His mind on Magda and the music. This was as it should be. This was as it *had* been. She was his inspiration, his muse. He focused on the figure forming under his hands. It was a young boy playing the flute. He could easily make it into Pan—the mythical Satyr who played tricks and the pipes with equal enthusiasm. Creatures of fantasy were good sellers, but somehow he didn't think this boy would turn into Pan. The expression on this child's face was haunting and reflective like the music.

He stopped working, covering the unfinished sculpture with a damp sheet and plastic. The music had started out light and cheerful, but it had gotten progressively darker as the morning lengthened. He could almost feel Magda pull away from him with each successive song.

"How about a break?" he asked, washing his hands in the sink. "We've been at it all morning, and I for one could use a walk."

Magda didn't answer, but she began cleaning her flute. The effects of a night spent not sleeping were taking their toll. The optimism she'd felt this morning had ebbed as lunchtime approached, and the songs she played had reflected her growing feelings of melancholy.

"We'll stop by the deli and have a picnic in the park." David acted as if she had agreed to go with him.

Declining would take too much effort. He would ask her why, and she'd need to come up with a reason she didn't have. It was far easier just to go along. Besides, what difference did it make where they ate? She shrugged in passive agreement.

He took the freshly swabbed flute from her and set it in its case. "Come on," he urged, grabbing her hand. "It's the perfect day for a picnic."

He was right.

Once outside on the sidewalk in front of the brownstone, Magda felt better. The sun was bright, and the breeze, clean by Manhattan standards, was warm. It was a perfect summer day.

David led her by the hand into the corner deli. "Pick out the drinks, and I'll order the sandwiches."

She selected two large Snapples from the glass case and joined him at the counter to watch the woman mound corned beef and coleslaw on thick slices of black rye.

Magda's stomach growled as they left the deli.

"Don't worry. We won't go far," he laughingly assured her.

"I guess I should have eaten breakfast," she said, smiling sheepishly.

They sat on a bench in Central Park and unwrapped their identical sandwiches. Magda took a big bite of hers, loving the combination of creamy coleslaw and corned beef. She'd made sandwiches such as this at home in Kirkinwall—hollowed out loaves of bread stuffed with meat and pickle. She'd taken them along to eat with Davy on summer days long past. She chewed thoughtfully, smiling despite the unshed tears in her eyes.

Would she ever see Davy again?

"This has got to be the world's best combination," David said, calling her back to the present. "Don't you think?" he asked, taking a big bite.

A glob of coleslaw escaped from his sandwich to plop in his lap.

Magda laughed. "It's the favorite of launderers everywhere."

"Launderers?" he teased, scooping up the errant slaw with his finger and bringing it to his mouth. "Aren't we being politically correct."

"Couldn't say 'washerwomen' now, could I? Not with the way you load the machine. Wouldn't be right."

"Damn straight."

"Now, about the dryer …" She grinned at him. "Its door is not that much different from the washer, and you don't even have to put in soap. Then when the buzzer sounds …"

"Uh, uh," he protested. "I know all about the dryer—wretched machine. You take things out of it, and they need to be folded and put away. I'm much better off leaving it alone."

She laughed. Laundry was such an easy chore here that she honestly couldn't find any reason why David even started the machine for her. Not that she was going to offer him that information. The household chores, with all the machines that actually *did* the work, were really quite negligible by her previous standards. However, running most, if not all, of them still seemed to fall to the woman.

"I made good progress today," David told her a bit farther into his sandwich. "Say you'll play for me again this afternoon."

Magda bit her lips to keep from smiling and shook her head sadly. "Can't. There's too much laundry to fold."

David barked out a laugh, beaming at his wife as if she were the cleverest woman ever. God, he'd missed this.

"Oh, all right," he grumbled, making certain that Magda saw his smile and knew he was playing. "I suppose I could sacrifice art to cleanliness just this once."

Magda grinned, teasingly. "How about I get the clothes from the dryer, *and* fold them, *and* put them away, *and then* I'll come check on you. Would you like me to bring you a snack? I could probably make cookies."

He raised his eyebrows. The game had turned serious. She hadn't baked for him since the hospital. "Chocolate chip?"

She nodded. During lunch she'd regained the feelings she'd had that morning. Once again she felt good about herself and almost at ease with him. She wanted to give him something to show him that. She wanted to show him that she was trying.

"Okay." His voice caught around the word. He cleared his throat. "I'd like that."

# Chapter 17

"Magda," Davy whispered in Maggie's ear, waking her as he ran a possessive hand over her warm body.

"Mmm," she sighed in response.

He smiled, cupping her breasts in his large palms. He teased her turgid nipples, rolling them between his thumbs and fingers until she gasped.

He wanted her again with a ferocity that he didn't care to examine. Pressing his erection against her soft bottom, he made his desires known.

She responded predictably, pressing back against him with a moaning sigh.

He scattered wet kisses along the side of her neck, sliding a hand down her body to part her thighs.

"Mmmm, Davy," she moaned approvingly as he touched her. She was already damp with desire, but he set his fingers to work until her breath came in heated pants, and she whimpered his name again.

"I love ye, Magda," he whispered, as he buried himself in her with a gliding thrust.

Maggie didn't correct him.

The following morning, Davy went with Maggie to the kirkyard, carrying a basket full of samples of their first fruits. Others were there as well with baskets similarly laden with eggs, leeks, peas, small carrots, asparagus, wool, and other early harvests. Some led young animals or toted small limbs full of nearly spent apple, peach, or pear blossoms.

Father Toddy was in his element, roaming around blessing individuals and their baskets as they arrived.

"I see the acorn has dragged the oak to the kirk this morning," Father Toddy said by way of greeting Davy.

"'Tis a festival, and I'm expecting festive news from yer mouth," he told the priest. He refused to think of Magda as Acorn. She was Magda and yet somehow not his Acorn. He refused to contemplate why, preferring to simply block the thought from his head.

Father Toddy laughed. "Dinna fash, son. God and man will smile on this blessed day."

The McClellan arrived with most of his household in attendance. Rob was present, but Sanna was conspicuously absent.

"Where's Sanna, I wonder?" Davy said to Maggie after Father Toddy had blessed their basket and moved on.

"Maybe she's not feeling well," Maggie speculated, not knowing who Sanna was.

"'Tis a bit early to be her time. She is meant to have a few more weeks, same as ye."

So Sanna was pregnant. Not knowing if she and Sanna were friends, she kept her comments generic. "Babes come in their own time. Not everyone knows what day they're conceived."

"Excepting ye and Sanna that is," Davy agreed with her. "Ye knew the instant, and Sanna knew the day. Maybe it's something else that keeps her away."

"Probably." *Magda had known the moment of conception, huh? How?* Maggie wished she could remember that. She wished, yet again, that she had Magda's memories.

Father Toddy started Mass, interrupting her thoughts. Since this was a festival, the readings and sermon were those of thanksgiving.

As Maggie listened, it dawned on her that though she knew her song cold, she didn't know when to play it. Beads of nervous sweat dampened her palms. She wiped them on her skirt and watched the priest closely, hoping for a sign.

She shouldn't have worried. A few moments later, Father Toddy looked her in the eye and nodded once. Flashing a thankful smile, she raised the flute to her lips. As always, the first few notes took her from herself. Music poured from her as if siphoned by the flute. She didn't return to herself until the last note had faded.

There wasn't the thunderous applause that frequently marked the end of her performances, but her audience was clearly appreciative. Many smiled at her as the Mass continued and came up to her after it had ended.

"Did the good Father bless these first fruits?" a woman with gray-streaked hair said, putting her hand on Maggie's belly. There was dirt embedded under the fingernails of her grimy hands as if she'd just pulled her first fruits from the garden and hadn't had the chance to wash her hands clean. Her scent told Maggie that the woman's hands weren't the only part of her that needed a bath.

"I think he'll wait until after it's born," Maggie said, wondering the identity of this pungent woman who felt entitled to pat Magda's belly. She automatically stepped away from the woman.

"Ye have yer man call me when it's time," the woman said, as her hand left Maggie's belly. "I'm off to the castle. Sanna seems to think she'll be a bit early, but I dinna think she's right. She'd just been nervous this week past, not as I'd blame her. Ye dinna muck with a witch." She shook her head, smiling. "Though the likes of Sanna never get what they've got coming, now do they? Much as we'd like otherwise." The lady cackled, elbowing Maggie as if they shared a joke.

Maggie looked for Davy to come rescue her from this disturbing woman, but she couldn't catch his eye.

"Yer not to worry, though," the greasy woman continued. "I heard yer prayers today same as everyone. Listened to them real good, I did." She nodded. "Yer safe as can be. And I'll tell anyone who's a-wondering, not that anyone would be, mind. Ye'r good as gold like yer mam. Built like her too. Yer gran helped her with ye, or I'd have been to yer birth." She paused, remembering. "But I'm for Sanna's now. She may come early, but ye willna. Yer bairn's still high as can be. She should n'er have mucked with that witch. Dangerous thing that."

Maggie watched the midwife go, silently vowing that she'd have her baby in a pit in the field before she'd let Davy call that woman.

Visions of her squatting in the dirt, having her baby in the field like the Chinese woman O-lan in *The Good Earth* flashed through her mind, filling her with dread. *Oh, God!* There were no hospitals here. Women gave birth at home with midwives—midwives like that horrible woman.

Women *died* giving birth in conditions like this.

# Chapter 18

David met Todd at the handball court for their weekly game.

"Is that a smile I see?" Todd asked, looking at his brother-in-law. "What happened?"

David couldn't keep the grin off his face. "Nothing really."

"Nothing?" Todd raised his brows in disbelief. "Come on, a goofy smile like that? You're getting some, aren't you?"

"God, Todd," David scolded. "You're a priest."

Todd shrugged. "Yeah, I know. Next you'll tell me Maggie is my sister. What of it? I'm still human, and I'm not blind. She's let you back into the bed, hasn't she?"

Shaking his head, David pulled a handball from his pocket. "Not yet, but we're dating."

It was Todd's turn to gape. "Each other, right?"

David laughed, pulling open the door to the brightly lit court. "Of course, each other. In fact, she's letting me take her on a carriage ride through Central Park later."

"Really? I thought I was coming over for dinner."

"You are." David bounced the ball on the floor and caught it. "You're just leaving right after. You've got a meeting or something you can't miss."

"So tell me," Todd said as David entered the serving square. "What happened? A week ago she was claiming to be Magda McClellan, and you were worried about divorce. Now you're grinning like a fool and dating your wife. What happened?"

David grinned, but he didn't answer.

"So you're talking?"

David nodded once.

"And holding hands?"

David grinned.

"And what else? You said she wasn't sleeping with you."

"Let's just say we aren't in need of your counseling services at present." David smiled sheepishly and bounced the ball again.

"Oh, come on!" Todd complained. "She's my sister. I need to know if Mom has any chance of grandkids."

David snorted. "Well, Uncle Toddy, fertility issues aside, Magda and I are getting to know each other better. I'll just leave it at that."

"Magda, huh?"

David served the ball. "Magda."

Magda greeted David at the door with a brief hug and an affectionate peck on the lips. It was an impulsive act that she immediately regretted when she noticed Todd behind him.

Blushing profusely, she pulled out of David's embrace.

"Don't mind me," Todd said, dropping his athletic bag near the wall and heading to the bathroom.

"I … I'll just check dinner," Magda said, turning to the kitchen.

"It's okay, Magda," David assured her, lightly grasping her arm.

She turned back to him, but she wouldn't meet his eye. "I really should check dinner."

"I liked the way you greeted me." David gently pulled her into his arms.

"You did?" She looked up at him uncertainly.

"I did."

She blushed again, but smiled.

"You can greet me like that any time." There was a controlled hunger in his eyes as he smiled into hers. "When I leave the room and come back … any time." She used to, he remembered, pushing aside the thought and the raging desire that accompanied it. This was Magda, he reminded himself. He had to take it slowly.

Magda's blush intensified. She looked at his lips as if contemplating another kiss.

As David lowered his lips to hers, the bathroom door opened. Magda jumped back and fled to the kitchen.

"Sorry," Todd said, looking from the swinging kitchen door to his brother-in-law.

"It's okay," David said, smiling.

"She acts younger," Todd commented softly.

David looked at Todd. "I think she is."

"You really think she's Magda and not just deluded?"

"You tell me; you're the therapist."

"I know. I guess I just haven't been taking her claims seriously. I still think this was caused by the anesthetic."

"I'll agree that that's when this began. But the more time I spend with Magda, the more I see the differences."

"Differences?"

David nodded. "Granted there are a lot of similarities. But it's really as if she's a different person, or maybe the same person with different experiences so that her frame of reference is different. It's hard to explain. I'm not even sure I understand it. But take kissing. Being caught in my arms, kissing me, even a little peck like the one you saw, seems to have been a big no-no in Magda's past. It seems that only loose women or married ones kissed, and then not in public. And since Magda doesn't consider me her husband ..." He waved off the rest of the comment with his hand. "Come on." He nodded at the kitchen door. "She'll be wondering what's taking so long."

Magda feigned being busy, tossing the already mixed salad. "Are you ready to eat?" she asked, glancing over her shoulder at the men.

"You and David are married," Todd announced. "I was there. You've got a photo album of it here somewhere."

David groaned. For a counselor, Todd was sometimes too stupid for words.

Magda blushed. "Thank you. I've seen it."

"I didn't mean to make things worse." Todd looked to David for help but, getting none, turned back to Magda. "I just thought if you knew that I considered you two married, that you wouldn't feel embarrassed that I caught you kissing David."

Magda looked at David accusingly.

"God, Todd," David groaned, glaring at the idiot priest, "I think you need a refresher course in diplomacy."

Todd looked at David. "Sorry."

Magda turned back to the salad.

"What can I help you with?" David asked, standing beside her. "Other than strangling your idiot brother, that is?"

She turned to him, a smile dancing in her eyes. "I suppose some idiocy should be expected with brothers."

"You've had some experience with brothers then." David meant it as a joke. Maggie, of course, had experience with Todd.

"Not until just recently."

Her response surprised him.

"No brothers?"

She shook her head, slightly.

"Sisters?" He'd asked the question automatically, but he hadn't really meant to. It was hard to fathom Magda having a past where she wasn't Maggie, but she appeared to have one. And sometimes that past affected things, like with the kissing.

She looked into his eyes as if trying to read him. Apparently satisfied with what she saw, she nodded and whispered. "One."

He nodded, trying to hide his surprise. He'd tried not to think of her past. It was too confusing, too disturbing.

"Oh." Did he believe her? Could he believe her? What should he say now that wouldn't destroy the fragile bond they'd made? "Do you miss her?"

Magda nodded. "She died with my parents in a raid years ago."

Years ago? Lifetimes ago. "I'm sorry."

She nodded, handing him the bowl of salad. "I'll get the soup."

"What are we having?" Todd's voice shocked David and Magda, who'd forgotten his presence.

"Cock a' leeky," Magda said.

"Cock a' *what*?" Todd asked.

"Cock a' leeky," she said, smiling indulgently. "It's Scots for chicken soup with onions." She'd been thrilled to find a recipe for it in a modern cookbook. Not that she needed the recipe. What she needed was the confirmation that not everything in the past was lost to her. She still had the music and the food.

The clip-clop of the horse's hooves against the pavement brought a rush of memories to Magda. In the shelter of David's arm, she closed her eyes and pressed against his side.

"What is it?" he asked gently, tightening his arm around Magda. It was the perfect evening for a carriage ride. The gentle breeze caused by the moving carriage eased the heat enough to make cuddling comfortable instead of sticky.

"Nothing." She opened her eyes. "Just memories."

"I suppose you rode in carriages a lot. I should have thought of that." And avoided it like the plague. When Magda remembered the past, she tended to pull away from him. Having her pull away wasn't what he'd planned for tonight. He wanted to go forward, not backward.

"Some. We walked a lot."

"Oh." He looked past the streetlights into the park, wondering how to reclaim her attention.

She looked at him. "But I don't want to think about the past, not tonight."

He turned his head, gazing searchingly at her. "Really. Maybe it would help if you talked about it." He nearly bit his tongue. What was he saying? Idiot. He wanted her to focus on him and now, not Davy and the past.

"Maybe." Magda smiled, watching David try to keep the disappointment off his face. Even she knew that no man wanted the woman he was with to bemoan a past love. "But not tonight." She looked around briefly before turning her eyes back to David. "It's too nice a night to be anywhere but here." Her gaze left his eyes, traveling to his lips.

It was all the invitation he needed.

His lips claimed hers in what he'd meant to be a gentle kiss, a mere brushing of lips. But as their lips touched, he knew he couldn't hold it to that. He wanted her too much and had denied himself too long. Still, he held himself in check the best he could, firming the kiss, but somehow managing to keep his mouth closed. She surprised him with her response, with the tentative brush of her tongue against his lips.

With a groan of pleasure, he tasted her.

Had she always tasted this sweet? Had she ever felt this right in his arms? He deepened the kiss.

Time fell away as Magda gave herself to him in the kiss. Davy. It was his kiss. With her eyes closed, she'd swear she was in his arms. She pushed aside thought and focused on sensation—the feel of lips against hers, smooth tongues gliding together, the press of his body around her and the cushions behind her, the feel of a hot hand cupping her breast.

It was the hand on her breast that brought her back. Or rather, it was the desire to have that hand on her naked breast. She broke off the kiss.

He blinked at her, dazed, before resting his forehead against hers and looking into her desire-clouded eyes. "Too fast, I know. I'm sorry."

She stared into his green eyes, not Davy's deep brown ones, and felt the prick of tears. "Not here," she said, pushing against his chest.

He flopped back on the seat, tipping his head to look at the starry sky. The horses clopped on, their driver silent.

"I love you, Magda."

When several seconds passed without a response, he tilted his head to look at her.

"You know that, don't you?"

She nodded sadly before finally looking at him.

She loved him too. He could see it in her eyes. He'd have swept her back into his embrace and resumed their kiss had that been the only thing he saw. But it wasn't. He saw sadness in her eyes, a deep, smothering sadness.

She loved him, and it made her sad.

# Chapter 19

Davy lay in bed, his hand resting lightly on his wife's belly as she slept.

*Magda.*

His baby pressed firmly against his palm as if it knew he needed the reassurance of its touch.

*Magda.*

They'd made love again last night. As if the mating of their flesh made her more truly his wife, more truly Magda.

Breathing in the familiar scent of her, he nuzzled her head, kissed her hair. They were the same, both scent and hair. Her kisses tasted the same. Their desire was the same. Everything. Everything was the same. And yet ...

*Acorn.*

Again, he tried the name in his head and rejected it. It didn't fit. Staring into the darkness of their room, he tried to avoid thoughts of why it didn't fit. He mentally wrapped the memory of Acorn in a thick quilt and locked it in a trunk in the back of his brain. He'd leave the memory of her there, safe and secure, but locked up tight. Thoughts of her brought doubt where there should be no doubt. He stroked his wife's belly and consciously turned away from the imagined trunk.

Magda was Magda.

He closed his eyes, giving into the pull of sleep. In the morning she'd be a day closer to delivery and still be Magda.

"Sanna's had a son," Davy announced, walking into the cottage with a bundle of supplies several days later. He swung the bag of flour from his shoulder to the table with a thump.

"That certainly took a while. I thought she was laboring during the festival."

"It was a false alarm. Good thing, though—early babes are tricky."

"But it's still early."

"Not by much. A fortnight isna early, really. Our babe's dropped. Ye could go any time."

She didn't want to think about it. Though physically uncomfortable, she certainly didn't feel ready for delivery—at least not in a world without hospitals. Lack of prenatal care and the high infant and maternal mortality rates weren't things she wanted to dwell on. And yet, she didn't seem to be able to stop thinking about them.

"Are they both all right?" Maggie asked, concerned.

"Word is that he's a healthy lad, just bit scrawny," Davy answered, tugging at the string on the flour bag. "It willna take long for the wet nurse to feed him round as a berry." He carried the opened sack to the flour barrel in the corner of the pantry and poured it in, raising a pale brown cloud.

"And Sanna?" Maggie absently opened the bundle on the table. The fact that a wet nurse would feed the woman Sanna's son instead of his mother fueled her worries.

Davy frowned. "Scheming as usual and acting like the lady of the castle rather than the second wife of the laird's brother-in-law there on suffrage. Lady Marian's been patient with the chit. Who knows how long that will last? She's never been Sanna's fool."

"But she's healthy, right?"

Davy put down the empty flour sack he'd been folding to pull Maggie into his arms. "Ye'll do just fine." He hugged her tight. "Yer fit and healthy. Both ye and the bairn will be just fine." Looking down at her worried eyes, he reassured her. "Ye'll not be alone. I'll fetch Ellen when the time comes."

Maggie forced a smile. Was Ellen the old gossipmonger at the festival? It didn't matter. When the time came, she'd need help. She couldn't give birth by herself.

A sudden rap on the door startled the couple. They exchanged puzzled looks as they ended their embrace. Davy answered the door.

Auld Annie stood in the sunlit yard.

"I've come to make me apologies. Meant to get here sooner, but this land's not the easiest for an auld witch to get around in," she told Davy. "Now quit yer gaping and let me in." She elbowed her way past him into the house.

"By the Goddess," she swore, looking at Maggie. "Yer still here? Why are ye still here?"

Davy was the first to recover. He turned on the witch. "What are ye about? Be gone, witch. *In nominee Patris, et Filii, et Spiritus Sancti*—" His right hand touched his head, breast bone, left and right shoulders in the sign of the cross.

"—Amen. Now, hush," Annie scolded, interrupting Davy's Latin prayer. "I'm no bride of Satan. Ye'll not banish me with yer words." She turned to Maggie. "I came to say I was sorry if I frightened ye in the switch, and here ye are still switched. Why? What have ye done?"

Maggie stared incredulously at the old nurse. "What have *I* done?"

Annie blinked. "Yer right, of course. It's Magda I should be asking."

"But she is Magda," Davy protested, defensively.

Annie eyed him silently for several moments before nodding thoughtfully. "Aye, and yer right, Davy. She's Magda, but not yer Acorn. Ye've realized that, have ye not?"

Davy blushed.

"Dinna fash, man," Annie told him. "Ye weren't to know the difference. It was to have happened so fast here that it should have seemed more an odd dream than anything else."

"I dinna understand," Davy admitted.

"Neither do I," Maggie added.

"Time is different here than where ye come from—slower. Something's gone wrong."

"Obviously," Maggie said. "Maybe if ye explain how it should have gone, what ye meant to do, we'd be farther along."

"Now then," Annie said, pulling a chair from under the table and lowering herself into it. "A pint of ale wouldna go amiss."

Maggie crossed the room to fetch the ale.

Once the ale was served and they were all seated, Annie took a long draw from her mug. Sighing in obvious delight, she set her nearly empty cup down with a bang. "That was good."

Davy and Maggie watched her impatiently.

"All right then. Ye'll both ken that I owed Magda a wish." She waited while both Maggie and Davy nodded. "Yet Magda claimed she had all she wanted in this life. It's hard to get a wish from someone who is happy with her lot, so I had to look elsewhere. The two of ye are mostly blessed. Aye, ye've troubles to add spice, but no real hardships. All yer lives, yer mostly happy with no real wishes of the kind needed to settle the score. Then I found a Magda with a wish. Yer not meant to have bairns every lifetime. Most times, ye dinna mind. Ye took in foundlings or focused on each other. This time, ye seemed to mind.

So I switched one Magda, one that could conceive easily, with the other for a bit. Should have been a short while, just long enough to be bedded. That's never been a trouble in any of yer lives. Lusty pair ye are, one of the true love matches."

Auld Annie eyed Maggie critically. "But something went wrong. Yer still here." She turned to Davy. "Have ye not bedded her then?"

Davy frowned, blushing at the thought of what he'd done.

"Oh, dinna fash, man," the old witch scolded. "Yer meant to bed her as she's meant to be bedded. Trouble is, yer Acorn must not have realized that yet. She needs bedding to make the bairn, but it seems she hasna been yet."

Davy paled. Magda hadn't given into temptation, but he had. And it was her strength and morality that was keeping them apart. He wasn't sure how to view that. He'd been fine, having convinced himself that Maggie was his wife. He'd been able to ignore, for the most part, the differences caused by lack of memory by believing the woman who sat across the table from him was Magda, if not fully Acorn.

Now, he couldn't do that anymore. Auld Annie had made it clear that it was Maggie he'd been sleeping with, been making love to. His stomach clenched uncomfortably at the thought, and he pushed away his cup. How was he to treat her now? His confusion must have shown on his face because Annie suddenly waved her hand in front of his face. "Forget the confusion of the past hour. Stand and go into the yard to care for yer horse. When ye return, ye'll not remember me visit. Ye'll know 'tis Magda sitting here."

Davy's face was blank of thought and emotion as he stood and left.

Maggie watched him go. "W ... w ... what did ye do to him?"

Auld Annie frowned after him until the door swung shut. "Oh," she said, dismissing her small magic with a wave, "eased his mind somewhat so that he will accept ye as his until I can get ye switched back. It willna harm him none."

Maggie stared at her with wide eyes. She swallowed heavily, glad that Annie felt she owed her something rather than the other way around.

Annie didn't notice Maggie's discomfort. Instead, she frowned at Maggie. "But ye," she said, shaking her head. "Who'd have thought ye'd resist yer mate in any time?"

# Chapter 20

David and Magda rode through Central Park as both the twilight and silence deepened.

"You picked a nice night for a ride," the carriage driver said. Unhappy couples tended not to tip well regardless of the reason for their unhappiness. "It's supposed to rain tomorrow, but you wouldn't know it to look at the sky. Not a cloud up there, now. Just look at them stars, will ya."

David ignored the man, taking Magda's hand in his. "It's all right, Magda. I know I was rushing things."

She looked at their joined hands. "It's not that."

He used his other hand to raise her chin until she faced him. "Is it me or is it Davy?" he asked her quietly.

"It's me."

"You don't want me?" he asked, knowing that it wasn't the truth, but fearful that she wouldn't acknowledge it.

She shook her head, a sad smile briefly playing on her lips. "No. That's the problem. I want you, but it feels as if I'm betraying Davy. I look at you, and I forget his face. I close my eyes at night, and I see you. I used to share everything with him. Now, I come home from the studio and need to tell you of my day. I used to rush through chores to spend hours watching him carve wood. The smell of cedar, the curl of oak before his chisel, the rasp and pound of carpentry, the tang of his sweat—those were my life. Now the slap of clay with its cool earthy scent ignites my blood. I live for the pound of the mallet, the smell of hot metal, the look in your eyes. The love I once felt for him is yours. The desire, yours."

"And that makes you sad?" he asked, caressing her cheek.

She avoided his eyes. "It's as if I've lost him."

"And I've taken his place. Is that so bad?"

"No. Yes. If you'd just taken his place, as a second husband would a first, it wouldn't be so bad. That I expected. That I'd welcome. But it's as if the two of you have blended in my mind and my heart. What made me love Davy is what makes me love you. What I felt in his arms, I now feel in yours. It's as if I can't tell you apart anymore."

He realized that her confession should have bothered him. Had he truly believed that Magda was a different person than Maggie, it would have. But he didn't. Magda was Maggie after drug trauma. He never believed they were different people. He'd tried, and there were times he could believe, but not for long. Calling Maggie "Magda" was just a way of pacifying her until her memory returned. No matter what she wanted to be called, she was still the woman he loved and had married. So, in his way of thinking, the fact that he'd blended with her memory of a husband in her mind and heart was a step in the right direction. Maybe whatever blocks the anesthetic had put on her memory were dissolving—and she was healing.

"I don't mind," he said.

"But I do," she protested softly, but she didn't pull away.

"Why?" he asked, watching her mouth.

She licked her lips in unconscious invitation.

"Because ..."

Her reason was lost in his kiss. Distracted by the press of his lips and the strength of his arms around her, she'd have been hard pressed to come up with any reason at all. If being one with Davy didn't bother him, why should it bother her?

The carriage stopped at the appointed place, but they didn't notice. It wasn't until the driver cleared his throat several times that they noticed that they weren't moving. Magda squirmed out of David's embrace, blushing crimson. David frowned at the interruption and then smiled in male smugness as he dug a couple of twenties from his pocket and handed them to the driver.

They were inside their front door before Magda would look at David's face.

"Sleep with me tonight," he said, pulling her into his arms.

"I ... I ..." His suggestion caught her off guard.

He interrupted her protest with a kiss.

"You want to," he told her, when they came up for air. "And God knows I want to."

"S ... sleep. Just sleep, right?"

"And if it should lead to other things." He pressed her against the front door, kissing her senseless.

She didn't protest, instead letting his hands wander up her sides to cup her breasts. *Davy*. She arched her back, pressing against him, feeling the hard ridge of his erection against her belly, tempting herself. *David*.

Finally, reluctantly, she pushed against his shoulders, and he released her.

"I want to, but I can't. Not tonight."

David frowned at her, puzzled. He'd been so sure. Her response had been so accepting. She'd never been a tease. Not before. "Why?"

Magda colored again. "It's my...." Her color deepened. "My ... uh ... period," she said, remembering the term at last. "I began today and ..." She looked at him hopefully, willing him to understand how uncomfortable it made her.

"Oh," he paused. "Your period. I see." She wasn't teasing him after all. "Then we will just *sleep* together until it's done."

"Are you sure?" If they'd tumbled into bed to make love and then stayed there, it would have been easier. Then she'd have had passion to blame. Now it was a conscious decision, the ultimate betrayal. If she went to bed with him now, it was because she wanted to, not because she had been weak. Once she'd slept with him, there'd be no going back. By saying yes to this, she was saying yes to future lovemaking. It was premeditation, not passion.

He seemed to understand without her saying a word. "Magda, I want you back in our bed. I don't sleep well without you in my arms. I love you, and I know you love me. We belong together. Sleep with me just for tonight. If tomorrow you decide it's too much, that we are moving too fast, I'll understand, and I won't press the issue. I promise. Just say you'll sleep with me tonight."

She looked into his eyes. Her heart ached.

"Say, yes," he prompted.

Closing her eyes, she pressed her cheek into his chest. "You've never begged before." She and Davy had struggled to keep her virginity intact until the wedding.

"I would have if I needed to."

She wanted to make love to him now, despite everything.

He kissed the top of her head. "It doesn't matter. The past doesn't matter. All that matters is now. Say yes."

Magda hesitated only a moment before giving in. "Yes."

Magda stood in front of the open dresser drawer and stared at the assortment of nightclothes as she wondered if she'd made the right decision about sleeping with David.

"Magda?" David said from the other side of the closed bedroom door. "Are you ready? Can I come in?"

"You can come in, but I'm not ready."

He opened the door to look at her. "What's wrong?"

"I don't know what to wear," she complained, sitting on the bed with an irritated bounce.

"It doesn't matter. Wear anything."

"Wear anything," she snorted, returning to the drawer. "Like what? This?" She pulled a flannel nightgown from the drawer and held it for him to see.

"Well, it's a little too warm for that," he admitted.

She dropped it on the bed before turning back to the drawer. "Or this?" She held up a lacy little nothing.

"Maybe not tonight," he admitted.

She dropped that as well. "How about this?" She pulled out a red satin pajama set that was a Victoria's Secret version of men's pajamas.

"Hmmm," he said as she added that one to the pile. "I see what you mean. What have you been wearing to bed?"

"It's in the laundry."

"So wear what you've got on."

She sighed, looking at the shapeless t-shirt and elastic-waist shorts she'd put on after her shower. "I wanted to look good."

"Then wear that lacy thing," he suggested. "You look amazing in that."

She frowned at him. "And we're just going to sleep?"

"Right." He looked from the crumpled negligee to Magda. "Shorts and a t-shirt—or maybe that flannel thing. Do you think it's too warm for a sweat suit? We could turn up the air conditioner." He grinned, shaking his head. "No. Just wear the t-shirt and shorts. I'll behave myself."

She smiled, at ease with him again.

"Come on," he said, grabbing her hand. "Let's go to bed." He drew her to the mattress.

Her nervousness returned when he released her hand to pull the comforter from the bed, revealing the summer-weight blanket, sheets, and pillows.

"Are you going to wear that to bed?" she asked, pointing to his shorts and t-shirt.

"It's this or nothing," he said.

"Oh."

"Relax, Magda. You may not remember it, but we have slept together before."

She remembered how sleeping with Davy often had been more than simply sleeping, and she blushed, imagining it would be the same with David. Maybe she wasn't ready for this after all.

"Perhaps—" she began, but she was interrupted.

"Perhaps we'd better get into bed before you talk yourself out of it again."

"How did you know?" she asked as David slid between the sheets and drew her after him.

"I know you, Magda."

"Do you?" she said, allowing him to turn her away from him and spoon behind her.

"Yes," he whispered into her clean hair. "Now relax."

It was disturbing how easy it was to do that. Even as he spoke, she'd felt her body melt into position. She remembered it on so many levels. This was the way she and Davy slept together, spooned close with his manhood pressed against her backside and his arm around her. She sighed and pressed back into him.

His cock surged forward, welcoming her. She noticed its rigidity and size, but she tried to ignore it.

"Just sleep," David reassured her. "I promise."

She smiled, feeling safe in the comfort of his arms. She closed her eyes, preparing for sleep.

His hand rested warm against her belly.

She yawned, curling her hands next to her cheek.

*Comfort.* The thought swirled in her sleepy brain. She hadn't felt this level of comfort in months. Even the firm cock pressed against her was reassuring rather than threatening. She felt safe and loved, trusting her heart and body to David.

As sleep stole her conscious thought, David moved his hand from her belly to her upper arm as if trying to find a comfortable roost.

She moaned softly.

He lay consciously still, trying not to disturb her. Holding her was wonderful, completely comfortable except he couldn't seem to figure out what to do with the hand that usually cupped her breast while they slept. He'd promised no sex, but what would she think of his hand on her breast when his penis already pressed against her in foolish optimism?

He moved his hand back to her belly.

"Mmmm." She protested his movement.

"Sorry," he whispered. Maybe if he lay still long enough she'd fall asleep, and he could put his hand where it needed to go.

They breathed in near-tandem, Magda sleeping, David lying tense.

He'd almost decided that it was safe to slide his hand into place when she stirred. Reaching under the covers, she grabbed his hand and drew it up to cup her breast where she left it with a satisfied sigh.

David smiled, relaxing at last. Now he could sleep.

After the first night, sleeping together became both easier and harder. Magda was no longer nervous about cuddling with David. They went to bed earlier to talk and pet. The pressure of intercourse was gone, having been postponed by nature and mutual decision. The knowledge that he wouldn't press the issue helped Magda relax and accustom herself to intimacy with David.

On their fourth night together, they found themselves in bed before supper, stripped down to their underwear.

The scent of baking chicken was ignored as they concentrated on each other. David raised his lips from Magda's swollen nipple and moaned, "Magda, I don't know how much longer I can handle this."

She guided his mouth to hers. "Tomorrow," she said against his lips. "Tomorrow."

He groaned, deepening the kiss and pressing his body against hers.

She opened her thighs, wrapping her legs around his hips as he ground himself against her.

"Now," he suggested as she matched his rhythm.

She was about to agree when the phone rang.

"Ignore it," he said, when she stiffened.

"I can't," she protested. "Brian is supposed to call to tell me how the mix sounds." The oven timer's buzzer joined the phone's ring. "And that's dinner."

David cursed, crawling off his wife and out of bed. "I'll get the chicken; you get the damn phone. But no matter how the mix sounds, you're spending all of tomorrow in bed with me. You can tell Brian you're sick."

Watching David's backside as he left the bedroom, she answered the phone.

"Magda?" The old woman's Scottish lilt startled Magda, dispelling her thoughts of making quick work of Brian's call and luring David back to bed.

"Who …?" she managed before the old woman continued.

"Ye'll be knowing how to get with child, lass. Ye did it before."

Magda froze. "Who is this?"

"Ye want to go home to yer Davy, dinna ye?"

Magda's eyes grew round as saucers. "Auld Annie."

"Dinna ye?"

"Yes," she answered automatically, even while her heart froze in her chest. Her stomach dropped. She'd fallen in love with David, almost given herself to him and now … now came the chance to go home to Davy. Magda bit her tongue to keep from yelling at the old witch.

"Then spread yer legs for the man. It's naught but a giggle and a poke."

The line went dead before Magda could think of anything to say. *It was naught but a giggle and a poke.* She pulled the covers around her nearly naked body. Sex had never been a giggle and poke for her. It was making love in the truest sense of the phrase. She hadn't been able to seriously contemplate it with David until just recently. And now that she could, now that it *was* love, she was to spread her legs for a giggle and a poke and go home to Davy? She paled.

Go home to Davy.

How could she make love to David and leave him?

How could she love Davy and not go home to him?

Oh, God! What was she to do?

David went back to the bedroom when Magda didn't come to his call that dinner was on the table.

"Dinner's read—" The words died on his lips. Magda was huddled against the headboard, wrapped in a crumbled sheet. Tears flowed down her cheeks and glistened in her red-rimmed eyes.

"What happened?" he asked, frozen just inside the door. "Are your parents all right?"

She nodded.

"Is it Todd? Oh, God, don't tell me some thug finally got him."

"No," she said in a choked voice. "Todd's fine. Brian's fine. Everyone's just fine."

David frowned, puzzled. "Then what's wrong? Who called?"

She didn't want to tell him. What would he think? What would he do? Did he truly love her as Magda? Or did he still think of her as Maggie, despite his assurances? Would he want Maggie back and think nothing of a quick bounce to achieve that goal? What would she think of him if he did? How would she feel if he didn't?

"Magda? Talk to me. Who called?" he insisted, joining her on the bed.

She nearly flinched at his touch, unsure how she should react toward him. She wanted him, needed him, and yet …

He ignored her hesitation, pulling her close. "Talk to me, Magda."

She clung to him, desperately sobbing.

"Magda, tell me who called." His voice was gentle, but firm, clearly an order instead of a plea.

"Annie," she said into his chest. "Auld Annie."

David disentangled himself enough from Magda to look at her face. "Who?"

Wiping her face with a handful of sheet, she faced him, still stricken. "Auld Annie," she repeated. He didn't understand. She could tell by the confused look on his face. "The witch," she clarified. "The one who took Maggie and sent me here."

"Oh." His tone was skeptical. He hadn't really believed that. He had tried. There were some things to which there seemed no other explanation, but he couldn't totally swallow Magda being a different person from Maggie. Mostly he tried to focus on the here and now instead of puzzling about events he couldn't quite fathom. As far as he was concerned, Annie was the strange old nurse they'd seen that day at the fertility clinic and Magda's identity confusion was the strange result of the anesthetic. Sometimes he felt as if he were pretending, humoring Maggie by calling her 'Magda.' Other times it was less of a ruse.

Mostly, he didn't think about it. He didn't dwell on what he didn't understand; he just lived with what he did. Magda or Maggie. In his mind, they were the same. One was as much a wife to him as the other.

"What did she say?" he asked, his voice quavering uncertainly as he spoke.

"I …" she hesitated, still not wanting to tell him.

The silence stretched.

He waited, watching her.

She stared pleadingly into his eyes, silently begging him not to make her talk.

He squeezed her hand encouragingly, but he never broke eye contact.

Magda closed her eyes and sighed in reluctant acceptance.

There'd be no reprieve.

David was still watching her in patient expectation when she opened her eyes.

"She told me how to get back."

His brow wrinkled in confusion, and his grip on her hands tightened. "What? How?"

She mumbled, "I'm to get with child."

His face cleared instantly. "That's good then."

"Is it?" Now she was the one who was confused.

"It's what we've always wanted. It's why we went through the GIFT in the first place, remember?"

She didn't.

"We did the GIFT because we weren't getting pregnant any other way."

"What other way?" There was but one way to get with child that she knew of.

He laughed, kissing her firmly on the lips. "What I don't understand is, if that was all she said, why it upset you."

He didn't understand. She was taken aback by the thought. "Because I love you."

He kissed her again. "I love you too, but I still don't understand. I thought you wanted a baby."

"I, uh, do. It's just …" She looked at his face reading the amused confusion. "It's just that I don't want to leave you."

"And you're worried that you'll leave me if you get pregnant?" he asked.

"That's what the witch said."

"Oh, honey," he laughed, kissing her again. "We've been trying to make a baby for seven years. If God wants us to have children, he'll give them to us, but I wouldn't hold my breath. We might very well try another seven years without a child."

"But I'm fertile," Magda protested.

"Well, actually, on day five of your cycle, chances are you're not. We've been doing this long enough for me to have your fertile days memorized. We've another week before there's much of a chance at conception."

She hadn't known about that. If she'd thought about it at all, she'd have thought that each encounter brought the chance of pregnancy. "Then I shouldn't worry?"

He hugged her close. "About getting pregnant and losing me? No."

She sagged with relief, snuggling against his chest.

He kissed her again. This time, she parted her lips, kissing him back.

"What about dinner?" she asked, coming up for air.

"It's chicken," he murmured, pressing her into the mattress. "It's good cold."

# Chapter 21

Maggie struggled out of bed, cursing the slack ropes that made getting up in the morning a climb. She had awakened tired and irritable after a night spent trying to get comfortable enough to fall asleep. Davy had gotten up with the sun, as usual, and greeted the new day with disgusting cheerfulness. She'd growled at him when he insisted she stay in bed a little longer and try to sleep. It was a futile task. She was simply too large—too large and too uncomfortable.

Her breasts were heavy and tender resting against her chest, making her sweaty where flesh touched flesh. Her belly, which seemed to grow hourly, rested on her lap as she sat. Her legs ached, her back ached, her feet ached, she was hot, she couldn't sleep, she had to pee constantly, and Davy was so damned solicitous that she wanted to rap him upside the head.

She waddled to the washstand, tugged off her clinging nightgown, and drenched a washcloth with the water in the pitcher. The cool cloth raised goose bumps on her heated flesh as she swabbed her body.

*Who'd have thought being pregnant would be this uncomfortable or unattractive,* she thought, looking at herself in the glass. Her areolas were huge and dark, her nipples puckered with cold. And her breasts … she sighed, lifting them to wipe beneath. She remembered the smallish breasts she'd had while in her own body. Had she ever really wanted large breasts?

Looking at herself in the mirror, she knew that it wouldn't be long, couldn't be long, before the baby came. Her belly couldn't get any larger. Already it felt as if the skin were pulled tight enough to rip in places. She rubbed ointment on her distended abdomen to ease the tension.

She hadn't made this baby, and she wasn't looking forward to delivering it. As the time drew nearer, she found herself silently urging Magda, *Hurry up and bed that man!*

It wasn't that she didn't love Davy or this baby. She did. The thought of leaving them was a physical pain. But ever since Auld Annie's visit, she'd known that her time here was limited. At first, knowing she was going to leave soon had made her desperate, but now it made her sad. How could she mentally and emotionally separate herself from David as Davy? She couldn't. All she could do was silently urge Magda to do what was necessary to put things right.

She wished she'd advised Annie not to tell Magda how to get home. In this case, ignorance might be the only way to make things right. She didn't know if she could have made love to Davy, knowing that by doing so she'd leave him. Could she create life knowing that by doing so she'd leave the man and the child behind? No. She couldn't. And if she couldn't, how would Magda manage?

She finished washing and tugged on a shift, wishing that it were proper to wear it alone. She was hot all the time now, even on days when the breeze was cool. Today there wasn't a breeze. She stuck her head out the window. No. Not a whisper. Still she had to wear a dress over the shift. She pulled the full cotton gown over her head, buttoning it closed before grabbing the basin of wash water and leaving the bedroom.

The cottage was empty. An empty cup and crumbs on the table proclaimed that Davy had eaten breakfast before leaving. Setting down the washbasin, she tied on an apron and cleaned up the small mess without thought before going outside. A small pain, more of a tightening low in her belly than real pain, surprised her as she sloshed the water over the garden plants. *Was it labor?* she wondered. Probably not. It was most likely gas. She'd had more than her fair share of that lately. She strode to the hen house, tossing a handful of feed to the chickens before ducking into the coop to gather eggs. She placed the warm eggs in her apron, counting as she did. Three dozen.

Back in the kitchen, she felt the tightening again. It wasn't pain really, more of a cramp. *Not labor*, she told herself. The thought of possibly being in labor thrilled and frightened her. As much as she wanted the baby to be born, she was worried. She hadn't had prenatal care. There just wasn't any here. No prenatal vitamins, no check-ups with the doctor. Nothing. And she was so small. Well, not her stomach or her breasts, but everything else. Okay, maybe not her ankles either, but that was just lately. They'd been slim when first she'd seen them. Now they were puffy like the rest of her. She had small bones and puffy skin.

She transferred the eggs to a cloth-lined basket and started making oatcakes. No, she decided. She didn't want to go through labor, not unless she got to keep the baby. It wouldn't be fair otherwise.

Maggie cracked two eggs into the flour in the bowl. *Hurry up, Magda,* she silently urged her counterpart. *If you want this baby, you'd better hurry up.*

# Chapter 22

Cradled in David's arms half-naked, Magda opened her eyes. Sunlight filtering through the window shades and the sound of traffic signaled morning. Last night, they'd driven each other wild, touching and tasting. Still they hadn't made love. She hadn't offered. He hadn't pushed. Her period had nearly ended yesterday. Before Auld Annie's call, Magda had been ready to discount any residual mess and give in to her burning desire. But after the call, even after David's reassurances, she'd been nervous. What if she made love with him and disappeared? Would she really return home to Davy in Kirkinwall? Could she? She'd been gone for six months. Her baby would be crawling. She didn't know its name. She didn't know if she'd had a son or a daughter.

So much had changed, not just in Kirkinwall and New York, but also within her. She'd mourned and buried Davy. Or rather, he'd melted and reformed as David. The whole concept disturbed her. As many times as she tried to tell herself that Davy and David were different men, they had somehow blended in her head and in her heart. She'd accepted David as her husband. He'd replaced Davy so completely that it was almost as if he'd become Davy. As much as she tried, she couldn't reconcile that. She'd betrayed Davy so thoroughly that she couldn't go back to him. Sorrow and self-loathing clawed at her heart.

No longer able to bear David's touch, she slid from the bed.

What was she to do? She wanted to be with David as a wife should, and yet she couldn't allow him to impregnate her. Could she say she didn't want children? Would he believe her?

No. He wouldn't believe her. She'd told him too much about the phone call, and he and Maggie had tried for too long. He wouldn't believe she didn't want children. Given this body's track record, he wouldn't believe her claims of fertility either. He'd said as much last night.

Did she believe she was fertile?

She thought of her own body in Kirkinwall. It hadn't taken long to get with child. But this body, here in New York? Was she fertile in this body? It brought back the old question. Was she herself or Maggie? Was her identity defined by her body or her soul? If the soul defined the person, then wouldn't it follow that she was Magda? Magda was fertile. However, if there were something in Maggie's body that made it incapable of becoming pregnant, then the body wouldn't become pregnant no matter what. Right? She didn't know. It was too confusing. As with the Davy/David issue, her mind shied away from delving too deep.

She stepped into the shower. Warm water cascaded down her body. She soaped and rinsed herself clean, trying to avoid the crisis of identity that threatened on the edge of her mind. What should she do?

She was about to step out, when the shower curtain opened, and David stepped in.

"Today's the day." He smiled at her, reaching for her.

She frowned.

His smile faded. "It is, right?"

"Oh, David," she moaned, falling into his arms.

"What?" he groaned in pleasured pain as his naked body came into contact with hers.

"Annie." The entire issue was explained in that name.

"Oh, honey." He kissed her wet head. "Forget her. Forget what she said. We've been trying for seven years to get pregnant. Raging fertility is not an issue for us. Not in that way. Trust me." His penis surged joyously against her softness. "It's not a danger. We'll make love and you'll see. You won't go anywhere, I promise."

"But how can you promise?"

"Because I know our bodies." His hands roamed over hers, pushing her away enough so that he could caress her breasts. "I probably know your body better than you do."

She moaned as he teased her nipples. "After last night, maybe," she conceded.

He'd known it much longer than that, but he wisely didn't say so, focusing instead on getting reacquainted again. He slid a hand between her thighs, moaning when he encounter the slippery evidence of her arousal.

"Trust me, Magda," he said, sliding his fingers inside. "Please."

Lost in the wonder of his touch, Magda forgot her argument. They made love in the shower.

"See," he said when they were semi-dry and in bed for a second round, "You didn't disappear."

"No," she admitted, between kisses. "I didn't."

# Chapter 23

The pains continued irregularly all morning. By the time Davy came in for the noon meal, Maggie was beginning to think that she might be in labor.

"How was yer morning?" Davy asked, carrying in a bucket of water. "Did ye sleep in a bit?"

"A bit," Maggie admitted, smiling at him. "Thank ye for letting me." Somehow, as the morning progressed, her mood had improved. She felt happy. That in itself was odd, since she was actually a bit more physically uncomfortable. Still, she didn't feel as tired as she had when she'd gotten up, and perhaps that accounted for her good mood. It was as if each tightening of her abdomen gave her energy. The thought of birthing a child still frightened her, and she wasn't quite willing to admit to being in labor, but she couldn't deny the feeling of excitement and anticipation that had been building inside her all morning.

He set down the water and gathered Maggie in his arms for a kiss. "What are yer plans for the afternoon?" Davy asked, caressing her belly.

She laughed. "Are ye asking me or the baby?"

He smiled at her. "Ye, of course, unless the baby has something to say." He eyed her speculatively. "Does it?"

She shook her head. "Not yet." She ignored the small voice in her head that suggested that she might want to tell him of the pains. "Not yet," she told the voice, the baby, and Davy. She wasn't ready. "I think I'll make a nice mince pie. Uncle Father will be coming for dinner tonight if I remember right."

"Aye, it's been two days since he last was here. Too bad Rome willna let the priests marry like the Presbyterians do. 'Twould do him good to have a wife to care for him."

Maggie laughed. "Dinna let him hear ye say that. He'll worry for yer soul for certain."

Davy snorted. "No more than he does already." He released Maggie and sat down at the table. "Are ye sure ye feel up to having him here, Magda? It's nearing yer time. I thought it would be today for sure when ye woke up so owlish."

"Owlish, was I?" she said, smiling. Her grin faded, suddenly. Another pain was coming. She could feel the tightening begin, and she sank into a chair as it grew.

"Are ye feeling poorly?"

She waited until the tightness passed before answering him. "Fine, fine. A bit of gas, is all."

He narrowed his eyes at her. "Yer sure yer not wanting me to ride for the midwife?"

Maggie's eyes grew wide. "No, not her. I dinna want anything to do with her."

"Ellen? Why not?"

"She's a fraud. Knives under the bed willna cut pain."

"I've my doubts about that as well, but she's delivered many a babe. I think it would be good to have someone with that experience with ye when yer time comes."

She crossed her arms under her chest. "Not her."

He raised a brow. "Who then?"

"There must be someone else who knows about giving birth."

"Most know about birthing animals, Magda, but we've only one midwife in Kirkinwall. Ye ken that."

She thought a moment. In an age where personal hygiene wasn't a big priority and medicine consisted of herbs and potions, she didn't hold much hope of there being any reliable help if she ran into problems during delivery. It would be best if she simply didn't do it.

"Well, it's not an issue today," she lied—as much to herself as to him.

"Best think on it, though, Magda. It willna be long before you'll have a need."

"You could deliver it."

He paled. "No." He shook his head. "I dinna think I could manage it."

"Dinna be silly," she insisted, serving him sliced beef with gravy. "Of course, you could."

"No," he insisted. "When the time comes, you'll have women to attend you, if not the midwife."

The afternoon sped by as Maggie attempted to ignore the tightness that gripped her abdomen with increasing frequency and intensity. She minced dried fruit and meat for the pie. She had just finished sealing the crust when another contraction began. She held onto the edge of the table as the tightness built, stealing her breath. They'd gotten too intense to work through. She stood still, closing her eyes and panting softly as she focused on the building pain. It started slow, a little tightness low in her belly, and then spread like a wave until her entire abdomen was cramped. Then, just when she thought she couldn't handle it any more, it would begin to lessen. Gradually the tightness loosened, sliding away until there was nothing, and she could breathe deeply again.

Davy stuck his head in the door to see his wife clinging to the table, pale and sweaty. "Magda, I ..." His words died as he rushed to her side. "It's time, isna it? I'll go for the midwife."

"No," Maggie gasped, shaking her head. The pain was almost over. A moment later, it was gone. She took a deep breath and sighed it out, relaxing. "No, Davy. I'm all right."

"Of course, yer all right," he reassured her, putting his arms around her. Birthing a baby was by no means a risk-free venture. He knew it, and she knew it. There was no need to dwell on it, but he grew pale regardless. "And ye'll be all right." He kissed the top of her head. "Why dinna ye lie down in bed while I fetch the midwife."

"Not yet," she said, holding him tightly. "Please. There's plenty of time." Actually, she had no idea if there was or wasn't, but she hoped there was. As difficult as it had gotten to deny it, she still didn't want to acknowledge that she was about to give birth to a baby she couldn't keep. "I need to put the pie in the oven, and then, I'd like to go outside for a while. Will ye walk with me?"

Davy held her at arm's length. "Of course, I'll walk with ye. We'll take one turn around the yard, and then I'll go for the midwife." His expression told her that he'd brook no argument. With her safety and that of their child at risk, he would humor her just so far. He wanted Magda to have help during the birth and knew he wouldn't be any. He couldn't stand to see her in pain, especially not when it was his fault. Seeing part of one contraction had been enough to tell him that he'd be less than useless during the birth.

She slid the pie into the open brick oven before the next contraction arrived. There was just time to grab the table again as it took hold of her.

Davy rushed to her side, trying to help, but unable to do anything but stroke her arm and murmur words of endearment.

"I dinna think we've time for a stroll around the yard," he told her, when she whooshed out a breath at the end of the contraction. "I'll be off for the midwife."

"No," she grabbed him, fear showing in her eyes. "Dinna leave me alone. What if it comes while ye're gone?"

Kissing her firmly on the lips, he disentangled himself from her grasp. "I willna be gone long. First babies take a while I'm told. I'll be back in plenty of time." He took several long strides to the door, but he stopped before going outside. "How long have ye had pains?"

She didn't answer him right away, which was an answer in itself.

"From when ye woke?" he asked, though he knew the answer.

She nodded once.

"Why did ye stay silent?" he asked softly.

She shrugged, staring pleadingly into his eyes for understanding.

He went back to her, holding her closely. She'd been afraid. She was still afraid. "I love ye, Magda Mary."

"I love ye, too," she whispered, clutching him as another contraction began.

He kissed her head and extracted himself from her grasp once again.

When she made a noise in protest, he stilled, noticing her breathing. "Ah, Magda," he crooned in sympathy, worrying that he might not be able to fetch the midwife in time after all. He waited for the contraction to finish before saying anything else.

"It's gone," she said with a cleansing sigh.

He gave her a brief hug before heading for the door again. "I'll go quickly then."

She nodded, wishing she could tell him no, wishing she could deny the impending birth just a little bit longer. This wasn't how she'd imagined giving birth. In her world, she'd have known a due date and been to the doctor for checkups and birthing classes. In her world, labor would prompt a call to the doctor or a certified midwife and a cab ride to the hospital. There'd be excitement, not fear. And David would be with her the entire time.

Through the open door, she watched Davy run to the barn.

In her time, there'd be qualified doctors, midwives and nurses in surgical gowns. There'd be sterile instruments and a pediatrician. There'd be the knowledge that she was with experts who'd delivered thousands of babies. There'd be baby monitors and pain medications.

She watched as Davy rode off on his unsaddled horse.

In her world, her family would be with her until the delivery and then after to welcome the new baby.

She looked around the deserted cottage.

Her water broke in a rush, trickling down her legs and soiling the rushes on the hard dirt floor.

A sob escaped her lips.

In her world, she'd get to keep the baby.

# Chapter 24

Later that morning, as they dozed replete in bed, Todd called.

David grabbed the phone on the third ring. "Hello."

"I'll need you at noon," Todd said without preamble.

"What?" David asked groggily.

"Are you sick?" Todd asked.

"No. Napping."

"Napping at ten in the morning?" he asked. "Oh … *oh*. 'Napping.' Right," he laughed. "Sorry, buddy. I'm glad you and Mag are finally 'napping' again, but you promised you'd help with the party at the mission, and I need both of you here by noon. You can wear a stupid grin, if you like, but be here." He hung up before David could say another word.

"Who was that?" Magda asked, pressing her sleep-warmed body against David suggestively.

"Your brother."

"What did he want?" Magda asked, nibbling on David's neck.

"I can't remember," he said, capturing her mouth in a mind-numbing kiss.

It was 11:58 when David and Magda, with their arms full of grocery bags, walked into the old concrete-block building that served as a mission. The building sat next to Christ the Savior Church in a lower-income neighborhood in upper Manhattan. Ten blocks away were the burned-out cars and drug houses of some rough sections in Harlem, but it was clear that Father Todd and the Christ the Savior Mission held sway here. The streets were fairly clean, and the local children were in school rather than hanging out on street corners smoking.

Todd met them inside the door, taking the bags from their arms and handing them to other volunteers to unload.

"I'm glad to see you're on time. Schools are out at three, and there's a lot to do before the kids get here." The mission sponsored a Halloween/All Saints party for the neighborhood. Todd put Magda and David under the direction of their decoration coordinator and promised to check on them later.

It was nine o'clock and dark outside when the last ghoul and fairy princess left. Cleanup took another two hours, so it was past midnight before Todd and Magda found themselves back at their brownstone.

"I'm beginning to have second thoughts about having children," David said, pulling open the door.

"Okay," Magda quickly agreed, walking into the house. Despite David's reassurances and the fact that she was still in New York hours after making love, Auld Annie's words still worried her.

"Does that mean you're too tired?" David asked, pulling her into his arms.

"Maybe." She *was* tired. Every muscle ached, and her feet throbbed, but was she *too* tired? She thought of lying in David's arms. Too tired? Probably not.

"Maybe?" he teased, giving her a smacking kiss. "How about I lock up here while you slide into a hot bath? Then, after I've opened a bottle of wine and joined you, we'll see just how tired you are."

# Chapter 25

Davy was back home before Maggie, resting on a kitchen chair with a dishtowel pressed between her thighs, had decided whether or not to change her gown.

She heard the horse and then footsteps before Davy swung open the door.

"Are ye well?" he asked.

"My water broke. Yer back fast."

"I met yer uncle on his way here and sent him off for help instead." He reached down and hauled her to her feet. "Let's get ye to bed."

She smiled at his concern, but she shook her head. "I'm too restless. I need to walk."

Davy would rather she were in bed surrounded by women who knew about birthing, but until they arrived, he'd have to do what she said. "Are ye certain?"

She nodded, taking his arm. "Just around the room a couple of times." She took two steps before freezing as another contraction began to build.

He watched her through furrowed brows as she paled and panted. "I think we'll walk around the bedroom instead."

She surprised him by nodding.

As soon as she was able, she began her slow shuffle into the bedroom.

"You'll need to strip the bed," she told him, transferring her grip to the doorframe. "And you'll need to cover it with oil cloth and an old blanket." She leaned against the wall as another contraction began.

Davy watched her helplessly for several seconds before moving.

It took a while to get everything ready. Davy, usually confident and competent, needed direction and reassurance every step of the way.

"Are ye all right, then?" he asked her after each contraction until she told him to stop.

"I'm fine, Davy," she snapped. "I'm trying to pass a pumpkin through a keyhole, but I'm fine. Now will ye quit asking me how I am and get the bed ready?"

She was newly settled in the bed when the sound of horse and wagon, accompanied by women's voices, filled the late afternoon air.

"Get ye gone, man." A bustling, stout matron Maggie recognized as Polly, the barmaid at the pub, barged into the bedroom. "Katie's setting yer dinner on the table—minced meat pie by the smell of it. Go oot and keep the good Father busy, while I look to get the pie oot of this oven." She turned her back on Davy, dismissing him. "I hope ye dinna mind me being here, Magda. Years ago, yer mam made me promise to tend ye whene'er yer time came and not to let Ellen at ye."

"Thank ye. I told Davy I dinna want her."

"There's not many as do, but she's the only true midwife around. Lucky she was tending some poor thing when the good Father came. So now ye have the likes of me, and she'll not bother ye none."

"Thank—" A contraction interrupted.

"Yer having a pain?" Polly asked. "Good. I'll just wash up a bit, so I'm ready for the next one. Best to check ye during one, ye ken."

Too busy concentrating on not panicking, Maggie said nothing.

Polly rolled up her sleeves and soaped both arms past the elbows. "There," she said, drying herself. "Now, if yer done with that one, let's get ye ready for the next one." So saying, she pulled the blankets off the end of the bed and lifted Maggie's skirt.

"Broke yer waters, did ye?" she commented, removing the sodden towel. "When ye start again, ye tell me. I'll slide me hand inside and feel for the head." She left Maggie exposed to rummage in a sack she'd left on the dresser. "Best grease myself up good," she said, pulling out a jar of rosemary-scented salve and spreading it on her hands and forearms.

Maggie groaned as another contraction began.

"Ah," the woman said, recognizing the signs. She slipped two fingers of her right hand inside Maggie and pushed, feeling around while Maggie grunted in pain. "Ye've a ways to go yet," she informed Maggie, removing her hand and wiping it on the bedclothes. "Close yer eyes and try for a few moments' rest. Ye'll be sure to need it afore the night is through. I'll slip oot and get some supper. Would ye be wanting a sip of something?"

Maggie shook her head.

"Rest then," the woman said, leaving Maggie.

Maggie hadn't thought sleep was possible, but she closed her eyes anyway. She found, to her surprise, that in the few minutes in between contractions, she was able to relax and even doze.

Outside, the shadows lengthened as the afternoon wore on.

# Chapter 26

Lying naked in David's arms, tired and warm from the bath and their loving, Magda knew.

"We've made a child," she whispered.

David squeezed her in sleepy response.

"If I leave, know that I love you."

"Mmmph," he snorted, already asleep.

*Will he know?* she wondered. Would David know the woman he woke with tomorrow was not the same as the woman he'd made a child with the night before? Her eyes filled with tears over the curious mixture of joy over the new life they'd created, sorrow for her impending loss, and a deep abiding exhaustion. Still an unwilling player in this game of fate, she fought sleep. *Will they realize what I've given them?* She thought of the baby newly growing in her womb and of the baby whose birth and first months she'd missed. Was the gain of one a fair trade for the loss of the other? She thought of Davy and David and her love for each of them. Unacknowledged tears dampened her pillow. Would anyone ever realize what the trade had cost her? Would anyone but she and Maggie ever realize there was a trade? And what of Maggie? Would she mourn the loss of Davy and the babe, rejoice in David and the new pregnancy, or both? Magda reviewed what she'd leave behind—David, the child, her heart. It was too much.

Despite the tears and mental turbulence, sleep called, its voice seductive and insistent. A respite from thought and strife, it beckoned. With a shaky sigh, Magda gave in to it and lost the struggle to stay awake.

A sudden, clenching belly pain woke Magda. It was like the worst gas she'd ever had, intense pressure and cramps, and it was growing. She opened her eyes to the cottage in Kirkinwall.

"Mother Mary," she groaned, her hands touching her huge belly. She was in labor.

The bedroom door opened as Polly came in with Katie.

"Getting stronger, are they?" Polly commented, washing her hands at the basin before going to Magda's side. "Ye had a bit of a nap, though," she chattered on. "Just what was needed, and now we can get to work."

Magda had time for a few panting breaths as one pain faded and the next began to build.

"Davy?" she asked, eyes wild. She'd been gone six months. This couldn't possibly be her second child, could it?

"Pacing the yard with Father Toddy, waiting to see what ye'll give him," Katie answered, helping Magda sit while Polly stripped the covers off the bed and readied herself at the foot of the bed.

Magda's knees were high and her thighs spread wide, exposing her naked private area. The pressure between her legs was too intense to even contemplate anything else. Polly looked closely, sticking her ointment-slick fingers inside Magda's straining body.

Magda growled angrily at the invasion. She needed to push.

"Ah." Polly beamed at her encouragingly. "Head's just there. Push a bit, next pain."

*Push a bit,* Magda thought disgruntled. *I'd have pushed during this pain if yer hand hadna been in the way.* The pressure was so intense and the urge to push so great that she could do nothing else.

Pushing was the best pain she'd ever felt.

Sweat dripped from her brow. Her face turned from red to purple. She groaned and pushed. Her body threatened to rip apart. And then, it gave. The baby's head made way for its shoulders, and with a growl from its mother, the rest of the body slipped out.

"Good lass." Both Polly and Katie congratulated her.

"You've a lusty lad," Polly laughed, as the slimy child let out an angry cry.

"Give him here." Magda reached between her legs for the child.

"In a minute, Mam," Polly said, tying a bit of twine around the umbilical cord.

Katie pushed down on Magda's stomach.

Magda growled irritably at her.

"Yer bleeding, Magda. Needs get the afterbirth out."

Katie's pushing stimulated another contraction.

Magda pushed and Katie, reaching between Magda's legs, pulled on the cord. The birth sack came out in a gush of fluid and blood.

Polly quickly propped pillows behind Magda and moved to the end of the bed to help.

The women cleaned the room and wiped down both mother and child before taking their leave.

"Born mother, that one," Polly told Davy when she finally allowed him into the room.

"We'll take care of the linens and bring them round tomorrow," Katie told him. "Congratulations."

Alone at last, Davy walked hesitantly to Magda's side. He peered into the bundle in Magda's arms.

"A son," Davy beamed. "We'll call him Brian William for our fathers."

Magda smiled at him, teary-eyed. Her heart was full to overflowing with love for her son and his father, and yet it ached at the loss of David.

David. Tears poured down her face at the thought of him. She'd left him after all. Closing her eyes, she could see his handsome face smiling. She could see the love they'd shared reflected in his green eyes. She was gone. Did he even know she'd left? Would he know how much she loved him and what it cost her to leave? Would he miss her? Had he ever truly loved *her*?

Davy kissed her cheek, calling her back to the present and its well of questions. How long had she been gone? What did Davy know? Was this child their first?

"Magda." He held her hand, clearing his throat. "Every man wants a son, me included," he said, looking at the child. "But there's part of me wishes it'd been a girl, so we could call her Acorn."

"Acorn?" Magda blinked at Davy. "Why Acorn? That's what ye call me."

Davy looked at her, stunned. "Acorn?" he whispered, hopefully. He'd never called the new Magda that. Never.

"Aye," she said, through the tears. "I've been yer Acorn since we were no more than bairns. Ye canna give that name away, Davy. It's mine."

He scooped her into a hug, crushing mother and child until both protested.

"Thank God," he breathed it as a prayer, loosening his hold, but not releasing them.

Father Toddy poked his head around the door.

"Dinna tell me ye've finally decided to believe in God, Davy? This birth was truly a miracle."

Davy laughed. "I always believed in God, old man. But ye have it right. This birth was a miracle in more ways than one. It's given me back my Acorn."

"Now, now," Father Toddy, scolded, shaking his head. "I ken that God said, 'Be fruitful and multiply,' but ye should give my poor niece a bit of a rest before acting on that impulse."

Davy gaped. Magda blushed.

"Come now," Father Toddy chided them both. "I'm a priest, not a eunuch." He looked around as if to make certain no one else was listening. "I ken where bairns come from," he said in a stage whisper.

Davy laughed. "Do ye now. Ye surprise me, Father."

Father Toddy snorted a laugh. "Enough from the pagans; now let me see that grand nephew of mine."

# Chapter 27

Morning light streaming through the window woke Maggie. For a split second she didn't know where she was. In that moment all she knew was that she was naked and entwined in a man's arms instead of dressed in a nightgown and in full labor. It took her only a fraction of a second to recognize her bedroom in New York and the arms as David's. Still, it was a shock to go from full labor to peaceful slumber, but not as much of a shock as Magda was sure to have experienced going from peaceful slumber to full labor. Come to think of it, during both trades, she had awakened naked in the arms of her husband while Magda had awakened to medical situations—first post-op and now labor. She couldn't help but think of her Magda self as suffering both ways; both times she'd left behind a wanted pregnancy.

Maggie didn't know how she knew that she was pregnant, but she did. It wasn't because she believed what Annie had said. No, it was something deeper. It was as if her body knew that a new life had started. Tears filled Maggie's eyes. She was pregnant, and she'd get to keep this baby. It was hers. She knew that in every fiber of her being.

*Thank you, Magda. Thank you, Annie.*

She nudged David awake. "We're pregnant," she whispered to him.

"So you said last night," he said, still half asleep. "What makes you so sure?"

How could she explain it? How much did he know about what had happened? "I just know."

He smiled, kissing her on the lips. "Well, I'm glad." He kissed her again. "And look, you're still here."

# Book Club Discussion Questions

1. Magda asks David and Todd what makes them who they are. What do you think makes a person uniquely his/herself? What do the characters think? Do David and Davy share the same belief? Magda and Maggie? Father Toddy and Todd? What does their point of view say about them?

2. Bradley keeps the Scottish dialect to the chapters that take place in the 18<sup>th</sup> century. Why do you think she did that? How would it have affected the story to have Magda speak with the accent throughout the book?

3. What was Auld Annie's intent when she switched Magda and Maggie? Why didn't it work out the way she thought it would?

4. How did Davy and David react to the switch? What do their different reactions say about the ages they live in? Would the story have worked as well had their reactions been the same? Switched?

5. Is Magda's reluctance to accept David into her bed true to her character? Why didn't Maggie share her reluctance? Are there times in your life when you would choose one course of action and times when you would choose its opposite? Explain.

6. Is Madga a changling? Do myths and folktales have their bases in fact? Can you give an example of how a myth or folktale explains an actual phenomenon?

7. Davy asks Father Toddy about faith and fairness. Davy comments, "Seems all too often those that do good are rewarded with pain." What do you think? Are good deeds always rewarded?

8. What do you think happens after the book ends? Are Maggie and Magda able to adjust back to their own lives? What do you think happens with their relationship to David/Davy the day they switch back? Five years out?

9. Was Maggie right to let Davy think she was Magda? What would you have done in her place?

978-0-595-40948-8
0-595-40948-2

Printed in the United States
79335LV00004B/55